The only thing [barcode: D0356731] **was that his mout** **fit against hers for maximum pleasure.**

And that the heat of his body felt like a fantasy in which she was granted everything she had ever desired.

It never worked like that in real life. Not even with a healthy dose of magic tossed in for good measure.

But never in her life had Zoë felt so connected to a man she didn't even know.

Sighing into the kiss, she tilted her body towards Kaz's aggressive stance, and as their hips met, he drew his fingers down her spine, coaxing her even closer with his touch. Chest to chest, she melted against his heat and strength. He made her feel delicate and pretty and so, so desirable.

A girl could become bewitched by such a kiss. And a bewitched witch was a rare thing.

Also available from Michele Hauf

Harlequin Nocturne

*From the Dark #3
Familiar Stranger #21
*Kiss Me Deadly #24
*His Forgotten Forever #44
Winter Kissed #52
"A Kiss of Frost"
*The Devil to Pay #55
+The Highwayman #68
+Moon Kissed #72
**Angel Slayer #90
**Fallen #109
The Werewolf's Wife #133
Vacation with a Vampire #139
"Stay"
Forever Werewolf #145
This Wicked Magic #153
Beautiful Danger #164
& The Vampire Hunter #175

*Bewitching the Dark
+Wicked Games
**Of Angels and Demons
&In the Company of Vampires

HQN Books

Her Vampire Husband
Seducing the Vampire
A Vampire for Christmas
"Monsters Don't Do Christmas"

LUNA Books
Seraphim
Gossamyr
Rhiana

MICHELE HAUF

has been writing romance, action-adventure and fantasy stories for more than twenty years. Her first published novel was Dark Rapture. France, musketeers, vampires and faeries populate her stories. And if she followed the adage "write what you know," all her stories would have snow in them. Fortunately, she steps beyond her comfort zone and writes about countries she has never visited and of creatures she has never seen.

Michele can be found on Facebook and Twitter and at www.michelehauf.com. You can also write to Michele at P.O. Box 23, Anoka, MN 55303.

THE VAMPIRE HUNTER

—

MICHELE HAUF

HARLEQUIN® NOCTURNE™

Recycling programs
for this product may
not exist in your area.

ISBN-13: 978-0-373-88587-9

THE VAMPIRE HUNTER

Copyright © 2014 by Michele Hauf

Printed in U.S.A.

Dear Reader,

I'm a little obsessed with *Breaking Bad*. It's the characters that get me, not the subject matter. And yet, I couldn't help but wonder what it would be like if *Breaking Bad* was smashed together with vampires. Toss in a witch and a few faeries? It could make for an interesting story. So I did just that. No meth in this story, but the faery dust the vampires are dealing is similar.

Once I got beyond the mechanics of the story, I was once again drawn to the characters. Kaz and Zoë push and pull at each other in ways that made me smile, lift a brow in concern and sometimes even cheer. Life is about trust and belief and learning to trust when there is no belief.

I hope you'll enjoy their story.

Michele

Prologue

The thing came at him so quickly, Kaspar had little time to react beyond putting up his arms to block the crazy long teeth that gnashed for his neck.

He'd been minding his own business, digging in the garbage behind Madame du Monde's dance studio. He'd found a broken chair and had screwed off one of the wooden legs. If he whittled down the serrated edge he might use it as a weapon. Call it a sixteenth-birthday present. Living on the streets a guy needed all the protection he could get.

But after nearly two years of street life, he'd usually seen the attack coming. This maniac had lunged at him from out of nowhere, and it was as if he were on drugs because he growled and shoved Kaz to the winter-wet tarmac, then jumped on top of his chest, compressing his thin rib cage with a hard knee.

Twice as big as Kaz and dressed all in black, the attacker snarled, revealing teeth that belonged on a monster. Kaz yelped and swung the chair leg before him. The man batted it away.

"No way!" Kaz yelled. Using all his strength, he managed to kick the crazy guy off him, leaped to his feet and swung the weapon wildly. "Get away from me, you creep!"

"A tasty little boy," the guy muttered like some kind of

menacing villain a person only saw in the movies. "I can smell your blood. Starved for sustenance as you are, I'll squeeze a few drops from your skinny neck."

The man lunged for him, gripping Kaz's shoulders and sinking sharp teeth into his neck. It hurt so bad, worse than all the times his dad had used him as a punching bag. Kaz kicked and yowled; he didn't want to die. He was too young. He may not have much to live for, but—no, it wasn't going to happen this way.

Pushing the thing off him tore the long, pointed teeth from his neck. Kaz whined at the pain, yet he didn't take his eyes from the attacker. His blood dripped from the maniac's mouth. With a hungry smirk, the thing again lunged.

Without second thought, Kaz swung around the chair leg, jamming the serrated end into the guy's chest. The creep growled and swore at him, cursing him with all the bad words Kaz had learned to use to vent his anger, and then some.

And then a blast of ash formed where the guy had been speared with the end of the chair leg. Dark gray flakes formed the shape of a man, then sifted to the ground, leaving behind a pile of clothing—and no vicious attacker.

Swinging down the hand that still clutched the chair leg in a painful squeeze, Kaz stumbled backward, hitting the steel garbage can in a clatter, and slipping to land on his butt.

"What the—?"

Another man swung around the corner of the brick building, gripping the wall to stop his running pace. He wore a plaid vest over a fancy shirt and pants, and looked like one of those rich guys Kaz always saw escorting pretty girls in and out of shops on the Champs-Élysées. "You got him, kid?"

Got him? Got what? What *was* that thing? It…it had dissolved right before his eyes. There wasn't even blood in the pile of ash. Human beings didn't do that. And it had—Kaz slapped a hand over his neck—bitten him.

The man approached him carefully, hands held out in placation. "I'm not going to hurt you. I'm one of the good guys."

Kaz drew up his legs as the man squatted beside him. He was too scared to run, and he didn't want to stab at him. One pile of ash was weird enough. Had he just murdered someone? He didn't want to go to jail. He'd take the cold, tough streets of Paris over jail any day.

The man inspected Kaz's neck with probing fingers that made him wince. "How old are you, boy?"

"Si-sixteen. Today's...m-my birthday." Kaz shivered because his windbreaker jacket was never warm enough for February. "Who are you?"

"You can call me Tor. Happy birthday, kid. Looks as if you got the grand prize. I didn't expect to run into any action tonight. You're lucky I was in the vicinity."

"I'm luck— Really?" Kaz held up the bloody chair leg. "*I'm* the one who took him out. What...what was that thing?"

"You're right. You took care of the longtooth all by yourself. That was some incredible work, kid. What's your name?"

"Kaspar," he murmured. His eyes scurried over the ash and clothing. He couldn't process, didn't want to listen, but the man's next words pulled him into focus.

"Kaspar, you just slayed your first vampire. And here's the good news. Even though you've been bitten, and normally a bite will transform a mortal into a bloodsucker, if you kill the one who bit you, then you're in the clear. You won't transform."

A worried noise scratched at the back of Kaz's throat. Transform?

Tor pointed over his shoulder to the pile of ash. Apparently, not transforming meant he wouldn't turn into a vampire. Was that some kind of twisted birthday present?

"The bad news," Tor continued, "is monsters exist."

Ah, hell. Kaz had always liked monsters. They'd not slept under his bed when he was little because his mother had chased them away with the broom. But then she died, and his world had, as well.

Tor picked up something from the ground and studied it. He held the bloodied key before Kaz. "This fall out of your pocket?"

Kaz swiped the old brass key and nodded, shoving it deep in his jeans pocket.

"Key to your house?"

Kaz shook his head. "Don't have a home anymore. I'm on my own and doing just fine."

The man nodded, and stood. "Damn right, you are. You're one tough kid." Hands at his hips, he peered over the destruction, then began to shuffle the ash toward the garbage bin, spreading it out. He picked up the singed clothing and dropped it in the trash bin. "My job is to ensure others don't start believing all the myth and legend that really does exist. No one will suspect those bits of ash were once a creature of the night. You going to tell anyone what you saw, Kaz?"

Kaz tucked his head against his elbow and closed his eyes. He shook his head. He wasn't even sure what he'd seen. What he'd done. He'd killed a vampire?

"You have a talent with the stake," Tor said. "Homeless, eh?"

Kaz nodded minutely but didn't look up at him.

"Well, you'll need the wound cleaned up so it doesn't get infected. And…to be totally up front with you, I don't have a home for you or a means to help you."

"Don't need your help."

"Course not. But there is a man I know who would be

interested in talking to you. His name is Rook, and he heads an organization of knights who protect humans from creatures like the one that attacked you."

"Knights?"

Kaz looked up into Tor's eyes, blinked and saw...the truth. Along with the truth, he also saw a deep and concerned kindness he'd not recognized for years. So without thinking it through, he grabbed Tor's offered hand and stood up, wobbly, yet not out for the count by any means.

"You can trust me," Tor said, "though I know you won't. You're a smart kid and know how to protect yourself and that's how it should be. But do you want to learn how to use that thing the right way?"

Kaz looked at the bloody chair leg he still gripped. The man was offering him something he hadn't known in a long time—trust. And he wanted it with every breath he inhaled.

"Come on," Tor beckoned.

And Kaz took his first steps toward chivalry, something he wouldn't comprehend until many years later.

Chapter 1

The vamps were fast, and he—well, he wasn't much faster, but he was skilled. A human matched against a vampire must wield some mean martial-arts skills or he had better be a track star. Kaspar Rothstein possessed the former, but right now he was contemplating the run.

Yep, best to go for the run.

The sickening heat of a vampire's breath skimmed the back of his neck as he raced down an alleyway in the eighteenth arrondissement near Paris's shadowed Montmartre Cemetery. His goal: to lure the four vamps far away from humans and curious eyes. Rushing into an open cobbled courtyard behind closed businesses far from any tourists, Kaz stopped abruptly, planting his steel-toed boots.

With a confident grin teasing his mouth, he swung around, catching one of the vamps in the chest with a titanium stake. The vamp ashed before him, forming the shape of a person out of fried vampire flesh, bone and clothing.

"Happy birthday to me," he muttered his victory claim. Wasn't his birthday, but who needed cake to celebrate?

The three remaining vamps grinned at him. Kaz had expected the idiot longtooths to actually share a brain among them and run for their lives. But if they wanted to stick around for the party games...

"Come on," Kaz encouraged. He tucked away the stake and put up his fists. He hadn't gotten in a workout this morning. Time for some fun.

The first vampire charged him. Kaz managed to grab him by the scruff of the neck, and swung the gangly tormentor toward another of his rag-tag pack. Their skulls cracked, both swore, and they collapsed on the cobblestones.

The leader swung around with a punch that Kaz stopped with his open palm. "Nice to meet you. I'm Kaz. Vampire hunter. I'll be ashing you this evening."

"Wiseass," the vampire cracked.

Kaz gripped the miscreant's fist, twisted, and with a swing from the waist, rocketed up a high sidekick to his jaw. The heavy boots delivered damage by breaking jawbone. The attacker dropped, growling and spitting blood. The other two charged him with fists. Kaz immediately dropped the one on the left with a wince-inducing gut punch.

A female scream alerted him. A woman clung to the limestone wall not thirty feet from their little soiree.

"Get out of here!" he yelled at her, and caught a punch across the jaw. He tasted his own blood, and shook his head to chase away the bluebirds spinning about his skull. That one could have led to his death had it been a knockout.

Enough play. Best to stake them before they beat him to a pulp. But—hell, not in front of an innocent.

Frozen in fear, the woman watched their antics with wide eyes. Chills scurried up Kaz's spine. He delivered another kick and landed a vamp at the hip, sending it stumbling backward. He had to keep the vampires busy and away from her until she grasped her senses and ran. Only then could he ash these idiots.

Out the corner of his eye, Kaz alternated his attention between fight and female. Was she scared—or interested?

She leaned forward from her position against the wall, her bright eyes following the action. A vampire charged him; he landed a kick to a particularly vulnerable part of its anatomy, bringing it down.

Licking her lips, the woman seemed to marvel over the show.

"Go!" Kaz shouted at her, but too late he realized the command had alerted one of the vampires to their audience.

He swung a fist at an attacking vamp and took him out cleanly. The other vampire raced toward the woman and pinned her to the wall by her wrists. She didn't scream. That was good and bad. A scream would call attention to this altercation and alert other innocents.

But why didn't she scream?

Must be scared voiceless.

Wishing he could stake the attacker from behind, Kaz left the stake clipped at his hip. He ran toward the vamp, grabbed him by the head and shoulder and peeled him away from the woman.

"Wow," he thought he heard her say, as he landed on his back on the cobbles, bringing the vamp down with him.

Twisting to straddle the vamp, Kaz punched him repeatedly until the longtooth's lights went out, his hand sprawling across the toe of the woman's lace-up boot.

Springing up to stand in the center of the fallen vamps, Kaz looked over his mayhem. Fists still coiled at his sides, brows drawn and serious, he was ready for another four, or even a whole gang.

But the vampires were only out, not dead. They wouldn't stay down long. He had to get rid of the girl.

Lifting her chin, the woman looked up at Kaz with wide and wondering eyes. He had rescued her from a bite, surely. But the less she knew, the better. And if he could contain this slaying then he wouldn't have to call in Tor to do spin.

"Impressive." She stepped over the sprawled vampire and slowly approached him. Strangely, she clapped, giving him due reward. "Like a knight who fights for his mistress's favor."

Kaz arched a brow. He was a knight. But he couldn't tell her that. Why hadn't she screamed and run? That was the normal MO for unknowing humans who stumbled onto a slaying.

Something wrong with this chick?

As he looked her over, he took a long stroll over her black hair, streaked on one side with white. Her heart-shaped face was shadowed by the night. A soft gray blouse rippled with her movements, hugging a narrow figure. Black, high-waisted slacks emphasized long legs that ended in heeled boots. Sexy, in a business kind of way. If her lips hadn't been thick and plush and so pink, Kaz would have marked her off as just another accountant or pencil pusher.

But that mouth. All pink and partly open and—he swallowed—kissable. That mouth distracted him.

"Generally," she said, unaware of his distraction, "when the knight defeats the bad guys, his mistress grants him a favor, such as a ribbon or piece of her clothing for him to proudly display."

He rubbed his jaw and chuckled softly. "I'm not much for ribbons." But the moment jumped on him like a blood-hungry vampire and he went with the next move. "Guess that means I'll have to take something more fitting."

Kaz wrapped his hand about her neck and curved his fingers against her silken hair as he bent to kiss her distracting mouth there, in the mysterious shadows of a city he would never feel comfortable calling home. About them, the vampires showed no sign of coming to, yet he remained aware.

Two magnets, he thought, as their lips crushed, com-

pelled to one another. Soft and wanting. The burn of her
mouth against his flamed his tongue with the sweetest fire.
The connection gushed through his veins and swirled in
and out of his being. Made him feel alive, more so than
even battling vamps did.

As well, this kiss claimed a certain void within him
that suddenly breathed in, wanting to capture it all. To
experience it all.

Really? Why had he suddenly started thinking like
some kind of romance hero? It was just a kiss. He'd kissed
lots of women. He'd admired many a pretty mouth, had
shared breath with— Hell.

He'd never kissed a woman who felt quite so...right.

She wobbled on her tiptoes, and Kaz gripped her shoulder to steady her. And when he pulled from the kiss to dart
a look back and forth between her blue eyes, he suddenly
knew. He had never sensed such immediate connection
before. Destined? No, he wasn't tumbling completely over
the edge. But there were no coincidences in this world.
People didn't just stumble into another person's life ran-
domly. He'd believed that since the night Tor had found
him behind Madame du Monde's.

Everything happened for a reason.

She fluttered her lashes and looked aside. "Nice."

Nice? It had been more than nice. That kiss had been...
transcendent. Yet maybe she was too shy to wax as po-
etically as his brain was right now. No, not shy, but flus-
tered. Her cheeks had pinkened and her lashes fluttered
as she tapped her mouth. Kaz liked that he'd disturbed
her with a kiss.

"Once more?" he asked on an aching tone.

This time when she tilted up her face to meet him, he
hooked his thumb along her jaw, his fingers spreading over
her cheek. His calloused fingertips touched a raised line

of skin. Felt like a scar. She didn't flinch. Perhaps it was merely makeup or his rough fingers.

She moaned into the kiss and wrapped both hands about his waist beneath the long leather coat he wore. A greedy touch that he felt honored to receive. She wasn't like any other woman who had selfishly clung and groped at him while seeking to satisfy her desires. Kaz pulled her tight against his body. This woman fit there as no other woman had fit before. She felt right. Felt different.

Felt dangerous.

Right, man. Don't forget: vampires surround you. Get rid of her now if you want her to live long enough for another kiss.

Kaz broke the kiss. She nodded and smiled sweetly. Stepping back, she deftly navigated through the fallen men over to the backpack she'd dropped by the wall. She picked it up and hooked it over a shoulder. Kaz watched her, his lips parted, his eyes following her every move.

"I…" she began. A sweet smile struggled with uncertainty. She raked her fingers through her loose sweep of hair. "Suddenly, I don't know how to walk away from you." Her brows pulled together as she wondered about that confession.

The statement reached in and clutched Kaz's gut. It was so intimate. She didn't want to walk away? He could get behind that sentiment. He'd like to wrap her in his arms and take her home with him and leave the world behind. Unfortunately, the real world had begun to groan near his feet.

"Just put one foot in front of the other," he said, regretting the dire need to send her off.

The woman chuckled and touched her lips, as if testing to see if his warmth was still there. "What's your name?" she asked.

"Kaspar Rothstein." He walked around the circle of

vampires starting to come to. "Kaz to friends and those I tend to kiss. And you?"

"Zoë. Uh, Zoë to friends and those who tend to kiss me."

At that moment, he fell, right into her stunning blue eyes and lush pink smile. Once again, his life had changed.

"Where do you live, Zoë? In case I feel the calling to beat up a second pack of idiots in order to claim another kiss from you."

She smiled at the suggestion.

Kaz really did know about this one. *Mine.*

"Down the street." She pointed in the direction she was headed. "Cerulean door. Can't miss it. But don't follow me. You've already been granted spoils this night for your heroic act."

"As my lady wishes." He bowed grandly, sweeping out an arm as if a knight genuflecting before his mistress.

Yeah, so he had his goofy moments.

The broad grin curling her lips matched his own as Zoë turned and strolled away, casting a look back over her shoulder.

She walked with a sensuous sway to her hips that he could imagine shifting side to side between his roaming hands as he danced with her. Kaz learned a lot about a person when dancing with them. It was safe, too, when surrounded by others on the dance floor and not all alone. Alone was fine, but only after he got to know the girl. Which, unfortunately, happened rarely due to his job. Ash in his hair and bloody stakes littering his apartment tended to turn them off.

A few groans alerted Kaz. He tugged out a stake with his right hand, and reached for another with his left—missing. He patted his hip where the stake was holstered—

No stake? He swung his gaze about, sweeping the tarmac, even as the first vampire rose to his feet. Had it fallen out when he'd been fighting? Had one of the vamps grabbed if off him?

The only one who had been close enough...

"Is that so?"

He chuckled and swung toward the vampire, a direct hit dusting the air with a fog of dark vamp ash. Before the other two could even rise, Kaz jumped over each one, planted the stake over their heart and finished them in succession. Four kills.

"But no closer to the prize," he muttered. For he was on a specific mission that required he locate a one-fanged vampire who had murdered innocents.

A glance down the street didn't spy Zoë. Kaz patted his back pocket, ensuring his wallet was still there.

"Interesting."

She hadn't gone for the cash, but instead for the one thing he should never allow to fall into the hands of the uninitiated. She'd called him her rescuing knight? The woman had no idea she'd gotten his title correct.

And the distraction of that kiss wasn't putting him any closer to the vamp he needed to get his hands on. He hadn't much to go on, but how many one-fanged vampires could there be in Paris?

Once he found the culprit, he needed to go deeper, to the source behind the vampire's attack. Someone was trafficking in a dangerously addictive substance in the city of Paris. Similar to faery dust but more like faery dust times ten. Humans were not safe from the addicted vampires who went after them.

"I will put a stop to it," he muttered, and strode down the street in Zoë's wake. "First I need to get that stake back. But not until I figure out what cerulean is."

Sid sat on the marble worktable, his big green eyes intent on every move Zoë made beneath the glass cupola capping her little tower in the sky. Purrs filled the room; the cat's resonance harmonized with Zoë's work.

The seventeenth-century mansion she lived in was narrow, yet high, soaring three stories. The third-floor tower room had confirmed her decision to buy the place five years ago. Perfect for a spell room. The curved, paned-glass roof let in the moonlight and opened the room to receive from the elements of air, earth and water.

She practiced all elemental magic, save for fire, a witch's worst enemy. Though some witches were talented with fire magic, Zoë had decided to focus on a more powerful magic that could alter the molecules of any object, even living, breathing flesh. Such magic was her father's specialty, and he'd taught her the basics before he'd had to go into hiding a decade earlier.

Because of his chosen study, the witches of the Light had declared her father, Pierre Guillebeaux, warlock. The Light did not approve of molecular magic. Witches must not alter living beings in any way beyond using magic to speed up the body's natural healing process. Only shape-shifters and demons were sanctioned to physically alter their bodies. But Zoë's father believed in the healing capabilities of his magic—that someone could heal himself or herself or otherwise alter their very being—something no witch was able to do. Instead of sacrificing the study of it, he had willingly become warlock.

She missed him. Though she hadn't seen him in ten years, she knew, wherever he was, he was well, yet that didn't dispel the emptiness in her heart. Since her mother's death when she was thirteen, her father was her only family, and though she had many friends, she craved an intimate relationship.

In the center of her spell room, before the round, marble-topped worktable, she carefully went about the process of alchemizing the faery ichor that was delivered once a week from an unnamed, but obnoxious source. Zoë didn't have to like the delivery girl; she just had to take the ichor and in return hand over the finished product. It was a smooth system that had been working for the few weeks she'd been engaged in this endeavor.

The vampire Mauritius, leader of tribe Anière, had been buying her blend to distribute to his fellow vampires. He had seemed eager to spread it around, assuring her it would do well within the vampire community. He couldn't seem to get enough of her blend—which was to be expected in this neighborhood that overlapped FaeryTown—so Zoë was kept fairly busy producing the concoction.

But it must be fresh, and only produced in small amounts. That ensured efficacy. The shelf life was about a week, she figured, though she hadn't done field experiments to verify that, and had only her best friend's usage report to judge how well it actually worked.

"I can't wait to see Luc," she whispered.

She leaned forward next to Sid to watch the ichor in the alembic dance and coruscate as if stars captured under glass.

It had been two weeks since her best friend, Luc, had been around for a visit. He had been her guinea pig for the dust blend. Luc mentioned her project to his tribe leader, and Mauritius had been very interested.

Zoë set the kitchen timer for four minutes. She had to let the dust formulate a short time before adding the key ingredient.

Noticing the backpack she'd hastily dropped beside the door, she spied the steel cylinder spilling out that she'd nicked from her rescuer. So she had a habit of snatching things. It was a better vice than drinking or practicing malefic magic, wasn't it?

She retrieved the cylinder and looked it over. Was it some kind of weapon? On second thought, it might not be steel. It was light, almost like aluminum, but she suspected the metal was strong and wouldn't dent. It didn't have a product name or brand anywhere on it. On one end was impressed a symbol of four pointed bars crossed over one another in the center of a circle.

The opposite end showed a cross slit that might open if some kind of button were pushed. Narrow black pads about three inches long stretched each side of the cylinder, like grips, and when she squeezed—

A sharp tip pinioned out the end of the column with such force that Zoë let out a gasp and dropped it. The deadly thing skimmed her boots, cutting a scar in the aged black leather, and clattered onto the white tiled floor.

She bent to grab it—but didn't touch it. Its apparent use grew obvious now that the tip was fully ejected.

"A stake?"

It looked like a weapon some kind of hunter might use to stake vampires. What other purpose would it serve?

"He had been a skilled fighter. Hmm…Kaz," she whispered, her thoughts wandering.

He'd reminded her of an action-movie hero. He hadn't looked vampire or werewolf, though she would expect as much only because of the crowd with whom she normally hung around. He must have been human, because the others who had fallen at his fist had looked like standard street thugs.

There were times Zoë preferred vampires to humans. At least with vampires she knew where she stood—either as a friend or lunch. Humans were a mixed bag of nothing but misplaced mischief and accidental danger. Humans generally didn't appeal to her, yet never had one shown her such chivalry. In those moments after she had stumbled onto the fight, she had felt the damsel.

Standing amongst the men, Kaz had been outfitted in a sleek, black leather duster coat and dark clothing. Night shadows had concealed most of his face, save for bullet-like eyes that had homed in to Zoë as if there were no other place he could see. He'd tilted his head, catching the moonlight on his devastating smirk and then had shouted for her to leave. The hero protecting the damsel.

His voice had been rough and deep, yet had eased into Zoë's pores with a soul-stirring tingle. He'd spoken English, though it had been accented with something other than her native French. German, to guess from his surname Rothstein. His brown eyes had moved over her face, landing on her lips, and then along the scar that curled across one cheek—yet hadn't lingered there—till finally they'd locked onto her gaze.

If only the moonlight had been stronger, she may have seen much more, and might have gazed for endless hours at the sexy man who had defended her with muscle and might.

The timer dinged and Zoë shot upright, leaving the stake on the floor. The next part of the blend recipe must be enacted immediately.

"Now for the magic."

She tapped the glass with her matte-black-polished fingernails that were tipped in white. A smidge of secret potion was added to the faery ichor from a long, narrow vial—*tap, tap,* the iridescent particles fluttered into the alembic—and then she recited the spell that she'd worked for months to perfect after dozens of hours studying the family grimoire.

"Feé substitutuary lente."

This kind of molecular magic tended to zap her energy. All other magics barely taxed her system, though she did have difficulty wielding any magic in public. Call it a lack of confidence, or never having been taught to use her magic around others.

"Dissimulate," was the final word.

The ichor in the alembic turned purple and she knew the process had been a success. Now she need only reduce the ichor to dust, package it in vials and hand it over to Mauritius's courier, who always arrived on Sunday morning, bright and early, despite the fact she was a vampiress.

Reaching for a tray of glass vials, Zoë paused and tilted her head to listen. She eyed Sid. The cat's ears also perked.

Someone knocking on her front door after midnight?

"Unusual. Absolutely unprecedented, actually."

Leaving the spell room, she carefully locked it with a snap of her fingers. Sid pussyfooted in her wake down the iron spiral stairs that landed but a few paces from the front door, and assumed his protective stance behind her legs.

Confident of the protective barrier that shielded her threshold from vampires, werewolves and faeries, Zoë gripped the doorknob and opened it to reveal a sexy smile and beaming brown eyes.

Her rescuing knight said, "I've come for another kiss."

Chapter 2

Leather coat draped over one arm, Kaspar—or rather, the man who allowed those he kissed to call him Kaz—stood in her doorway, not crossing the threshold. Zoë could usually feel her wards tingle when an unwanted visitor activated them. Not even a *ting* in the air. He was human; she was sure of it.

Yet it was well past midnight. She never received such late callers.

"You found me," she stupidly said, glancing over her shoulder and up the stairs. The dust mix needed to sit for an hour before she reduced it, so she could manage a chat.

He rapped the bright door. "Figured out what cerulean looks like. It's so bright it glows even in the dark. Nobody could miss it. You going to invite me in?"

"Depends on what you want."

"I like a cautious woman. Smart. Especially this time of night. I've already said what I want. Another kiss. In fact, I figure I should get one kiss for every one of those bastards I laid flat. Four down. Four kisses."

"You've already taken two kisses."

He stepped up to the threshold, towering over her, but not making her feel small in any way. "Two left."

And too many ways she imagined those kisses. Long

and lush, deep and delving, hot and achy. But she hardly knew the guy.

Zoë leaned up and kissed him quickly. "There's one."

"That wasn't a kiss!"

"You didn't specify length."

He beat the door frame with a fist, but as a sign of his own frustration, nothing threatening.

"We'll call that one half a kiss," Zoë conceded, because she wasn't going to deny herself this man's delicious kisses. She may be a bit of a recluse, but she wasn't a hermit. And oh, but this felt like some kind of faery tale when the handsome prince showed up to woo the princess with glass slipper in hand.

Not that there was any slipper she could see. What girl could walk on glass, anyway, without breaking it? She preferred to keep bloodshed out of her faery tales.

Zoë crooked her finger, inviting him inside with a silent dare. Her normal cautionary inhibitions slipped away as she stood in Kaz's intent brown gaze. Sort of brown and gold blended together, she decided of his eye color. Freckled eyes alive with expression. She could stare into them all night long.

Kaz walked her up against the wall, and braced a forearm against it, paralleling her head.

"Your hair is interesting," he noted in a bemused tone. He swept his gaze down the white streak that spilled from roots to tips in an inch-wide swath.

"Does it bother you?"

"Not at all. It's pretty to look at. Like your mouth. Your lips are soft and pink and when you dash out the tip of your tongue like that I want to taste it."

"What's stopping you?"

Kiss number three landed on her mouth with a sigh and a press of skin to skin, yet it encompassed things about her that felt needy and wanting. Kissing usually happened in the dark, and during a heated race to sex. She rarely enjoyed a kiss merely for the sake of it. And the thought of starting a race felt wrong.

Such luxury he gifted her. And wrapped in a dreamy kind of faery tale she wanted to read all night long.

Inviting him to taste her breaths, Zoë opened her mouth a little wider. Kaz's tongue explored and caressed hers. Slow, lazy, he moaned as he placed his palm against her back, gently affirming his control.

And then suddenly the kiss was not there. Instead, Kaz beat the wall beside her head with a fist.

Rudely startled from the amazing fall into bliss, Zoë gaped up at the stranger she had foolishly allowed across her threshold.

"There's another reason I'm here," he said. Now his look admonished, yet curiously. "About a matter of something gone missing from my, er…person."

Zoë flashed him her best innocent cat-burglar smile, and followed with a flutter of how-can-you-not-forgive-me lashes tossed in for good measure. "Something you were carrying *before* the fight?"

"Yes."

"Whatever it was, you probably dropped it while beating on those idiots."

"Possibly, but I looked around and couldn't find the missing item. I'm inclined to believe this a case of sticky fingers."

"Huh." Zoë made a show of looking at her fingers. "My fingers are not at all sticky and—" Was that faery dust embedded in the whorls on her fingertips?

"Sparkly?" Kaz noted the shimmer despite the spare light in the hallway.

She rubbed her hands down her pants legs. "You know us women. Always putting sparkly stuff on our faces and skin. Just some glitter."

"Give me back what you took, Zoë. Please?"

He said it so gently, and yet with a sure tone of command, she simply nodded and pointed over her shoulder.

"Up there?" he asked.

With a guilty shrug, she offered, "Sometimes I can't help myself. It's a habit." It was also fun, daring and the only way she could find a thrill lately.

"I need it back. Can't buy those things at the supermarket."

"I'll uh, go get it. You wait here."

But he didn't wait in the foyer, and instead, followed her up the spiral staircase. Zoë ran the steps, beating him to the fuchsia door and turning to put up her palm.

"This is my private—" She couldn't call it her spell room. Kisses aside, she didn't know him well enough for that yet. "Uh—study. You can't go in there. You'll mess up, uh…like my vibes and stuff. I'll grab it and come right out."

There was no belief in the doubting look he gave her. The things she did to protect the magic were very necessary.

She opened the door and slipped inside, locking it behind her as she did. "Just give me a minute to find it!"

The thing she had taken sat on the floor beside her backpack. Too bad she had to return it. Whatever it was, she liked it. And well—it was *his*. He had held it in his wide, strong hand. She stroked the column, imagining his grip about it, and then her thoughts strolled to Kaz's fingers stroking her skin. Slow and soft, like his kiss. Yet also needy, as his kiss had proven.

She clutched the metal column to her chest. Could he be the rescuing knight she'd never known she needed? Did she need rescuing? Well, no. She was perfectly fine, not in any danger. But the idea of him, so masculine and take-charge—who would shove that out their front door?

A rap on the door spoke his impatience. If she were going to claim kiss number four, she'd better play nice and give him back his toy. Besides, the clock was ticking. She needed to tend the ichor blend soon.

Slipping out, without opening the door so wide he might glimpse her spell work, Zoë held out the thing with a sheepish grin.

"The tip popped out accidentally. Sorry. Is it some kind of weapon?"

He claimed it with a snatch, and compressing the side paddles, the stake part snapped back inside the column. "Something like that."

"You always carry such an interesting weapon on you?"

"Always."

"Have you…ever used it on anyone?"

"Many times."

So he was more than an innocent stranger who had happened to pick a fight with four idiots. The man knew how to handle a dangerous situation. So much so, he was always armed.

"Are you like some kind of avenging angel who rescues those in need? Have you ever killed anyone with that thing? The point is very sharp. It's less like a blade than something you would stab—"

He silenced her curiosity with a punishing yet much-desired kiss. *Don't mess with me*, the kiss seemed to say, and *don't ask stupid questions. But do let me take what I want.*

Zoë was cool with that. Very cool with that.

The man's hand glided along her jaw, sending titters of heat down her neck and chest where her nipples tightened in a pleasurable squeeze. He dived deep inside her mouth with his tongue, tasting, touching and divining. She gave him all that he wanted, and he wanted a lot.

She knew nothing about Kaspar who liked to be called

Kaz by friends and those who tended to kiss him. Save that his mouth knew exactly how to fit against hers for maximum pleasure. And that the heat of his body against hers, so wide, hard and strong, felt like some kind of ridiculous fantasy in which she was granted everything she had ever desired.

It never worked like that in real life. Not even with a healthy dose of magic tossed in for good measure.

But who was she to argue a moment of serendipity? Because truly, the stars had aligned above her home and the clouds were clearing. Never in her life had Zoë felt so connected to a man she didn't even know. The thought should frighten her, but instead, it made her want to race to the end to get to the happily-ever-after part because she didn't want to go through all that harrowing middle stuff.

It was always the middle stuff that screwed up the relationship. Secrets were revealed, bad habits discovered, kinky quirks—

Don't move so quickly forward. Stay in the here and now, Zoë.

And so she would.

Sighing into the kiss, she tilted her body toward Kaz's aggressive stance and as their hips met, he drew his fingers down her spine, coaxing her even closer with his touch. Chest to chest, she melted against his heat and strength. He made her feel delicate and pretty and so, so desirable.

A girl could become bewitched by such a kiss. And a bewitched witch was certainly a rare thing.

I want to know bewitchment.

Kaz slowly pulled away, holding her gaze as if the connection of their lips could continue in their eyes. As his thumb traced the scar on her cheek, he studied it, but didn't say anything or ask the usual questions. She didn't mind answering, but was impressed that he wasn't so hung up on the outer surface. Or maybe he was being polite.

Finally, he exhaled, stepped back and tucked away the weapon inside his coat.

"Thanks for the kisses. I've work to do," he declared in that deep, commanding tone that cued her to nod and touch her kiss-burnished lips.

He skipped down the stairs, leaving her floating on a euphoric cloud of desire and wonder, and stretching out a proverbial hand for him to return to her arms.

She was on her way to happily ever after. Her rescuing knight needed to get on the same page as her.

Once at the door, Kaz called up, "I'll be back!"

"Uh..." What to say to make him stay?

After the front door shut, Zoë fisted the air and growled. Way to drop the ball. She'd had him, and then she had not. He'd wandered out as casually and as quickly as he had appeared.

She shifted her body against the spell-room door, bending her legs to squat, and sat with her legs sprawled out across the floor. Sid nuzzled against her thigh, rubbing a kitty hug along her black pants.

She touched her mouth, still warm from Kaz's remarkable kisses. She could feel him there and imagined the sensation would not soon leave. Not if she fixed it to memory. Memory was a special kind of magic that anyone could access but few could master. The key was in sorting the good memories from the bad and never letting them intertwine.

She had her share of bad memories. A mother gone too soon, a father forced to leave her life, a friend who had once been a tormentor. But some new memories were forming, and those could only be filed under "spectacular."

Standing on his back legs, Sid nudged his head along her jaw until Zoë patted him and pulled the fat ball of fur onto her lap to snuggle.

"That man certainly knows how to kiss, Sid. And he will be back, because he won't be able to stop thinking about me. And that's not magic, that's just—" she sighed "—wishful thinking."

Sid agreed with a meow.

And Zoë decided that the bewitchment had commenced.

Kaz double-stepped it down the sidewalk that paralleled the street before the Moulin Rouge. The red-and-gold neon lights spinning round the iconic mill wheel flashed across the faces of passersby. As he turned to walk along a row of buildings that reflected the pink, green and yellow neon, he spied the informant he had earlier in the day arranged to meet walking across the Boulevard de Clichy.

He knew he was late. He should count his luck the vamp was still in the area.

Hustling and turning the corner by the Magnum club, Kaz gained on the vampire, who strolled down the Rue Lepic, hands in his pockets, oblivious to the stares he received from the passing women dressed for a night of flirtation and fun. Kaz could have called out, but he wasn't stupid. Shuffling around a couple walking hand in hand, he landed beside the vampire and slowed his stride.

"You're late," the vampire said, not glancing aside.

"Apologies. I got sidetracked."

Sidetracked kissing a gorgeous kleptomaniac. She could roam those sticky fingers all over him so long as she didn't steal the merchandise.

And why the hell hadn't he turned tail and run from her arms? He never followed a woman he'd just met around like a puppy dog. That was not his MO. The job always came first.

"Don't rush off," he tried. "I need a few minutes of your time."

The vampire stopped before a black Aston Martin. Kaz eyed the gorgeous vehicle and deeply regretted his decision to remain carless.

"V12 Zagato," the vamp offered. "Hot off the production line less than a month ago."

The curves were insane, not to mention the deep color inlaid with mica flecks that captured the glowing neon lights and flashed like some kind of supernatural conveyance.

"That is—was—a sweet ride," Kaz corrected as his gaze landed on the smashed front quarter panel, and followed the scrape that arced over the wheel well to end in a crunched side mirror.

"Still is sweet," the vampire offered. "Just a few dents."

Dents? More like a major crash. Kaz couldn't believe the tire was still attached to the axle, let alone in the shape of a circle.

"Get in before someone sees me talking to you, hunter."

Thankful for the invite, Kaz slid inside the car and had to bend his knees and shift a hip to the side to fit properly. He almost reached to adjust the seat back, but a man never touched another man's car unless he was directed to do so. Folding his hands across his knees and curling his shoulders slightly forward, he decided to mark this particular model off his wish list. Not that he needed a car to get around Paris. The Metro served him just fine. And a hunter who took the time to find a parking spot would never claim a kill.

Before he could ask a question, Kaz suddenly remembered an important detail about this particular vampire.

Twisting a frantic look over his shoulder, he scanned the backseat, down to the floor and then up along the center divider, and somehow managed to check near his feet, though it was difficult to bend too far forward.

"Green Snake is at home," the vampire provided. "Chill out, man. Don't tell me you're afraid of reptiles?"

Kaz dropped his shoulders, yet they remained slightly

curled forward in the cozy confines. "I don't like surprise reptiles, is all."

The first time he'd met the vampire, a green mamba snake had curled about his ankle as he'd unknowingly sat in the back of a limousine talking about local vampire tribes. Those things were poisonous. Apparently, though, not to vampires.

"So, Vail—"

"No names!"

He met the vampire's blue gaze, and did not miss the warning glint of fang between his compressed lips.

"Fine. Sorry."

It wasn't as if he hadn't talked to Vaillant before, and had once even had a drink with him at the Lizard Lounge, sans reptiles. Kaz made a premeditated choice to cater to this vampire's quirks to stay on his good side. Besides, they weren't all evil.

"So, Mysterious, Dark-Haired Man Who Has Never Taken A Driving Lesson And Who Wants to Give Me Information, what do you have for me?"

Vail tapped the steering wheel with fingers bejeweled in dark metal and diamonds. Black clothed him from boots to slicked-back hair. He was a vampire who had grown up in Faery (not by choice) and had returned to the mortal realm to claim a dysfunctional family (including a werewolf twin brother) and a faery dust addiction. He was supposedly clean now. If anyone had a finger on the pulse of what was going on with vampires and the dust connection, it was Vaillant.

"This dust blend you told me about is very new."

"Weeks," Kaz said. "Just hitting the market. Not many know about it."

"Exactly. Not sure there even is a market for it yet. When I mention the purple stuff fellow vamps give me a wonky look. Though the one vamp who did know what it was called it Magic Dust. And he was anxious for more. Had to beat him off with a stick."

Yep, that was the way it worked on vampires. Normal faery dust caused instant addiction. This new stuff compounded that addiction with an unreal craving for sparkly stuff. Only, sometimes the sparklies the dust freaks went after were pieces of jewelry attached to innocent humans.

"Magic Dust. Is that what they call it?"

"Yep."

Kaz hated that the substance carried an appealing name. Of course, that's how most drugs were named, to attract attention.

"You know it drives vampires crazy for anything that sparkles?"

Vail studied his knuckles, the diamonds glinting. "Nothing wrong with sparkly stuff."

"Unless it's wrapped around some human's neck, and the vampire decides to tear through it—and skin and bones—in an attempt to feed their addiction."

"You told me about your friends. I'm sorry, man. That's rough."

Robert and Ellen Horst had been murdered last week while in Paris on their honeymoon. They'd called the morning of their arrival, hoping to meet Kaz in a café to catch up. Kaz and Robert had both hung around Madame du Monde's Dance Emporium a decade earlier for reasons they'd kept to themselves.

Kaz had only arrived at the hospital five minutes before Robert had died. His friend had told him the attacker had fangs and had been crazy for his wife's diamonds and had growled about needing more dust to keep the high. As he'd exhaled his dying breath, Robert's hand had fallen open to reveal the fang he'd knocked out of his attacker's jaw as he'd fought for his and his wife's lives.

That tooth now sat in Kaz's front pocket.

"I have no clue where it's coming from," Vail offered. "None of the known dealers in FaeryTown, that's for sure. They're all sanctioned through the higher-ups, if you know what I mean."

"What does that mean, exactly? Does someone control all sales of faery dust and ichor?"

Kaz hadn't a clue about illicit drugs sold amongst the paranormal breeds, and the Order certainly hadn't an interest in it, either.

"Dust and ichor are two different highs, man. Do you even know how it all works?"

"It's a drug that makes my job a pain in the ass. What more do I need to know?"

Vail sighed and tapped the steering wheel, then turned to him. "So you've got faery dust and faery ichor. The dust is easy to obtain, and it gives a quick high. Very addictive. You get dust directly from the faery, but can also do something to the ichor to make it turn to dust. I'm not sure how that works. But it's dust form. Right?"

Kaz nodded. He understood that much.

"Vamps deal dust. But not ichor. The Sidhe Cortège controls that."

"Do I want to know what that is?"

"You should. They're sort of faery mafia that exist only in the mortal realm."

"Great." Yet another wrench tossed into his investigation. "So all ichor goes through this cortège?"

Vail nodded. "A vampire can only get ichor by going to FaeryTown and checking into an ichor den. Or he can find a willing faery and bite her. Ichor straight from the vein is amazing. Or it was. I'm clean now, man. And then there's the ultimate. The Neverland Fix."

"Explain."

"That's when a vampire has sex with a faery—you

know when a faery comes they sort of explode dust all over, right?"

He had not known that. Kaz wasn't sure he'd ever get the image from his brain.

"So if you bite them and suck out their ichor while they are coming in a cloud of dust it's like Neverland," Vail said. "Except, you ain't never coming back from that one. Total oblivion for the vamp. No chance of returning to sanity. But I've heard it's worth it."

"Is that so?" Kaz eyed his informant. He knew the vampire was a father and had many friends in the paranormal community. But how much was he keeping to himself? Did he have reason to protect those vamps who dealt dust?

"You going to some kind of AA, Dark One?"

Vail nodded. "Don't worry about me. Addiction is tough. Since I've gotten clean, I fight it every day. Good thing I have Lyric. She's a million times more appealing than ichor. But still…" He heaved out a sigh.

Kaz had never touched drugs or alcohol, himself. Too many bad memories harbored by those illicit substances. Vail's sigh said so much that didn't require words.

Kaz understood addiction because his father was an alcoholic. Okay, so he didn't *understand* it, but he did know it when it hit him in the face. The bastard was always ready to punch him whenever he got wasted, which had been all the time. Kaz hadn't seen him in almost fourteen years, and had no desire for a reunion anytime soon.

"Now that I let my mind wander," Vail started, "there is a vamp chick who slinks about under the radar. Always into something new. Not attached to a particular tribe, though she does tend to date tribe leaders. She deals dust and has been known to do wet work, as well."

Sex, drugs and murder? Sounded like a piece of work. "Name?"

Vail held up his palm between the two of them. "There

are only two or three vamps who have permission to deal dust in this city. Give me your word that this information did not come from me."

Kaz slapped his hand into Vail's in a gentleman's agreement. "You have my word. I know you supply me with information because you care about your breed. You don't want to see any of them addicted to the stuff."

"The vampire's name is Switch," Vail said. "I don't know where to find her, only that she moves around. She's tall and slender. Aggressive, but attractive in a hooker kind of way."

"Great. That describes half the female vampires in Paris."

"Yeah, but you should be able to pick her out by her hair. Half black, half pink, like some kind of cotton-candy machine gone over to the dark side."

A distinguishing hairstyle? Perfect. It would give Kaz a place to start.

"So you know the names of those two or three who sell the dust? They would be the ones giving Switch the work, right?"

"Yes, but…I don't have names. Isn't what I've already told you enough?"

It would be a start. "Thanks, Vail—er, Dark Stranger. Give my regards to your wife." He recalled the Order notes he'd reviewed before coming here tonight. "Did she just have a baby?"

"Our second," Vail offered with a note of pride. "Sweet little girl. I love her, even when she wakes in the middle of the night yowling like a banshee. Yeah, I'll tell Lyric you said hello. If you need me…I'll find you."

"Cool."

At the thought of a vampire baby, Kaz quelled the shudder that wanted to give his bones a good shake. Then he prayed he wouldn't have to stake the little flesh pricker someday.

After shaking Vail's hand, Kaz got out of the car, stroked the smashed front panel and walked away, hands in his coat pockets, without giving the vampire a glance back.

He lived on the left bank, far from the eighteenth arrondissement. Hopping onto the Metro at the Blanche station, he settled in for the ride.

Once home, he activated the inner wards by closing the four sliding locks on his front door. The Order ensured all their knights' homes were warded against vampires, werewolves and sometimes, if the knight requested it, witches. Between that and some personal wards he'd had tattooed on his body, Kaz felt relatively safe, even knowing the city of millions was populated with tens of thousands of paranormal critters.

Standing before the living room wall, plastered with a large Paris city map, he darted his gaze from the red pins, which indicated the location of tribal nests, to the white— individual vamps, to the few green pins—known wolf packs.

Plucking out a silver pin from the nearby pin box, he poked it in place in the eighteenth arrondissement.

"Zoë," he muttered. A smile was unstoppable.

"Will you find the source of the Magic Dust, little one?"

Coyote flinched at Riské's use of the possessive moniker. Yes, she was small. But she was anything but little.

"It's tainting our supply," Riské continued. The faery elder's feather headdress listed in the summer breeze that always surrounded him, even on brisk winter nights. "The idiot bloodsuckers are selling on our turf. This mortal realm is convoluted with lacking intelligence and those who would sell their very souls for another coin in their pocket."

"I've Whim sniffing out the trail," she answered, preening her left wing over her shoulder. Living in the mortal realm zapped her vitality, and she was ever concerned about her faded wings. "He's an excellent tracker."

"And what about the other one who is often stumbling about in your wake? Ever? Sever?"

"His name is Never. And he does not stumble. He's an ace marksman. My secret weapon."

"I thought *you* were my secret weapon?"

"I am, mon Grand Sidhe," she said, using the respectful title. Lately, Riské had been ignoring her for his many other consorts. She was fine with that. The sidhe lord was a fickle lover. She preferred those with a bit more devotion—and vita, which could restore the color to her wings that living in the mortal realm had drained. "I suspect the dealer is a vampire."

"Of course." He said it as if admonishing her for stating the obvious.

"I don't want to unsettle the fragile balance we have with the vampire community," she said.

"See that you do not. But do not allow this one who deems to step on my feet one moment longer of triumph. I will not accept failure from you, Coyote."

Meaning, he'd strike her dead with a look that could stop her heart if she returned without the vampire's head. Easy enough. Coyote always got her man. Or vampire. She just had to let loose her hounds, Whim and Never, and follow the trail.

Chapter 3

The knock at the front door was accompanied by a yelp.

Zoë smiled with self-satisfied glee. "I do love a well-tuned vampire ward."

She grabbed the plastic kid's lunchbox from the living room table and strode to the door with the usual spring in her step that the yelp always produced. The autumn sky was dark, promising imminent rain. Most vamps could handle the sunlight for a short time, though they did tend to grumble about it whenever anyone would listen.

A flash of pink swept before the narrow window that paralleled each side of her front door.

"Fashion nightmare," Zoë muttered before she swung open the door to grant her visitor a Cheshire Cat greeting. "You again, and looking so bright and cheery."

"Witch, your wards hurt."

"That's the purpose. You have my phone number. You can call when you're walking up the sidewalk and I'd meet you at the door."

The vampiress, tall and lanky, and built like a rock star with a permanent heroin hangover, cocked a hand to one hip, and swept back the pink half of her hair with a tilt of her head. Sunglasses concealed what Zoë guessed was a dagger gaze. She held out a waiting hand.

She was annoying, but also strong, and Zoë had no intention of pissing her off. The woman had visible muscles revealed by a sleeveless plaid shirt spattered with black ink and skulls. She wore enough silver jewelry to kill a werewolf just by being in his vicinity. And besides the head of hair that was half fluorescent pink and half Hell black, she sported a chain of earrings along each ear, henna tattoos all over her arms, a thick silver ring that looked like—and probably was—brass knuckles, and a visible knife blade sticking out her hip pocket.

Despite her many vampire friends, this one wasn't a vampire Zoë wanted to meet in a dark alley anytime soon.

Passing the lunchbox over the threshold, far enough to cross over the wards, Zoë held it there until the vampiress snatched it. Then she reached behind her leg and wheeled around one of those small, hard case travel suitcases. It was black, save for the white outline of Hello Kitty with a bright pink bow cocked above one ear. The vampire was into the iconic cat for reasons Zoë would not question.

"What's that for?" Zoë asked. "You going on vacation?"

"It's for you. The big guy wants more next pickup."

"More?"

"Dust. He said business is booming."

"Business? Well, that's…"

Awesome that her blend was being so well received. But that much more? The suitcase was six times the size of the lunchbox. She'd have to work on the blend every day until the next pickup.

Business? She'd thought Mauritius was distributing her blend free of charge. Well, perhaps he had to charge a small price to cover expenses. Ichor wasn't free—at least not in the form she required—and he did pay her for her work.

"There's cash inside to cover any additional expenses you might incur," the vampiress said. "Can I tell him you're on board?"

"Uh…" She'd hate to disappoint. And she had developed an amazing blend. It felt good to be in demand. For once in her life, Zoë had accomplished something important. Her father would be proud. "Certainly. I, uh, I've never made such a large batch. But I'll give it a try."

"You do that. Same time next week. I'd say it's been a pleasure, witch, but that would be a lie."

Lunchbox tucked under an arm, the vampiress strolled down the sidewalk and across the street toward the waiting car. She always arrived via the backseat of a fancy limo. Zoë didn't know her name. Only that she truly needed a stylist, because with a little work—and heavy metal removal—the woman could be stunning.

"Vampires," she muttered.

But she didn't follow with a scathing remark. She had many vampire friends. The very reason she made these Sunday morning meetings was for vampires.

"They need me. And I won't disappoint."

The Order of the Stake headquarters was situated in an old cathedral that offered tours of the nave during the week to tourists who had no clue a secret order devoted to extinguishing vampires existed just beneath their footsteps. An Order employee had been hired specifically for the tours and to handle the affairs topside.

While the Order dated back four centuries to inception, this building had been in use for a little over two centuries, and they'd had no problems with civilians discovering the truth bustling about beneath the stone floors.

Kaz swiped his key card and entered a secret door a few buildings down from the cathedral. He descended the stairs to the underground passageway that led to the main Order rooms.

It always gave him a shiver as he passed through the limestone passageway. It was cold down here and smelled

like death, always reminding him of the labyrinthine net-
work that ran beneath all of Paris. Hundreds of miles of
tunnels that plunged down as far as seven stories. So much
took place beneath the city proper it would stun, bemuse
and even frighten most mortals.

Here on the lower level were Rook's office, a gym and
training area and lockers. As well, the research lab offered computers that linked other worldwide Order posts
with a massive database of the paranormal breeds. While
vampires were their focus, they did like to keep tabs on
other breeds, because interaction often led to discovery.

The lab was quiet today. Kaz usually only ran into
Tor down here. The Order's spin master did a lot of research because his job required he know the breeds inside
and out—as well as how their legend and myth had been
formed in the minds of the mortals. Turning truth back
into myth was a tricky job, but someone had to do it to
protect the integrity of the organization.

The Mac computer silently flashed a screensaver of cir-
cles raked into a Zen sand garden. Kaz entered his pass-
word and opened the database. He also connected his cell
phone because the program would automatically update
his mobile files and kill stats. He loved technology, and
his phone was also hooked up to a funky security system
for his home, and everything was Wi-Fi.

In seconds he found a file on Switch that had been up-
dated within the past few years. A vampire created roughly
eight years ago, give or take a few months. Pre-vampirism,
Switch had been known to work odd jobs, such as auto me-
chanic, tour barge operator and even a stint at the Moulin
Rouge as a burlesque dancer. Once inducted into the league
of longtooths, she'd never officially joined a tribe, but preferred to hang with some of the local tribes for months at
a time before going off on her own again.

Vail had mentioned something about her hooking up with tribe leaders.

"The chick goes for the guy in charge. She's not stupid," Kaz muttered as he read further.

She was a bruiser and known to cause problems. No human losses had been associated with her vampiric activity—a good thing. Kaz did not like to kill females, but he would, if necessary. Yet Vail had also mentioned she did wet work. Did she stalk her own breed? Maybe she had a thing for taking out werewolves? The two breeds, though supposedly in accord with one another, could never shrug off their ingrained hatreds.

Werewolves were a breed Kaz avoided with a passion. When they shifted to their werewolf shape, he ran in the opposite direction. Most smart—and still breathing— knights did.

A few final notes detailed her possible age at midtwenties. Switch was most often found on the right bank, sixteenth through eighteenth arrondissements, so he assumed she must also live in that area.

Zoë lived in the eighteenth. Too close to the area he'd targeted for investigation.

Kaz sat back, closing his eyes from the screen strain, and smiled. "Cerulean," he whispered. "Who'da thought I'd like that color?"

His thoughts wandered, and the memory of Zoë's stunningly intense kisses broadened his smile. Zoë with the bright blue eyes that seemed to look for things inside him even he wasn't aware existed. Zoë with the mysterious scar dashing her cheek, which didn't lessen her appeal, but did make him want to learn how it had happened so he could crush the offender's skull. Ex-boyfriend? He hoped not. Maybe it had been a car accident?

Scars were plenty in his world; that was for sure. Kaz bore his own inner scars, and a few on the surface.

He could fight vampires fist to fist and win, but a well-matched fight usually ended in a new battle scar. And a pile of ash. His kill count was high, and would remain so, because the damned vamps kept making more.

He wondered if Zoë was aware of the paranormal world that existed around her, and then decided she was lucky to remain naive. Good thing he'd been able to avoid staking the vamps while she had been watching last night. He would have hated to introduce her to all things fanged and vicious in such an abrupt manner.

Despite every molecule in his being that warned how difficult it was for him to commit to any kind of relationship, he definitely wanted to see her again. Because man could not survive by the fight alone. He needed kisses, and skin contact and all that messy, exciting stuff involved with sex.

And how could the rescuing knight not return for the damsel?

Yet could he manage it without bringing along the danger of the world he lived in?

"Rothstein."

He hadn't heard Rook enter the lab, and stood quickly to face his supervisor. Initially his teacher, Rook had also become Kaz's mentor over the years. The man had a way about him. Stealthy and silent as the wind, Rook was a master of all martial arts. After Kaz had earned his trust and a bed in the Order's broom closet to sleep after a long, grueling day of training, Rook had trained Kaz for a year before he'd been knighted by the founder, King, and officially accepted into the Order. At seventeen, Kaz had been the youngest knight to take vows.

Live to serve. Serve until death. Die fighting. Words he lived by.

"Afternoon, Rook." The name was a moniker, he knew, and Kaz had no curiosity about his real name. In a job like this, a man had to protect himself with every measure available.

Rook leaned in and read the computer screen. "What's she up to? Is Switch involved in the faery-dust incident?"

"Possibly. It's a lead my informant gave me."

"She's all sorts of suspicious, but I'd never task her with human murders. Werewolves, on the other hand..."

That answered Kaz's suspicion about what sort of wet work the vampiress did.

"You know, I've been thinking about something since assigning you this job," Rook said. "If this new blend of faery dust—"

"They're calling it Magic Dust."

"Is that so? Huh. Well, if it is making vampires go after one another, maybe we should stand back and let them at it. That solves our problem, doesn't it?"

"But that's the thing. The longtooths aren't killing one another for this new blend. It's different than the usual stuff. It—I don't know—it won't let them go. It's as if it builds up in their system and never shuts off, which compels them to seek more of the dust."

"Like meth," Rook commented.

"Yes." Kaz had researched methamphetamine just days ago. "The drug turns on the dopamine in the brain and never shuts it off. It's like an overflowing faucet. Unfortunately, vampires on this stuff go ape-shit for anything sparkly, thinking it's faery dust. They murdered my friends, Rook. I *will* make it stop."

Rook crossed his arms over his chest, an uncharacteristic move. He was always on the alert, hands free at his sides, prepared. He shook his head. "Family and friends are never safe once ensconced in your world."

He knew that. And that was the toughest pill to swallow.

"Don't let sorrow for your friends jeopardize your focus out in the field, Kaspar."

Kaz lifted his chin.

"You want revenge for the death of your friends? I gave it to you with this assignment. But first and foremost, we need to get to the core of the operation and find the origin of this insipid drug."

"I will do that."

"Not if you take out the vampire who killed your friends in a blind rage. Keep your wits about you, man. You'll need him to lead you to the operation."

"I'm aware of that, and intend to do just that."

The knights vowed only to slay those vamps that presented a clear threat to humans. Of course, each knight had his own scale of gauging threat level. Kaz counted the vampire lethal when he killed, and not before then. The vampire who had killed his friends was still out there. And he had only one fang. That should go a long way in identifying his perp.

"Once this Magic Dust circulates and becomes easy to obtain," Kaz said, "half the vampire population in Paris could flip out."

Rook sighed and tapped the computer screen. "And you think Switch can lead you to the source? She's a hard one."

"So it seems. But it's the best lead I've got."

"Don't let this become a war. The last thing the Order needs is a human to see the veil pulled aside and witness hunters staking vampires."

As had almost happened the other night when Zoë had stumbled onto the slaying.

"Make it quick, clean and quiet, Rothstein."

"I will."

"Keep me apprised," Rook said, and he walked out, leaving the lab door open.

Kaz reread the info on Switch. There were a few details that would aid him in overpowering her. One being that it was believed a vamp from the Anakim tribe had created her (though that information was only hearsay). That tribe of vampires was not immune to sunlight.

Sunset would be the optimal time to go looking for her.

Walking home from the grocery store, Zoë inhaled the evening air. She loved crisp, cool autumn. In this kind of weather she often wore ankle boots and tweed slacks and a snuggly, solid-colored sweater, along with her mother's diamond pendant at her neck. Classic and cozy.

In her recyclable bag, fresh veggies nestled against a crusty baguette. The celery, leeks and potatoes would make a nice stew that should last her—and Sid—a few days. Now that she needed to increase production for her buyer, she would be working nights through the week.

Now, if only Luc would give her a call. She'd stopped by his apartment last week, but no one was home. She felt sure it was tough getting over a broken engagement, but to fall victim to such an addictive drug as faery dust? She'd thought Luc stronger than that, but then again, she knew he had a dark side that sometimes lured him to do things out of character. Best to give him the distance his very soul must require.

Turning the corner toward her house, she passed by the narrow alley that was heaped with the neighbor's discarded, bent-iron bed frame. Kicking the fallen leaves, she delighted in the *schushing* chorus that responded.

Grunts echoed from down the cobbled alleyway, and she paused, stepping back beside a shed wall so as not to be seen as she peeked around the corner of the building.

About fifty yards away, three men and one woman stood over a fallen man. In seconds the man who had been prone leaped to his feet and swiped a threatening weapon toward his attackers. With each movement, the tails of his long, black leather coat dusted the air like bat wings.

Clinging to the rough brick, Zoë recognized one of the

attackers. The vampiress with the bright pink hair—the very vampire she had hoped to never meet in a dark alley. She stood flanked by two others to her right and one to her left.

The other man, the object of the vampires' scorn, was human. She recognized him, as well.

"Kaz," she whispered, then checked herself to be sure she'd not spoken too loudly.

Why was he standing up to four vampires? And doing an excellent job of it, since he wasn't bleeding or dead.

Yet.

Did the man pick a fight wherever he went? He'd easily taken down four men the previous night. But tonight's opponents were vampires. They had double, or even triple the strength of the strongest human man, not to mention a supernatural agility and speed.

The vampiress chuckled and checked Kaz with an expert kick, which landed her high-heeled boot aside his jaw. Her henchmen followed closely with more brutal punishment. None went at Kaz alone; they attacked en masse. One wrenched Kaz's arm around behind his back, which caused Kaz to cry out in pain.

Kaz fell to his knees. The guy was outnumbered.

"I just want to talk," he managed, then spat blood to the side. "We don't need to do this. I made no move to harm you or your buddies."

Narrowing her gaze, Zoë saw that the weapon he held in his free hand was a stake. The very stake she'd stolen from him? How many people carried stakes on them unless they expected to get into a tussle with a vampire?

Why hadn't she considered the possibility he was a hunter last night?

You were too googly-eyed at the time, remember?

Right. Rushing head-on into happily ever after and kicking her glass slippers aside with abandon.

A kick to Kaz's back flattened him. His head was crunched under one of the vampiress's boot heels, and blood sputtered from his mouth.

Zoë cringed. The urge to rush for him, to help him in some way, had her teetering on the balls of her feet— but she wasn't stupid. If Kaz couldn't stand against the vampires, what could one feeble witch do but make it ten times worse?

From where she stood, she could fling some magic at them, but again, that would draw unnecessary attention to her. And she couldn't feel the magic that normally hummed at the tips of her fingers because right now she was anxious. She could never access her magic unless she was calm.

"Don't kill him," she muttered as the female bent and wrenched up Kaz's head by a hank of his hair.

Fangs exposed, the vampiress lunged for Kaz's neck, yet the tips of those fangs did not prick skin. Releasing Kaz as if electrocuted, the vampiress jumped back, cursed and smacked a fist into her palm as she again swore aggressively.

Spitting on the fallen man, whose eyelids fluttered, the vampiress hissed something Zoë could not hear. Then she marched off, her henchmen in tow.

They didn't intend to kill him? Rarely did a vampire let a human go free without, at least, a bite. And all encounters were usually removed from the human's mind with persuasion, a means to enthrall the memory from their minds. It hadn't appeared as if any of the vampires had taken the time to enthrall Kaz.

Zoë waited until the vampires were out of sight, then dashed down the alley and squatted beside the fallen man. He bled from his mouth, ear and his split knuckles. Apparently, he'd gotten in a few good punches.

The stake he'd wielded lay beside his head. Acting on

some sort of emergency autopilot, she shoved the stake inside his inner coat pocket, then lifted him by the shoulders. Her heel slipped on the leaf-strewn cobbles as her struggles nearly toppled her. He was heavy, and he wasn't helping her much because he was bleary. Zoë noticed his coat collar was edged with blades. She hadn't noticed them the other night. Strange fashion statement. She had to be careful not to get cut.

"You need to get out of here before they come back. I don't know why she didn't bite you. You're one lucky guy. Come on. I'm going to help you to stand, but you're a big guy. You gotta do some work, too. Kaz?"

With a mumbling grunt, he struggled to his feet as if drunk. She suspected that the bruise on his temple had him dancing in and out of consciousness. But he managed to hook an arm over her shoulder and stumbled along beside her. She had to abandon the grocery bag. With luck, she could run back to get it before someone nabbed it or a rat found the booty.

Zoë led him toward her home, maneuvered him through the door and deposited him on the couch in the living room. It took some delicate finessing to get the coat off his shoulders without cutting herself. His black T-shirt had torn to reveal a monstrous bruise below his ribs and along the side of his torso. A kidney shot. That one must have hurt like a mother.

"You're going to need a magical touch," she said. "Fortunate for you, I can help you with that."

She stood over him, spread her feet and smacked her palms together. Rubbing them slowly to heat her palms, she recited a healing spell, closing her eyes and focusing on the resonation of her voice as it touched the air. The healing she performed went beyond herbs and potions that most Light witches used. Her father had taught her this magic, and she used it in all aspects of her magical needs.

Words fading, but sound rising, she hummed deep in her throat, centering the vibrations in her chest as she laid her hands over Kaz's body.

At what she knew was an electrifying touch, Kaz's chest pulsed upward and his arms flailed. Alert, he moaned, looked down over what she was doing, then, still discombobulated, settled back into the couch. Zoë spread her palms over his chest and shoulders and down his arms and hands, humming constantly to maintain the magic's resonance. At his ribs, she concentrated the healing vibrations.

Sensing the shock of her magic as it permeated his skin, the man groaned again.

The healing had been laid upon flesh and bone. Now, to make it permeate. Rubbing her palms together again, she summoned a soothing numbness spell to tender his pains. Blowing the visible white mist toward his wounds, she noted that he blinked and opened his eyes.

The man saw the magic, and muttered, "Y-you're a witch?"

"Yes."

"Witches creep me out." And he passed out.

"Is that so?" Zoë righted, hands on her hips. "Well, this creepy witch just reduced your healing time from a week to less than half a day. Ungrateful bit of…"

She sighed. It was bad karma to be angry with someone who hadn't asked for it. He probably wasn't aware of what he had said. Pain often blurred rationality. She was thankful he was here, and not in the alley bleeding out, an open buffet for another vampire to come and snack on him.

But now a new problem had arisen. She may very possibly be harboring a hunter in her home. And for a witch who was friends with vampires, that was not a good thing.

Chapter 4

Kaz came to with a snort. Blinking his eyes, he squinted. Hmm, the ceiling was too high. The cloying scent of oranges and cinnamon concerned him, as well. His apartment usually smelled like the fake pine stuff the cleaning lady used during her monthly visits. And the couch he laid on felt hard and militant, not soft and lumpy like his.

Where was he?

He sat up abruptly, slapping a palm to his side where an ache pulled at his muscles and prodded his ribs. Curiously, that didn't hurt as much as he expected it should.

His shirt was off, and he poked at his side. One of the vamps had shanked him in the ribs with a steel-toed boot. The blow had battered his kidney, dizzied his senses and taken the fight from him. Yet why was he not doubled with pain right now?

Rarely was he bested by his opponents. Four vampires? No problem. And he'd thought he'd had an advantage over Switch, finding her as the sun was setting and catching her not at full strength. Not true at all. She hadn't been weak or seemingly fearful of the sun. And she'd had her henchmen, who hadn't fought fairly, going at him all at once.

Stroking his fingertips along his neck, he searched for the inevitable wound, but his skin was smooth, save for the two-day stubble that reminded him he needed to shave. No bites? He'd almost forgotten. He wore a ward against vampires behind his ear. Whew.

Suddenly, Kaz's vision landed on something soft and blue. Ruffles. The blue fabric danced around the hem of a black, pleated, wool skirt that stopped just above a pair of shapely knees. And higher, the narrow waist of that same black wool led up to a tiny blue bow centered between breasts that rose in soft mounds from the low neckline.

Mmm, now that looked like something that would eradicate the pain, if only he could touch...

Zoë's hair swished to one side as she tilted her head and flashed him a bright smile. "Rise and shine, Kaz. I have breakfast."

Breakfast? He had just been fighting.... But the room was light. Had he slept here on Zoë's couch all night?

"Chia pudding and blueberries."

She placed a bright yellow pottery bowl in one of his hands and held out a spoon, which he took without averting his eyes from her too sunny smile. Plucking out a blueberry from the bowl, she held it to his lips and, still trapped in a worshipful daze, Kaz opened his mouth to accept the offering.

Sweetness gushed across his tongue, even as he puzzled over the situation. As well, sweetness stood over him like some kind of Nightingale nurse rocking the schoolgirl look. What a sight to wake to. Unexpected, but he'd take it over what might have happened had he been left to lie in the alley all night.

Had he walked here on his own? He couldn't recall much after taking the kidney punch. Had there been white smoke and chanting involved?

"They're fresh." She tapped the bowl. "I picked them this morning."

Zoë sat on the coffee table before the couch. Her eyes

were brighter than the sky after a summer rain, and her pink smile looked almost sneaky. Or was she sizing him up, trying to figure what next she'd steal from him?

He wondered where his stake was, and if he should search her. Not a bad idea, running his hands over those soft swells, emphasized by that tiny blue ribbon. Her breasts looked so full and firm. Maybe if he sort of fell forward and collapsed against her and nuzzled his face against them...

Whew! Kaz shook his head. Apparently, he still didn't have his wits about him.

His fingers conformed about the warm bowl but he had no appetite for food, only a strange spinning at the fore of his brain, and a growing curiosity. "How did I get here?"

"You don't remember?" He liked the husky edge to her voice. Bedroom sexy, but smart at the same time. "You've slept all night. I watched the vampires attack you in the alley. Since my place was close, I helped you walk here. How's your side?"

She'd witnessed him take that hellacious beating? *Way to go, hunter.* Good thing he hadn't had the opportunity to stake any of them. He was slacking. And why was that?

Because a sexy mouth and a pair of enticing breasts kept luring him back to this woman who felt right. And what was wrong with that?

He eased a couple fingers along his torso. "Doesn't hurt as much as I think it should. I took a punishing shot to the kidney. Normally, I could have held my own against four miserable—er..."

"Vampires?" she offered sweetly. "I'm sure you could have," she said with a bit too much forced reassurance.

"Vampires? Come on. You've been watching too much TV."

"You don't have to put on an act for me, Kaz. I could plainly see they were vampires. The pink-haired one tried to bite you, but she stopped before sinking in her fangs. Weird. Most vamps would never pass up a free meal like they did you."

Kaz's jaw dropped open. Bloody hell, the woman knew too much. And he was damned if he didn't wish for some kind of persuasion like the vampires used so he could take that memory from her mind.

"You can sit up with little pain because of the magic," Zoë said. "It's a healing spell. Speeds up the healing process remarkably. Another two or three hours and you should be good as new."

Magic? Kaz now remembered bits and pieces of last night. Something about her chanting a spell as he'd groaned deliriously. Her hands had moved over his skin as if they were heated instruments designed to soothe and suck out the pain. He'd seen a white mist float before him, and had known it was magic, had just *known*.

"You're a witch."

"Aren't you perceptive."

Her snark didn't rile him. He could deal with anything a female put to him. Except, apparently, three surprise henchmen. Damn, he should have had those vamps last night. But he hadn't wanted to use the stake when his only intention had been to talk and get information. That decision may have proven a mistake.

Another blueberry plucked from the bowl was placed at his mouth, and Kaz dutifully ate the juicy offering.

"And you are some kind of vampire hunter, yes?" Zoë blinked sweetly, awaiting his answer with wondering blue eyes.

He hadn't wanted to reveal himself like this. A knight was more discreet. But she couldn't have pinned him as a knight from the Order of the Stake, so that important detail was still a secret.

"Something like that," Kaz replied.

He glanced to the table. Beside Zoë's thigh lay his leather coat, folded in half, and on top of that lay the titanium stake. Enough damning evidence right there. But she'd already held the stake in hand and she hadn't seemed to figure him out then.

"What's that?" She nodded toward his shoulder.

Kaz slapped a hand over the brand he'd received upon taking vows with the Order. "Just a teenage thing. You know, crazy dare. Something like that."

"Uh-huh," she uttered, tons of disbelief dripping from the nonwords.

"You know too much," he said.

"I know as much as any other paranormal breed should know about the world and all its wonders."

Kaz sighed and shook his head. She was a freaking witch. That put a new spin on the situation.

"You didn't kill the vampires. Interesting," she noted.

Kaz licked his lips. Her lips were the color of raspberries. Kissable, despite the fact she was a witch.

"From where I was standing, it appeared as if you didn't even try to stake your opponents. You were defending yourself, yet were unwilling to make a kill."

"There was no need to slay them. I only take out those who harm humans. And I only wanted to talk. Unfortunately, vamps don't like talking to hunters. So you're a witch?"

She placed a hand over his, which still clutched the spoon, on his thigh. "We're talking about you now, Kaz. We'll get to me later."

Something about her touch baffled him. And then it did not. He couldn't remember when he'd last been touched with such kindness. And that scared the hell out of him.

"So," she said, "what did you want to talk to the vampires about?"

"Can't tell you that."

"Secret hunter stuff?" She winked and those long, dark lashes devastated his need to remain unaffected by her sensual allure. And that annoyed him. Because she was forcing business to merge with pleasure and he didn't like to do that. It never ended well.

"I'll give you that," she said. "I suppose hunters have to be all secretive to get the job done. Like Batman."

Batman? "I don't have a cape."

"Too bad. I bet you could work the cowl-and-cape look with that handsome square jaw. The stubble is sexy, you know."

A flutter of those lashes and he wanted to grab the woman and kiss her soundly. Wrap her in his arms and crush her body against his. And taste her, lick her everywhere, until he memorized her flavor.

"So I creep you out, eh?" she asked suddenly.

"Huh?"

Zoë took the spoon from him, dipped it in the weird gray pudding stuff, and lifted it to his mouth. Kaz absently opened his mouth and let her feed him. A blueberry burst on his tongue.

"Last night when I was invoking the healing spell you said witches creep you out." She spooned him another bite. "And I assume, since I am a witch, that included me."

"No, you could never— I didn't mean—" He pushed away another spoonful. Stuff was…weird. And he was sitting here, being fed by a witch. "Well, hell. You're all kinds of surprises this morning, aren't you?"

He wasn't going to get into this argument with her. Witches were not his favorite creatures. Something about them did creep him out, but what was it? He couldn't recall the exact reason for his heebie-jeebies.

Kaz grabbed the spoon from Zoë, dropped it in the bowl and shoved it toward her.

"You need to eat. Build up your strength."

"I need to leave."

"Not for another few hours. I want to keep you here until I know the spell has worked."

"I'm fine." He pushed up and swung his legs over the side of the couch. His brain wobbled inside his skull, and briefly, he saw two witches sitting before him. "Why do I feel so woozy?"

"The spell is rushing through your system, doing its thing. It'll require all bits and pieces of you to work cohesively to heal the damaged parts. So you won't feel right until it's completed. Lie back." She shoved the bowl into his hands. "And finish your pudding."

She stood. Kaz's eyes veered directly to those blue ruffles above her knees. A dash of his tongue—right there—would taste the curve behind her knee, and he knew the flavor would satisfy him like no bowl of goopy gray stuff ever could.

"When you feel less dizzy, I've set out some towels in the bathroom. I'm washing your shirt right now. It was spattered with blood—probably your own. I could clean your pants...?"

"They're fine," he said quickly of his leather pants.

"You sure? I won't look."

The situation was getting intimate. Fast. And what was wrong with that?

You don't do the intimate with someone you hardly know. You screw them and leave. You know this woman. It's too late for a quickie, never see you again, sweetie.

She'd already nestled her ribbons and raspberry lips into a place in his brain. *Good luck getting her out, buddy.*

She turned and strode out of the living room.

"You don't creep me out, Zoë." He whispered the words as his brain fogged and his heavy eyelids fell shut. His grip softened about the pottery bowl.

"Pretty..." was the last word he could manage before

surrendering to his body's need to shut down while the spell worked to heal his wounds.

Zoë smiled to herself as she moved the clothes from the washer into the dryer. Pretty, eh? The man hadn't been all there in the head when he'd muttered that. As he hadn't been in full grasp of his senses when he'd muttered about creepy witches.

She hoped.

The blood had come out of his black shirt thanks to her homemade herbal detergent with an extra touch of earth magic. She tossed it into the dryer and sprinkled in some cloves to imbue a pleasing scent into the fabric, though she was a little sad she'd washed away the leather-and-licorice scent from his shirt. It still lingered on his skin, though. Goddess, but the man smelled like a treat.

But she had much better things to do than household chores and tending the sick, no matter how delicious the patient smelled. A whole lot of faery ichor needed processing and her time was valuable. But she couldn't work while the hunter was in her house because that might tempt him to climb the stairs to see what she was doing. Her work wasn't a secret. She just liked to keep her spell room sacred and never allowed others inside.

"Protect the magic," she muttered. "Always and ever."

Her parents had taught her that. One slip on her father's part had branded him warlock. It was a hard life to live in the shadows with few friends, but there were days Zoë suspected her father preferred such a life. He'd always been quiet, almost to the point of reclusive.

As she wandered into the kitchen, curiosity over Kaz's encounter with the vampires last night crept up on her. If he'd no intention of killing them, and had only wanted to talk with them, she wanted to know why. Because the pink-haired vampiress was involved in her life in an important way.

Had Kaz's curiosity anything to do with something "Pink" had done?

"Couldn't be related to me," she muttered, while setting the breakfast dishes in the sink. "I hope not." She and Pink had no relationship whatsoever; only business connected them. "I'm doing nothing wrong," she said with a lift of her chin. "And hunters don't involve themselves in the kind of stuff I'm working on, anyway. Do they?"

There would be no need to. Why, the hunter should appreciate her efforts.

She heard the shower running. The image of Kaz in the buff popped into her thoughts. Now, that would be a beautiful sight to take in. The way his eyes had danced up her legs and to her breasts after he'd first woken had made her feel as if he were drawing his fingers along her skin. Slowly, lingering, feeling out the curves on her body. And she'd felt every long gaze seep through her pores.

She smiled at the delicious notion that he had been assessing her charms. In that moment of assessment, she had wanted to kiss him, but he'd been out of sorts. Probably she misunderstood his interest in her as woozy discombobulation produced by the spell surging through his system.

She was rushing toward happily ever after and wasn't even sure the man was on the same page. Well, of course he wasn't. They'd only just met. But his kisses had definitely turned a few of her pages.

She placed the clean plates on the drying rack. She couldn't condone anyone causing harm to another living being. Not unless it was justified. If a vampire had harmed a human, or even killed them, then yes, she had no problem with a hunter ending their life. But not if the vamp was merely drinking from humans to survive—as they must do, for cold blood from blood bags did not sustain life.

If they did only that, never taking too much, and leaving the victim enthralled in a sensual swoon, then hell no, she would never stand for a hunter thinking he had the right to end that vampire's life.

Kaz was not the sort to irrationally take another's life. She sensed that. He wore honor like a flag, though he didn't wave it blatantly about as if he needed the accolades for his bravery. He'd only wanted to talk to the vampires last night. And she had plainly seen he had done his best not to harm them. To his detriment.

"I feel one hundred percent better."

Kaz strolled into the kitchen, dark leather pants low on his hips and droplets of water still glistening on his broad, wide shoulders. His short, wet hair was tousled this way and that, and where there had been bruises last night on his chest, ribs, jaw and temple, now there were none, save the fading mark over his kidney.

She studied the raised scar on his shoulder. It looked like a brand, some sort of symbol. Where had she seen it before? Recently. He'd gotten it when he was a teenager? The things kids did when they were drunk.

"How does your side feel?" she asked. "That was an awful injury."

"It's still tender, but I'm good to go. You have my shirt?"

"Another half an hour for the dryer cycle to finish. Let's sit." She strolled into the living room and sat, patting the couch beside her. "If it's still tender, I want you to relax until my magic has completed its work."

"It was a healing spell, eh?" he asked. "You witches are into that kind of stuff? Healing?"

She noticed his gaze strayed to her cheek, and the scar, and could read his unspoken thoughts. "Witches are enlightened beings. We're all about resonance, harmonics and frequency. As is the body both mortals and immortals inhabit."

Zoë again patted the couch.

With a sigh, he sat next to her, stretching his arms across the back. Zoë wanted to snuggle against him and draw in his darkly sweet scent, but, sensing she may not have judged him correctly for his comment about creepy witches, she sat forward, elbows on her knees, and twisted her head to the side to eye him.

"The paranormal breeds tend to heal instantly," she said, "or very close to that. Humans, on the other hand, take a lot longer. Without my magic you would have been swollen and groaning this morning."

"Whatever you did, I appreciate it. You're not at all creepy."

She smiled and that summoned a smile on his lips, which were oh so thick, and his teeth gleamed like some kind of movie star.

Kissable was the word at the tip of her tongue, but Zoë feigned disinterest.

"You must have encountered a creepy witch at some time?" she asked.

"When I got this." He tilted his head to reveal a curved tattoo behind his ear half covered by his hair.

Zoë inspected what looked like black tribal markings about an inch long and as wide as her finger. "Is that a spell tattoo?"

He nodded. "Keeps vamps from biting me. Not sure how it works, only that it does. Comes in handy in my line of work."

"I imagine so. The only witch who does spell tattoos is—"

"Sayne," he offered. "And if you don't agree that dude is creepy, well then…"

Sayne, an ink witch who had no known home and traveled the world, inked spell tattoos. He was known to be quiet and respectful and very wise. But as for creepy? Yes, she had to concede he was, for the witch's entire body was covered in tattoos. His face looked like a skull with black ink hollowing his eye sockets, and a partial brain exposed as if the top of his skull had been sawn off. The one time she'd met him, she'd been distracted by the inked image of a corpse worm crawling across that exposed brain.

"He is creepy, but kind," Zoë said.

"Apparently, I'm only one of two humans the witch has ever agreed to do a tat for."

"You must have charmed him."

"Either that or the thick stack of cash I whipped out had something to do with it."

"I'm glad you have the tattoo. Had one of them bitten you last night I might have had to rush out to save you. I wanted to fling some magic at them, but it tends to be less than reliable when I'm under stress."

"That would not have been smart. I held my own. Mostly. I'm a little embarrassed you witnessed what is a rarity for me."

"A rarity?"

"Getting my ass kicked."

"Your ass is fine." At least it looked well and fine in those snug jeans he wore. "It's your kidney that took the licking. If I hadn't been there you might have bled out in the alley."

The man suddenly sat upright, puffing up his chest. "I wouldn't go so far as to say *bled out*. I might have lain there in pain awhile, but eventually I would have pulled myself up and staggered home."

"But you prefer that I decided to toss in a little magical intervention?"

"Can't deny your touch made me feel better." His fingers stroked her leg and landed on the ruffle above her knee. "Pretty."

He'd said the same about her earlier. She threaded her

fingers through his and he turned his up to clasp within hers. Zoë felt a grin start deep in her soul. Holding hands was so simple a connection. Yet it quickened her heartbeat and warmed her skin.

"Uh, I should…" She gripped his hand tighter when she sensed he wanted to tug away. "…get going soon."

Why was he so insistent upon leaving? "Wait for your shirt to finish drying. Just a few more minutes."

"Right." He slapped a hand to his bare chest as if he'd forgotten he was half-naked.

Zoë had not.

She leaned across him to check his side. The bruising was almost gone. Take that, witches who daren't dip into molecular magic. Their healing touch would take much longer.

"Looks better," she said.

Their faces were close. She could feel his breath mingle with hers. And the only thing that could happen, did. They connected in a rush of need and desire. Spreading her hand across his chest, Zoë felt the steady pulse of his heartbeat as she deepened the kiss, wanting to take all of him into her being as if he were a new kind of magic she needed to study.

He pulled her closer, slipping a hand around the back of her head and into her hair. The possessive move sent a giddy thrill through Zoë's system. She liked the way he took control, coaxing, as if the only place she belonged was against him.

Her body moved of its own volition, one leg sliding across his lap, until she straddled him. Nibbling his thick lower lip, she smiled against his mouth and his return smile made her giggle.

But he suddenly bracketed her face and pulled from the kiss, his eyes searching hers. "This changes things," he said.

"What? This? You mean *us* this? Are we an us?"

"You. Being a witch. And me, being what I am."

"No, it doesn't. Why do things have to change? They've only just begun." She kissed him again. He did not pull away. He wanted this connection as much as she did. She wouldn't allow him to deny it. "I'm no danger to you."

"No, you're not, but whenever I think about you—and I think of you a lot—I thought you were human, like me."

She wrinkled her nose. "Is being human so important to you?"

"Maybe. I don't know." He leaned in for another kiss, but Zoë moved back, unsure now. "It's not important. Hell, yes, it is. It's just— I've never done this with anyone who was not human. Kissing, and…making out."

Trying not to be offended only made her all the more offended. Zoë began to slide off his lap when Kaz gripped her by the shoulders and, hands gliding down her back, pulled her to him forcefully, and landed a kiss on her mouth that she could not escape.

And did not want to escape.

While she did not care for any man who would rule out another breed as a potential romantic partner, she decided to give him the benefit of the doubt. If he'd not ever had a partner out of his breed, then his leeriness was justified. She wasn't different from the average human female, save that she could cast magic, press her body and mind beyond average mortal limitations and could have immortality if she chose it. She hadn't made up her mind regarding that life-prolonging measure yet.

"I said that wrong," he offered, his thumbs stroking her cheeks as his eyes flitted back and forth between hers. For a moment, his thumb stroked the scar and Zoë winced. Was it the scar? Did that turn him off? "I've been saying all the wrong things, and yet, you still want to kiss me?"

"Kaz, resisting your kisses is futile."

"I could say the same. Your mouth is better than blueberries in chia pudding, that's for sure."

"Maybe I can teach you that witches are nothing to be afraid of."

"I'm not afraid of you."

No, he wasn't. But something about her made him stumble over his words and she suspected what it was. "Does the scar offend you?"

"What? No. Well—"

"It does bother you." She pulled a strand of hair across her cheek, an involuntary action she'd developed after getting the scar a decade earlier. "I can't heal myself."

"Zoë, don't hide it like that. It doesn't bother me. You are—well, perfect would be boring. No one is perfect. What does bother me is that you obviously suffered to have received such an injury. I hate that someone did this to you, or something. Was it an accident?"

Zoë shrugged. "Kind of."

Sighing heavily, he nodded. "I get that you don't want to talk about it. I'm inexperienced with this conversation kind of stuff. I'm more of an action man."

"More kisses, less talk? Your kisses are toe-curlers. And as a hunter, you must know about all the various breeds, so it's not as if you're a bumbling human who has no clue about witches."

"True. You're as close to human as any breed gets. Though I'm not sure how all the magic works. Let's just say I'm much better at running away from things like this. Okay?"

Things like emotional stuff, she suspected. What guy was good about that kind of thing? But she wasn't going to award him any prizes for such honesty. If she expected more of him, he would give it to her.

"You haven't fled yet, so I'll mark myself as lucky."

"But I'm trying, trust me. I'd be at the door right now were you not sitting on me."

"That creepy, huh?"

He shook his head and kissed her quickly on the mouth. "I like you, Zoë. But there are things going on in my life right now that could complicate the good stuff happening between the two of us. And believe me, this is very good."

"Like things with vampires?"

"Always with vampires. I'm currently working a job that I don't want you to get tangled up in."

"I've no desire to tread the grounds a hunter walks. But…" She traced her fingers down his bare chest. "I do want to tread this. You can't work all the time, can you? Daylight doesn't seem the optimal time to track vampires."

"It's not, but—"

"Then kiss me again."

"Sounds good, in theory."

"You really are skittish."

He heaved out a sigh.

Zoë sensed a distraction from his deeper thoughts was a necessity. Leaning in, she lingered before his mouth, not touching, waiting to see if he would take what she offered. She dusted her lashes and they fluttered against his cheek.

Kaz's kisses touched her lips, her cheeks, the lobes of her ears. He explored down her neck and skimmed his tongue across her breasts' exposed curves. The square neckline did not allow for further access, and Zoë bemoaned the prim dress style.

But no. She did and she did not want to tear off clothing. While rushing into kisses, and tastes and touches could lead to sex, that was an entirely different chapter she hadn't even gotten to yet. Happily ever after would come with patience and a slower turn of the page.

She didn't want to scare him off. Especially when he'd confessed an urgent need for escape. Slow and exploratory felt right. Because she knew little about him, and suspected she had only peeled back the first layer of Kaspar Rothstein. Beneath, he harbored many layers that she would be wise to cautiously seek out and carefully explore.

The dryer beeped that the cycle had finished. Kaz nuzzled his kisses between her breasts and then up along her neck.

"You smell good. Peaches?"

"And cinnamon. You like? Men usually do like the food scents."

"Speaking of which, I'm starving."

"You should have finished the chia pudding."

"Yeah, I'm not so into all that healthy stuff."

"You should be." She bent to kiss his pectoral. "You want to keep these muscles hard as rocks, you should feed them properly."

"I eat well. Protein and veggies. But chia? That doesn't sound remotely foodlike."

"Okay, I'll give you that. It does require a certain palate. I can make you some lunch. Or how about I take you out for a bite?"

"Are you talking about vampires now, because I'm not sure…"

"The bites I have to offer don't involve fangs."

"A lunch date?"

She nodded, hopeful for his positive answer. "We can go Dutch. Come on, hunter. I dare you to be seen in public with a creepy witch."

His smirk wasn't so horrible; in fact, it was sexy shy as his mouth gradually caught up to the smile that already beamed in his eye. "Lunch, it is."

Chapter 5

Seated at a tiny table for two beside a window that over-looked the streets crowded with tourists, Kaz felt as if he were being watched. And not by the gorgeous witch across the table, who was digging into her crème brûlée. Her blue eyes flashed up to his and she smiled before forking in a generous bite.

"Want a taste?" She tilted her head. "Kaz? You seem distracted."

"Uh, sure, I'll take a bite. Anything that makes you smile that big must be great."

She served him a taste.

Kaz didn't indulge. Didn't have the time for it. Since joining the Order ten years ago, his life had become disciplined, and his diet militant. Picard's grocery was his usual stop for frozen meals he could pop into the microwave. He rarely ate in restaurants, unless he was on a date, and dates were few and far between because he never had a day off to actually meet women. He was always on call, which meant he didn't hang out in nightclubs or bars.

Instead, he had to beat up vampires to get the girl.

Apparently, that method worked for him.

Zoë devoured the dessert, and Kaz split his attention between her and his surroundings. It was difficult to completely let down his guard in public. No wonder his relationships never lasted long.

What was a relationship?

Whatever it was, it was beginning to appeal more and more. Had she been in many? Did he appeal to her as much as she did to him? Could a knight ever attract a woman looking for stability? Did she want stability?

Well hell, who didn't?

It had been a long time since he'd thought about that night Tor had found him behind Madame du Monde's Dance Emporium, bloody chair leg clutched in his white-knuckled grip. Man, had his life taken a one-eighty for the better since then. Though, most certainly a strange turn.

"Is it something outside?" she asked. "I've not had your full attention since the salad. I'm sorry to bore you—"

Dragging his gaze from the window, Kaz forced himself to pay attention to the only thing that he should have in focus. "It's not you, Zoë." She was all kinds of pretty to command his attention. "Do you know how exciting it is watching you eat? I'm trying not to stare at you so much you want to start calling *me* a creep."

"I could never do that. You're too handsome to be creepy."

He wished he'd never said that about witches. It would remain a sore spot for her, he felt sure.

"Do you ever feel like you're being watched?" he offered as a means to change the conversation. "I can't put a finger to it. I usually can tell when vampires are nearby. This feeling I'm having is…out there. That's not a good way to explain it, but it's the only words I can summon."

She nodded knowingly, and set down her fork. "You're sensitive to the paranormal breeds. That's why you can feel it."

"It? Feel what?"

"FaeryTown, of course."

"Faery—"

While the Order had only touched on faeries during training, Kaz did know FaeryTown existed within Paris. It was sort of a fourth dimension overlaid upon the mortal realm. A place where faeries lived amongst mortals, yet could not be seen by them. It was also where vampires in the know went to get their dust fixes.

"Why didn't you tell me where we were?" He darted his gaze around the small restaurant and out the window, but wasn't sure what he expected to see. Wings? "Right now?"

She nodded.

"I should have been told."

"Wow. You hop right up that anger scale with little provocation, don't you? I didn't think it necessary because it's not as if most people are aware of it. And you're not a vampire, so—"

"So, it's important to me to know these things, Zoë. Don't keep significant information like that from me."

She leaned back, toyed with her fork, but left her half-eaten dessert alone. He'd offended her, had spoken harshly when she could have no reason to understand his anxiety. It had been a bad idea to go out for lunch during a job. Did he want to hook up with her that badly?

Yes.

"Sorry." Kaz turned his focus to her pouty pink mouth. "Once again, I said the wrong thing to you."

"I'm not taking offense, but I am surprised at your reaction. So we're in FaeryTown. What of it?"

A lot of it, actually. Especially since Kaz was tracking the source of the Magic Dust. Could it be in FaeryTown? Made a hell of a lot of sense. Why hadn't he considered this angle of investigation until now?

Probably because he had no known way of accessing such a realm.

"Let's say I'm curious about my surroundings and this

very obvious feeling of unease I mentioned to you. I mean, can they see us?"

She nodded.

"But we can't see them."

"Not unless they want you to see them, which is rare. A faery could be standing right next to you, or even sitting in that very spot."

Kaz jostled on his chair, but didn't go so far as to stand up. The idea of someone sitting in the exact spot where he was right now... "You have to admit that's disturbing."

"Not if you don't think about it." She was so calm about the possibility their conversation was being observed.

Kaz propped a concealing hand along the side of his mouth and spoke quietly. "Isn't there some way for a human being to see faeries?"

Zoë smirked. "You do know some things, hunter. There is an ointment that will allow you to see into the sidhe realm," Zoë offered.

"And where does a guy—" he checked his tone and lowered his voice to a whisper "—get some of that?"

"From a faery healer, or someone in the know. Or...a witch." Zoë winked.

He held her gaze, discerning that she may be a witch with access to just such a thing.

It hadn't so much been the fact that the ink witch's physical appearance had creeped him out. It was that he—any witch—could command the elements, move things, change things, with but a few spoken words or hand gestures. That was a lot of power. And a guy never knew when said witch was going to whip out the magical words or gesture.

At least with vampires, Kaz could see the bad coming.

Zoë leaned across the table, speaking quietly. "What do you want it for?"

"Hunter stuff."

"It will cost you," she offered, and sat back.

Had he thought that little blue bow was pretty earlier? Yes, and he'd also thought the breasts behind the bow deserved an exploratory licking. Why hadn't he stuck around at her place longer?

Right. Hunger. And work. Which he really should get back to. The witch, and her delicious assets, would keep. Besides, much as he wanted her, he was still leery of the whole witch thing.

"So…" He dropped to a whisper again. "If I stop by later would you have some available?"

"Does that mean you're ditching me now?"

"I, uh, have to get back to work." And home, away from temptation so he could focus on what had become key—FaeryTown. "I've been gone all night, and I appreciate the care you've given me. Who would have thought I'd be completely pain free after the beating I took last night? I owe you one, Zoë."

"I will remember that. It's always an advantage to have an indebted hunter at one's call."

Yikes. Really? What had he just promised her?

"I've work to do, anyway," she continued. "It was fun getting to know you, Kaz. I hope this is more than just a returning-favors thing between us."

He rose and leaned in to kiss her across the table. She strolled her fingers inside his open coat and hooked them at his waistband. Some of her touches were kind while others were more focused on seductive danger. He liked both styles of touch. Lingering with their mouths together, Kaz wanted to make sure she understood this was more than a favors thing.

But not until he got his priorities in order.

"I like you," he whispered in her ear. "And you'll have a time trying to get rid of me from now on. But, uh, the job comes first."

He traced his forefinger through the creamy dessert and

tapped her lip with it. She licked it clean. He glanced aside. In Paris everyone enjoyed a sexy show, and the couple at the nearest table smiled at them.

But were the faeries smiling, as well? Too disturbed to put aside the nervous feeling that he was being watched, Kaz kissed Zoë quickly and told her he'd see her later. He filed through the closely spaced dining-room tables and turned to catch the witch's wink before exiting.

Why was she interested in him, anyway? He was everything wrong for her—any woman, really. The pretty little witch should find another witch or vampire, or whatever breed floated her boat, and forget about the trouble he could bring to her life. Because where a knight from the Order walked, trouble spattered the street in piles of ash.

Before crossing the restaurant threshold, Kaz shoved a hand into his pants pocket. His fingers curled about the old brass key. *Safe.* He could move onward.

Outside the restaurant, he scanned the streets, hoping to catch a glimpse of something, anything not right. He didn't know exactly what he was looking for, but sensed he might feel it.

Would he know if wings fluttered nearby or brushed his arm? What if a faery were standing before him right now, staring him down with a pair of violet eyes and a goofy grin?

This place was creeping him out more than a witch with a tattoo gun ever could.

"Later," he muttered.

He headed toward the left bank, where Order headquarters were located. He needed to scan the database and brush up on his knowledge of faeries.

Zoë had much work waiting completion at home. Of course, she was insane for thinking her work was more important than spending time with Kaz. She must have eaten too much dessert and now the sugar was messing with her brain, because who chose work over romance? Certainly not a damsel headed toward happily ever after.

But apparently, the knight did.

She wouldn't overthink this. So he had to work. She could accept that. They were just getting to know one another.

She hadn't far to walk home, and the afternoon served up a chill that made her glad she'd brought a long, gray sweater to wrap about her shoulders as she kicked her boots through a pile of fallen maple leaves cluttering the alley behind her home.

A flash of red caught her eye as she strolled up the back way through her garden. Her neighbor Lillian, who was also a witch, and who had seen the French Revolution—not to mention Joan of Arc's rise and fall—waved to her from amidst a tall crop of hollyhocks that had gone to seed.

"Hello, little one," Lillian called as Zoë approached. She never called her Zoë, having once explained she thought the name didn't fit her misplaced soul. Zoë wasn't sure why her soul was misplaced, but it sounded about right to her. Because really, her wanting soul should have found true love by now. "It's a lovely day."

"That it is. Collecting seeds for next year?"

"I've a stew to make for a certain gentleman suitor who intends to call later this evening. Hollyhock will clarify his thoughts regarding engaging in an affair with me."

"You have a sneaky way of getting what you want, Lillian."

"And I'd never deny it. So what's put the blush in your cheeks? And don't tell me it's the weather."

Leaning her elbows on the wrought-iron fence and toying with the dried head of the flower, Zoë managed to sprinkle the seeds into Lillian's waiting bowl as she detailed her adventures with the sexy hunter.

"You don't often date humans," Lillian noted.

"I don't think I've ever dated a human. And we're not dating. We've kissed and I've healed his wounds."

"Kissing is one of life's finest pleasures," Lillian said on a sigh threaded with experience.

"Kisses are delicious magic," Zoë agreed. "He took a shower this morning after spending the night on my couch in healing mode. Lillian, that man's muscles are remarkable. I couldn't even fit both hands around one of his biceps. I never thought I was into muscles until I saw those guns."

"I was once the courtesan to an English knight. Let me tell you about that man's muscle. It was always hard."

"Lillian!"

"What? Oh, you mean you were talking about some other kind of muscle. Pfft. The most important one is always the most interesting, yet men tend to keep it tucked out of sight."

"I haven't seen that particular muscle on Kaz yet."

"What's taking so long?"

"I told you I've only just met him. Half of me wants to take it slow while the other half is already picking out china patterns and writing happily ever afters."

"Oh, that's right, you always have been a bit of a freak in the dating department."

Zoë gaped at Lillian, but the older witch simply shrugged. "What about the ice demon?"

Zoë wasn't going to dignify that one with an agreement. So she'd learned that some demons took offense to her idea of a romantic date—snuggling before a cozy fire. The guy hadn't melted, but he'd had to activate some kind of cold sensors in his body and had really gotten hard. And not in a good way, either.

"And the familiar, Thomas?" Lillian tossed out.

Zoë rolled her eyes at memory of that particular alley

cat. "Don't remind me. I'm never keeping a familiar as a pet again."

"You're sure Sid isn't keeping something from you?"

"Positive. Sid is pure cat. When he sits on the edge of the bathtub watching me bathe, it's out of boredom, not lust. Oh, now you made me think of that!"

"I personally enjoy the idea of having a familiar around the house, always watching, and sometimes catching you in a most compromising position." Lillian winked.

The woman was a vixen. On the other hand, Zoë would be thankful merely to be in a compromising position, so she wasn't going to judge Lillian's industrious sex life.

"Fine," Zoë said, "so I tend to pick the wrong men on occasion."

"Always."

"Always," Zoë agreed and followed with a sigh. "But Kaz is different."

"He's human. That's about as different as it gets. And a hunter? Curious. You don't think that'll jeopardize your friendships with vampires?"

"I hope not."

"What's the name of that cute, dark-haired vamp who is always hanging around you? Come to think of it, I haven't seen him in a while. You should hit that, Zoë."

"Lillian, Luc is a friend. We'd never *hit* each other." She shuddered to even think of having sex with her friend. "He's on a sort of vacation right now. Actually, he's had a tough time of it since breaking up with his fiancée, and succumbed to a dust addiction."

Lillian shook her head sadly.

"But he's getting clean. That's why I haven't seen him in a few weeks. He wants to surprise me."

"Good for him. And sorry to have implied you two should…you know. Vampire sex is always a bit messy. The blood stains! Anyway, tell me more about this sexy hunter with the big muscles. Does he slay on his own? Is he part of an organization?"

Zoë shrugged. "I didn't ask. Is that important?"

"You don't often find a lone vigilante staking vampires. Not that it doesn't occur. It's just not common."

"What organizations are there?"

"There's a few. He hasn't mentioned any, shown you any weapons or secret handshakes?"

"I did snag one of his stakes. It was made of metal and was spring-loaded. And I got this."

She tugged the thing she'd nicked from Kaz while they'd kissed in the restaurant, and studied her find. Looked like a hi-tech tape measure, but when she pulled out the tape, she saw it was some kind of twisted cable.

"A garrote," Lillian remarked. "Wonder if there's any blood on it."

"Ugh." Zoë tucked the weapon back in her sweater pocket. "And he's got this mark on his shoulder. It's like a burn, but in a circle pattern. And inside are four marks in a radiating style. I've seen it before...."

"Like stakes within a circle?"

"Could be. Oh, yes, now I remember. The same mark was on the bottom of the stake he carries. Are you familiar with it?"

Lillian shuddered and pulled the bowl away from the flower head that had given up all its seeds. "Sounds like Order of the Stake. They're ruthless. Best you stay away from their knights."

"Knights?"

Lillian nodded. "That's what they call the hunters who are trained to extinguish any vampire who looks at them the wrong way."

"How do you know so much about this order?"

"I dated a knight once. Name was—well, I can't tell you or he'd have my head, for sure. Misogynist son of a bitch.

He had a thing for witches. But he was cold, so cold. Devoted to his work. He'd be making love to me while detailing the things he planned to do to the next vampire who crossed his path. Oh, this isn't good, little one. Don't let that knight cross your threshold again."

"But I told you he didn't attempt to slay the vampires last night. I have to believe Kaz would not kill just because his opponent was vampire. He only goes after those who kill humans."

"How can you know a man you've only met? A few knee-bending kisses have blinded you. Be wary. And whatever you do, do not introduce him to any of your vampire friends."

"I hadn't intended to. But I'm also not going to kick him out of my bed just because he's got some special title from a boy's club. I've never heard of the Order of the Stake. Sounds like something you do in a restaurant. I've work to do inside. I'll talk to you later, Lillian."

"If you need backup," Lillian called as Zoë strode up to her back door, "you know where to find me."

Thinking the old witch had finally slipped a cog, Zoë marched inside, collected Sid in her arms and turned into the kitchen to start a pot of apple cider.

"He's not a bad man," she said to the purring black cat. At least, she hoped he wasn't.

And a knight? Her fantasies were gliding along quite nicely, if she did say so herself.

Kaz had spent the afternoon and early evening reviewing the Order's files on faeries. There wasn't much, not even names of particular faeries known to the Order. Names were a powerful thing to the sidhe, and they never revealed their true name to anyone.

Within Faery, there was a hierarchy and various courts

such as Seelie, Unseelie, Bright and Dark, Summer, Winter, etc., but they existed in Faery, not the mortal realm.

He learned an interesting method to prevent faeries from seeing him. Turning his coat inside out. It was rumored to work, but no reports from Order knights confirmed it. Iron was another excellent faery repellent, though it had to contain pure, cold iron to cause death. Forged iron merely slowed them down a bit.

Following his computer research, Kaz checked the Order's arsenal and found an old iron blade, something from medieval times, and checked it out. The blade was heavy and short, but better safe than not. It was easy to conceal down the side of his boot, too.

Back at home, he showered and changed, then reviewed yesterday's events as he stood before the map in the living room. Talking with Switch had proven disastrous. He still couldn't believe he'd let the vampires get the upper hand, but suspected that Switch had immediately started in with the persuasion, luring him into a subtle thrall that had weakened his defenses.

He'd been trained to defeat the thrall. Where had his focus been?

He wasn't even going to answer that question.

On the map he tapped the location of the restaurant where he and Zoë had eaten, and muttered, "In Faery-Town."

Order records had confirmed FaeryTown was rammed up against the Bois de Boulogne, a city park that stretched along the western edge of the sixteenth arrondissement. That would make the FaeryTown area vast if it crossed from the eighteenth, through the seventeenth, and hugged the sixteenth.

He connected a few strings on pins and drew a line with them from the restaurant to the park. He'd adjust the borders as he learned more and familiarized himself with the area. To do that he needed to *see* the inhabitants of FaeryTown.

Dressing quickly in casual black jeans, boots and a warm gray sweater, he left the Order gear in the closet. He didn't want to appear threatening when walking the streets of FaeryTown, yet he stowed the iron blade in his boot. In his pants pockets he'd secured a stake, holy water and a small silver cross. He couldn't find the garrote he always carried. He patted the Order coat hanging in the closet, but didn't feel it. It couldn't have come unhooked from his belt—

"Really?" He recalled kissing Zoë in the restaurant and her sliding her hand along his waist. "What is it with that chick and her sticky fingers?"

But he could survive without the garrote. It was the weapon he used least often.

Kaz headed out to catch the Metro back to the eighteenth. Tonight he did not intend to allow his actions, successful or otherwise, to be witnessed by a curious witch. But first, he had to obtain a necessary ingredient if he was going to see the faeries with whom he wanted to chat.

The cerulean door made him smile. Behind that door lived someone equally as bright and intriguing. Kaz knocked and waited. From the noise inside, it sounded as if she descended the spiral stairs twisting skyward inside the foyer.

He wondered what was up in the tower room that she was keen to keep from his curious gaze. Was it a place where she conjured potions with jars of bat wings and mouse tails?

Did he really want to know?

Kaz shuddered. Probably not. This particular witch may not physically creep him out, but he had no idea what she did with her spells and cauldron. Just wondering about it put a little creep up the back of his neck.

Zoë opened the door and greeted him with an enthusiastic kiss. She wrapped her legs about his hips and clung. No sense in fighting the effusive show of affection. Their mouths crushed together, Kaz walked inside, carrying the lightweight witch along with him.

"You're certainly happy to see me." He closed the door, one sweetly smiling witch still wrapped about his torso. She smelled like apples and cinnamon. "Must be my winning personality, eh?"

"Could be, or it could be the weather."

"The weather?"

"Autumn makes me, um…well, lusty. Kiss me again, hunter."

He pressed her back against the wall and glided his hands down her arms while she maintained a leglock about his hips. The chick got turned on by the cooling season? He could work with that.

A kiss to her jaw and she tilted her head to the side. Her silky hair spilled over his fingers and he drew out the strands, marveling at the blend of dark and white. He liked it for its oddness. Add that to the scar cutting her cheek and she was unique and fascinating.

And horny. Go figure.

But really? When had he ever resisted a wanting female?

A kiss to her collarbone made her squirm. He wanted to pull down her shirt to reveal her breasts but he'd just come in from outside and even if the weather did turn her on, he felt sure cold hands would not.

She pushed her hands up under his sweater and Kaz sucked in a breath at the heat that seared his skin. Damn, she was hotter than summer.

"Your touch is more than healing," he said with a kiss to

her shoulder, where the neckline began on her black shirt. "It makes me..." He ground his hips against her, wishing she sat a little lower on him so she could feel his erection.

"It makes you what?" she asked. "Lusty, as well?"

"You think that's the only reason I returned to see you?"

"I know what you came for. But you're not going to get it until I've had my way with you."

"Is that a fact? Sounds like a worthy trade."

"Oh, the faery ointment is going to cost you real, hard cash, buddy."

"I brought my wallet. Unless you've stolen it already."

"Come on. I take one little thing from you and you think I'm a kleptomaniac?"

"One thing? I, uh, seem to be missing something else from my arsenal. Would you have any idea where it might have gone?"

She had the innocent-shift-of-eyes-toward-the-heavens look down pat.

"Zoë..."

"Oh, bugger. I'm sorry. I can't help myself. It's just—"

"That thing you do?"

She nodded. "Some things I just do without thought. Gives me a thrill. You know?"

"Maybe you should seek your thrills in another way?"

Her cheeks flushed and her raspberry lips curled seductively. Kaz was glad she'd made the connection to what he was suggesting.

"I can retrieve it right now, or..." She nibbled her bottom lip and met his gaze close up with a flutter of lush lashes. "We could fool around a bit longer. Touch me, Kaz."

Kaz dragged his hand down her shirt, and it came off her shoulder, exposing pale skin that smelled like herbs and spices. The house smelled like stewed apples. It was appealing in ways that teased at memory and hunger and desire all wrapped together. He bent to kiss and lick her shoulder.

"You're dressed down tonight," she said. "No blades at your collar. No slaying in mind?"

"Nope. And we're not going to discuss my work anymore."

"Fair enough. What do you want to discuss?"

"This." He licked a trail down from her shoulder to the rise of her breast. She wore no bra, and he dared to caress her breast and cup it in his hand. Her nipple hardened against his palm, and that sensation caused things on him to grow hard. "You make me feel like a teenager who is excited to touch a girl, Zoë. It's funny."

"Because you're touching my boob?"

"A little. I feel as if this is new, and I've never done it before and I don't want to do anything wrong or I'll lose you."

"Wow." She traced his hair with both hands, along his ears and down to caress the back of his neck. "I bet you've had tons of girlfriends. Why do *I* make you feel like this?"

"Not sure. You're different."

"Because I'm a creepy witch?"

"I think it's because you're so much more than another pretty girl."

"I'm not pretty. This scar—"

He kissed her right on the scar, tendering a soft touch to the raised skin that made him wince to think of the horrors she must have endured. "It is uniquely you, and you are pretty, Zoë. But can I ask, if you were able to heal me, then how come you couldn't…?"

"Heal myself? That requires much study with molecu— er, healing magic. I can heal others but not my own flesh. All magic has a price."

"That sounds so wrong, but I guess it makes sense."

"There is a price to be paid for all magics." She nudged

her forehead against his and closed her eyes, her lashes dusting his. "You really don't want to lose me?"

"Zoë, I don't know how to explain the way I feel, but losing you feels wrong. I just found you."

"Then kiss me again, and touch me all you like. I want your big hands roaming over me."

He bent and kissed her breast through the thin fabric, and gently tweaked her nipple, which stirred up her moan that resonated like a song in Kaz's soul.

For some reason, Zoë seemed to touch his softer side, the side of him that pined for a connection. A side that he, as a hunter, had deftly hidden away from all who might attempt to permeate that carefully protected part of him. It felt too good to push her away right now.

The witch shoved up his sweater and pulled him in closer so he could feel her hard nipples against his bare chest. There was some kind of rightness, he thought, in standing here making out like teenagers. He crushed up against her, moaning his own soulful song of desire, and found her mouth again for another long, lingering kiss.

Cupping her breasts, he squeezed the nipples, which drew a moan from her that echoed into his kiss. The sounds of her pleasure made him eager to harmonize with those whimpers and moans all night long. But he had work to do.

Just a few minutes longer…

"So, I know what you are," she said as he let down her legs so she could stand.

"What do you mean? About me being a hunter? Big surprise."

"You're a knight with the Order of the Stake."

"Ah." Kaz exhaled. Desire fell down the scale and landed with a splat.

How'd she figure that one? He hadn't worn the telltale coat with the bladed collar tonight, but she had probably closely examined it the night she'd helped him home to her couch. Some in the know would recognize the style, but she hadn't initially given any indication that she had.

She could have researched him on the internet, but— no, the Order took particular measures to ensure nothing about them was recorded online. Not on the mortal's version of the internet, anyway.

"My neighbor told me," she offered. "She's a centuries-old witch who knows everything and then some. That mark on your shoulder was the giveaway. A teenaged dare?"

Okay, he'd give her that one. He often forgot about that telling symbol.

"It's a brand I took when I said vows and was knighted into the Order. I was seventeen. My identity is not common knowledge, Zoë. I need to maintain secrecy or every Tom, Dick and Lestat will come after me."

"Don't worry about me. I just wanted you to know I'm in on it now so you don't have to lie."

"I've never lied to you," he protested fiercely. Realizing that had been a bit harsh, Kaz dropped the defiance a notch. "I keep some things close to my vest, is all. I can't reveal details about investigations. It would compromise both of us."

"Fair enough. But can I ask about this organized order of humans who hunt vampires for a living?"

"No."

She nodded. "Right. No questions. No lies."

"It's easier that way. Can you deal?"

She nodded. "I can, and I will. I suppose you need to get to work, then? I should run up and get the ointment."

As Zoë dashed up the stairs, Kaz exhaled and leaned against the wall. That hadn't gone over as well as it should have. But at least he was out, so to speak. A knight's best defense was his secrecy, yet he suspected Zoë would remain an ally in his silence. Until she had reason to use it against him.

Would she?

He'd known something the moment they had kissed in the alley that first night. And he still held that knowing as truth. So he didn't want to screw this up, didn't want to give her any reason to turn against him. Much as it wasn't his usual MO, he wanted to see where things went with the pretty little witch. He'd like to know her. All of her.

Did he deserve that? Hell, no.

But screw the right and wrong of it. This time around, he would take what he could get.

A few minutes later, she landed by his side and handed him the filched garrote, coiled into a neat ring. "You ever use that on a vampire?"

"Many times. Doesn't kill, but does shut them up for a while."

He pocketed the weapon, and Zoë took his free hand and placed on his palm a small, clear, glass container about the size of his thumb with an aluminum screw-on lid. The contents were black and sparkly.

"This is it?"

"You rub a bit under your eyes to see faeries. It's powerful stuff, so I didn't give you much."

Sounded wonky to him. Rubbing something sparkly under his eyes? Reminded him that he'd seen the vampire Vail sporting just such a look on more than a few occasions. But he wouldn't question magic, faery or otherwise.

"How much?"

She trailed her fingers down his sweater and snuggled up to him as her hand ventured lower, along his leg, but merciless inches away from his hardening erection.

"Zoë?"

She murmured that sweet little moan against his ear that reminded him how much he'd wanted to listen to her pleasure. "Just come back again. I'll be waiting."

Best deal he'd been offered in a lifetime.

"Tonight?" he asked.

"I've work to do that'll keep me up late, so why not? A goodnight kiss is the price you must pay for what you hold in your hand."

"Deal." He kissed her quickly, and she fisted hanks of his hair and pulled him back for a longer kiss that burned through his skin and summoned a sigh in his whole body. "Later, I'll give you the official goodnight kiss."

Pausing on the threshold, Kaz patted the key in his pocket. *Safe.*

He felt her gaze on his back as he walked down the sidewalk overgrown with sweet bluegrass and tiny white flowers. He wasn't about to let a woman interfere with an important operation. But he also wasn't willing to stay away from Zoë for too long. Because already his mouth felt cold and ached for the touch of her lips.

With every kiss she gave him, running away from the kleptomaniac witch felt less and less reasonable.

Chapter 6

With the black ointment rubbed under his eyes, Kaz worked the football-quarterback look. It would have to do.

He strolled quickly through the Pigalle, Paris's red-light district, which always seemed more filled with tourists looking for salacious sights than actual salacious sights.

He passed a store blasting out French rap music. He understood French, but German was his native language and his father had spoken it exclusively, despite their having lived in Paris most of Kaz's childhood. He preferred English, mostly because speaking English pissed off the locals, and he'd never lose the rebellious streak two years of living on the streets had carved into his soul. Musicians and wannabes hung around the neon-framed doorway and one high-fived him as he strolled by. So maybe he was working the rocker look more than the football star.

The moment he set foot in FaeryTown, he realized it. Entering the altered dimension overlaid upon the mortal world tugged minutely at his system. It felt as if he were being zapped from inside, not from a nerve twinge, but perhaps by something moving through him and swirling about. Had he not been aware, and had been on a casual stroll as a tourist, he might have marked it off as a sudden chill that tightened his skin and put up goose bumps, or maybe a brush up against a rude stranger.

Now as Kaz rubbed his hands together and felt the hairs at the back of his neck settle, he noticed the flickering winged beings that walked the streets. Others didn't walk but rather fluttered a few inches above ground, and here and there, some soared parallel to the rooftops. The faeries were solid and yet not. They appeared as human as the next, yet not. Some moved as if a movie film reel were missing a few cels, their steps jerky. Others with wings moved normally, as if out for a casual stroll—or flight.

Yet amongst them, the humans appeared slightly dull to Kaz, as if the colors of skin, hair and clothing had been lightly muted. They were unaware of the fantastical world that existed about them. If a faery wing happened to brush across a human's face, that person would merely sweep a hand over their cheek, perhaps marking it off as the wind.

"Amazing," Kaz muttered.

He'd never given faeries much thought, consigning them to the fantastical. Yes, even he, a man who slayed creatures of the night, had a hard time believing in faeries.

Until now.

Slightly disturbed by what he saw, and wondering how many times he'd walked this area unaware of the world overlaid upon his own, he marked it as a learning experience. A fascinating new adventure.

Shoving his hands in his pockets, he ventured down the sidewalk, passing regular mortal stores and shopfronts, but also noticing the occasional wildly colored, narrow shop tucked between two mortal shops that couldn't be anything but sidhe. Wing Healer? Yeah, that wasn't a mortal shop. Nor was the Lazy Troll Tavern that offered discounts to banshees.

The sidhe gave him little notice, going about their conversations and business as if the human realm they interposed upon did not exist.

Zoë had mentioned something about faeries only allowing a mortal to see them if they wished, so he had to wonder if they were aware he could see them now. Certainly the dark ointment was a giveaway. And if they did notice, did they care?

Kaz felt a compulsion to reach out and stroke his fingers along the veined, see-through pink wings of a passing faery, but controlled the urge by shoving his hand in a front pocket. The Order's information had detailed something about faeries' wings and touching them being a sexual overture. He didn't want to test that information.

Oddly, the air smelled sweeter, though he reasoned he couldn't possibly notice the difference beyond the gasoline fumes and crush of fall leaves in the gutters. He only had the ability to *see* faeries. The ointment didn't affect his other senses, did it?

He spied a neon sign that flashed a big, red V. In the dip of the V hung an I—no, closer inspection determined it could be a stake pointed into the crotch of the V. Interesting way to lure in vampires. Stretched out from the V were faery wings that flashed from bright green to yellow, then red. It was the symbol for an ichor den—that much, the Order had taught him. They were everywhere in FaeryTown, places vampires visited to get a faery dust fix, but he only noticed them now.

"Just the place I want to check out."

Kaz walked across the street and entered the open doorway beneath the V sign. The air choked him with a scent he couldn't place. Sweet, yet cloying, so much so, he blinked and his eyes watered. And he could taste something bitter at the back of his throat. He couldn't see any dust in the air.

He walked a long, bright hallway that seemed to glow of its own accord. It didn't necessarily sparkle; it just beamed. Kaz felt both eager and anxious. He had no experience with faeries that he knew of. What he did know for sure was that one should not mess with faeries. That was a conviction held by humans and paranormals. Any breed all the other paranormal breeds liked to walk a wide circle around, wisely incited caution.

He realized he was sweating. So he took his nervousness down a notch and focused on calling up the calm Rook had trained him to utilize in dangerous situations. Breathe in; breathe out. Slowly. Calmly.

He would touch as little as possible. Faery dust on his fingers shouldn't affect him as it did vampires, but who could know? As well, he had no clue what faeries could do to his mind. Could they utilize persuasion, as did vampires? Did they have magic like Zoë? Would he even see the hurt coming should he piss off a faery?

As a hunter who was merely human, he was out of his league. Most likely, he could catch the Magic Dust dealer without nosing into the affairs of the sidhe. Why had he come here?

Run away, Kaspar. It's what you do best.

Vacillating on his ill-thought decision to enter the ichor den, Kaz swung around to eye the open door through which he'd entered. Immediately before him stood a tall, abnormally thin woman with long, green hair and slitted eyes that gleamed silver-violet. Wispy-edged violet wings curled forward about her shoulders, like a soft shawl. She wore very little, and the few sheer strips of fabric wrapping her pale skin revealed body parts that Kaz was thankful were very humanlike.

The unabashed exposure teased at his need to remain in control, and he immediately snapped his gaze up to her eerie eyes.

"You've no business in this establishment, human," she said in a whispery voice that Kaz felt more than heard. The sound tickled his ears and throat from the inside, as if a sneeze was imminent. Everything about FaeryTown affected his insides, and he wasn't sure how to feel about that. "Are you lost?"

"No, I was, uh…curious."

He couldn't admit he was investigating illicit drugs. Nor could he deny he hadn't purposely chosen to snoop about with the black ointment, an obvious giveaway to his intentions.

"Is it all right if I look around? I'm fascinated."

"Of course you are. All humans are beguiled by our presence. Where did you get the ointment?"

"From a friend. A witch. We were talking about Faery-Town and she knows I like to explore and learn new things. I won't touch anything."

The faery smirked and her wings snapped out behind her, shimmering madly as if a disco ball hung overhead and beamed upon the gossamer appendages.

"Beautiful," Kaz offered, but as a means to ingratiate himself to her, who he suspected was suspicious as hell. And for good reason.

"Are you one of those who get off on wings?"

"Huh? Oh, no. I would never—" Really? Yes, he could believe some might have a kink for wings. They were certainly…intriguing. And did she smell like a summer meadow? "I've said the wrong thing. I have a habit of that."

A man stumbled down the hallway, using the wall for support, and clutching an arm across his bare, thin chest. At first glance, he looked a heroin addict, but Kaz knew he could only be a dust junkie. The vampire shoved past

Kaz, brushed up against the faery, and she turned and led him toward the door.

Using the faery's distraction, Kaz quickly stepped toward the hanging beads blocking a doorway. He slipped through the beads, wincing as they clattered. Not much time for reconnaissance. He made his way forward through the neon brightness of what initially appeared to be some kind of opium den with low, velvet couches and people lying on them in various states of disorientation.

Not people. Vampires.

He clenched his fist about an invisible stake. He didn't feel compelled to take the stake out of his pocket. A stoned vamp should give him little worry. Unless that vamp was high on Magic Dust.

Of course, if there were such a vamp in this place he would notice him because the vampire would likely be raging and begging for more of the drug.

But what Kaz did do was reach into his pocket to clasp the key he always carried. *Safe.* To him, the key was like a cross to some people, a symbol that gave him solace and hope.

His arm brushed a wing. Kaz turned to find a pretty faery with pink hair and wings, and nothing else on her painfully thin frame, smiling wearily up at him.

"You've come for me?" she asked meekly.

"Uh, no, sweetie. I'm looking around, uh, for a friend."

Her smile fell. Bones bulged through her skin. While a human's veins appeared blue beneath their skin, her arms were mapped with iridescent trails. She looked, literally, drained. He knew a vampire could bleed the ichor from a faery through a bite, a needle, or through an extraction process that would take greater amounts more swiftly. Poor thing.

He moved onward, hating leaving the pink faery. This was probably where she had come to die, because why else would a faery willingly submit to such torture? Did they get something out of the ichor extraction beyond pain and eventual death? It made little sense. Unless they were paid well? Perhaps to support a family in the realm of Faery?

Breathing in, he choked as his mouth began to tingle. The bitter taste returned to his tongue. Had he inhaled dust? He sucked at the insides of his cheeks to draw up saliva and swallow. The last thing he needed was a dust high. Despite not believing it could happen, he could not be sure—

A vampire lying on one of the low, velvet couches jittered so erratically, Kaz felt the urge to give him a shove so he wouldn't land on the floor. He stopped near the vamp, looking about for the faery that may have serviced him. He noticed the crushed vial of iridescent dust near the vamp's head.

The vampire's eyes managed to connect with Kaz's, even while his head shuddered back and forth on the flattened satin pillow. "Stuff isn't working," he said. "Need the magic."

"You looking for Magic Dust?" Kaz squatted near the couch, but slid a hand over the pants' pocket with the stake. "Where'd you get it last time? Here?"

"Not here." The vamp slapped a hand to his elbow where Kaz saw the track marks. That the needle punctures had not healed told him he was a regular customer. "Nothing from this shit, man!"

"Where'd you get the dust?"

"Not going to tell you. Stuff's hard to find. You'll buy it all up."

"No, I—"

An arm gripped him by the wrist. The long fingers were boney, and he felt, with a twist, the faery he'd encountered in the entry could snap his bones. He stood, raising his free hand in surrender.

"You are leaving," the faery commanded.

"I am leaving." Because he wasn't going to get anything from a dust freak in withdrawal. "I have to ask before I go.... No Magic Dust in here?"

Her violet eyes flashed wide and silver. He felt her anger in the tight coil of her wings forward about her shoulders. "Never. Now leave!"

"Forgive me."

Kaz made way whence he'd come, not wanting to aggravate or gain new enemies. But he was aware the faery had taken out a cell phone and now spoke hastily to someone. Faeries and cell phones? For some reason that didn't jibe with his idea of winged beings from nature.

He stepped outside the ichor den and inhaled the fresh fall air. Across the street a mortal restaurant emitted savory scents that mingled with those of nature. He made a beeline, and ordered water at the bar, and a beer. He didn't drink the beer, but he hadn't wanted to simply ask for water. He needed to clear his head because he felt a little muddy from the faery dust.

"Hey, buddy." Said in a French accent, the *bud-DEE* sounded ridiculous.

Kaz turned slowly, looking cautiously over his shoulder at the man who jittered like a dysfunctional video-game avatar. His eyes were black because his pupils were enlarged. His fangs were down. He was higher than the top of the Eiffel Tower. And stupid as hell.

Eyes darting side to side, and hands jammed into his holey windbreaker pockets, the vamp asked, "Did I hear you say you got some Magic Dust?"

Bingo. This wasn't a source, but the idiot was looking for the same thing Kaz was. Must have followed him out from the ichor den.

"Maybe." Kaz turned back to his water and tapped the glass with his fingertips. Turning his back to a vamp was not wise, but he sensed he had the upper hand with this one.

"I got cash, buddy. I need some, like seriously."

"Not in here," Kaz said, and stood. As he passed the vampire, he said, "Follow me."

Passing a gaggle of giggling faeries, Kaz merely shook his head. No time for fascination now. As soon as he turned down a dark alleyway, Kaz turned, stake in hand, and shoved the strung-out longtooth against the brick wall. The vampire took one look at the titanium stake and yelped.

"Yep, you picked the wrong guy," Kaz confirmed. "Answer my question and you won't feel titanium pierce your heart."

"Hey, buddy! Can't you see I'm jonesing here? I thought you had dust?"

"I have something that'll kill you more sweetly." He tapped the stake against the vampire's chest. "Right here is where it'll go. I can feel your heart racing."

"It's the dust, buddy. It's like a train that never stops. I want to ride it all night."

"Where did you get the Magic Dust?"

"I don't have any, buddy. Didn't you get that?"

"I'm talking about the stuff you bought before you needed to find more."

"Hey! Get that thing away from my heart, buddy. Ah, hell, I can't think straight with you acting like some kind of slayer."

"I am a slayer."

The vampire hissed and spread his mouth wide, threatening with a fanged sneer. But it was a little late for scare tactics.

"Not impressed." Kaz turned the stake upright and, inches from the vampire's face, depressed the paddles. The pointed business end of the stake pinioned out.

Again the vampire yelped.

"Where did you get the dust?" Kaz repeated.

"Not sure, buddy. It was somewhere on the right bank."

"That rules out half of Paris. Keep thinking. Focus on the stake. See that end? It's nice and pointy. Bet it hurts like a mother. You want this instead of the sweet high dust can give you?"

"No way! Uh…" The vampire bounced on his feet, but Kaz held him firmly. He was skinny, no match to Kaz, even unarmed. "I think it was in the fifth. Behind some kind of business building. I don't remember. The windows looked kinda red when the sun glowed on them. The chick had pink hair."

The vampire slashed his long nails at Kaz, growling viciously as he would expect from a violent predator. It was a brave effort at survival, but not against a slayer who wielded a stake.

"Pink hair? Excellent. Now, what to do about you?"

"Give me dust!"

"Dust, you say?"

The vampire nodded eagerly.

Kaz slammed the stake through the vampire's heart. The creature ashed and landed in a thick pile of gray dust and melting clothing.

"Happy birthday to me."

It had to be done. Had he let the creature go, he would have eventually torn at a helpless mortal wearing something sparkly in an attempt to feed his unholy craving.

Catching movement at the end of the alley where he'd entered, Kaz rushed to the street and scanned both ways. He didn't see anyone. Nor did he feel any of the weird sensations he'd noticed when first entering FaeryTown. Yet his heart raced.

The rush of something big moved swiftly through the air above him, painting a shadow across the cobbled street beneath Kaz's boots.

A faery? Why couldn't he see it?

Pain suddenly pierced his gut. He gripped his hip, felt the hard, metal object that had embedded in his flesh, and forced himself not to cry out at the agonizing pain of it. Instead, his eyes tracked through the night in the direction from which he estimated the weapon had been shot.

Nothing. No movement. Not even a stray tourist fumbling about.

Had it been a fellow vampire keeping an eye out for his buddy? Maybe. But Kaz felt such a strange and unusual tingling in his wound he could only associate it with Faery.

Eyelids fluttering, he fought to control his senses as the pain needled its way into his veins and traversed his nervous system. He would not pass out here in FaeryTown. He could not. Vampires may come after him.

Or worse, faeries.

Perhaps they already had.

With thoughts of Zoë's raspberry lips to focus on and lure him onward, Kaz stumbled into the street filled with humans milling before a jazz club, and brushed past the wings of faeries who gave him little notice.

His hand slid down his leg, aiming for the iron blade in his boot, but he couldn't bend far enough without crying out in pain.

Too late for defense. His attacker was probably laughing as he flew off into the night like some kind of sparkly bat. Clutching his gut, he stumbled onward, knowing Zoë lived not far off, and hoping he'd make it.

Chapter 7

Concocting the blend was a lesson in marvel. Atoms made up everything in the universe, and understanding that, Zoe knew how to access the very molecules of a living substance and align them through use of verse and intent. Combine that with resonance, the key to all magic, and she could do amazing things.

Zoë never forgot to give thanks to the universe for her skills and innate powers as well as for the years of study alongside her father, who had taught her unique magics. Through focus, and channeling her energies, her magic had become a well-honed instrument.

Touching the goggles she wore, she ensured they were a good fit. Safety first. She'd experienced too many spells gone haywire as a teenager not to have learned that lesson.

"Not a peep on how silly I look," she commented to Sid.

Sid curled his tail about his legs, his silence a possible agreement.

Moonlight glittered across the marble worktable, dancing in the glass vials and alembics and doing a saucy tango with the contents that glowed purple and glinted with all colors.

Faery ichor was a beautiful thing. It saddened her that it worked such horrors on vampires. Just so, though. Perhaps vampires should stay away from faeries. But since they did not…

She chanted the transformative spell. The ichor settled at the bottom of the alembic and now it must rest for an hour before she could reduce it to dust. She set the timer.

Pushing up the goggles onto her forehead, she eyed Sid and nodded toward the door. "You hungry? I could go for a late-night cup of tea and some cookies. I've your favorite Russian tea cakes."

Sid scampered down the stairs and to the kitchen before Zoë even flicked off the lights in the spell room.

In the kitchen, she put on a kettle of water and dug out the cookies from a glass canister. Breaking one onto a plate, she set it on the floor for the cat, who eagerly went at the powdered-sugar-coated treat.

The phone rang, and, with a glance to the clock—past midnight—Zoë hesitated answering. She got so many cold calls from salesmen. But this late? She owned a clunky, old, rotary-dial phone, so caller ID was out of the question. It continued beyond the polite four rings, so she picked it up.

"Mademoiselle Guillebeaux?"

It was Mauritius, the vampire who had hired her. She recognized the British accent. "It's late."

"Not for me."

Of course not. Vampires were notorious night creatures. Did they ever sleep? She wasn't tired herself, but the principle of such a late call miffed her. Without question, vampires had entitlement issues. She let it go. Not worth the argument.

"Is there something I can do for you?" she asked. "I got the order for an increase in volume."

"Which you can handle?"

"Yes, I think so. We'll know for sure by Sunday."

"I trust you've the capability to produce. I've heard startling news regarding my liaison."

The pink-haired vampiress? "What's that?"

"She was attacked by a hunter last evening."

Attacked? More like Pink had sicced her henchmen on Kaz, while she'd stood back and watched the carnage ensue.

"Do you have any idea who could have done such a thing?"

"Why would I?" She wasn't going to hand over Kaz's name to a vampire who could erase him from the planet. Or, vice versa, alert a hunter to the vampire who was helping her to effect change in the vampire community.

"The woman is annoying," Zoë continued. "She probably looked at the hunter the wrong way and there you go. And that is what hunters do, isn't it? Stalk vampires? Anyway, can't she handle herself? Or is she dead?"

"No, not dead. I'm looking into things. I like to keep a tight rein on business."

"Business?" There was that word again. "Are you distributing my blend widely?"

"Oh yes, indeed, I am."

"I hadn't really considered it a business. More like charity."

"Business, charity. We all use different terms for the same thing."

"Sure." And all because Luc had hooked her up with Mauritius. "I haven't heard from Luc for weeks. He's not at his apartment."

"I understand he's been staying with…uh, someone who can help him overcome his addiction."

"Do you have a number for him?"

"Mademoiselle, as I've explained, your friend Luc doesn't want to speak with you until he's completely clean of dust. You understand? He wants to surprise you."

"Sure." But still.

It wasn't like Luc to disappear, no matter the circumstances. Though he did like surprises. They'd had a terrible beginning, but once they'd grown comfortable with one another, Luc had revealed his mischievous side to Zoë with late-night flower-picking excursions in the park and trips to the nearest cemetery to help her collect items for her spells. But not even a phone call?

"If you're sure you've no information leading to the hunter?"

"Don't be ridiculous, Mauritius. I don't cast a very wide net. It's just me and the cat here, and we pretty much keep to ourselves."

"Yes, you do live in a bit of a bubble. Works for me. Good evening, Mademoiselle. I'll be in contact soon."

She stared at the receiver after he clicked off. Why did her living privately work for him? The man was mysterious and annoying. But he was doing a good thing for his breed, so she overlooked the weirdness.

Sid jumped onto the kitchen table and rubbed his cheek along her arm. "Another cookie? Fine, but on the floor, Sid. No cats on the table."

The cat obeyed, parking himself by the plate with the crumbled cookie. Not a flake of powdered sugar remained, though the black cat did sport a smart white mustache.

Kaz spied Zoë sitting on her back steps amongst a froth of tall flowers that transformed her backyard into some kind of midnight wonderland tucked amidst the sooted gray landscape of Paris. He stopped at the wrought-iron gate, slapping a palm on the flaking curve of metal. The pain at his hip challenged clear thinking.

He considered turning and leaving. She hadn't noticed him yet. It was late, and he should have gone home. But he didn't think he could handle the trip without passing out on the Metro.

The thing stuck in his gut had securely clamped onto flesh and muscle like a homicidal squid. He'd twisted on it while stumbling here, but it had hurt like a mother, and knowing nothing about faery weapons he decided against yanking it out. A careful removal was necessary. And someone who practiced witchcraft might know a means to remove it.

Good thing she wasn't already tucked in bed. For a moment, his thoughts cleared the pain and replaced it with a woozy, dreamy wonder. He bet her sheets smelled like her, all fruits, spices and flowers. He could imagine nuzzling next to her in the morning with the sun beaming over their skin, both of them exhausted from making love.

Zoë challenged his need to walk away. Since meeting her he'd walked toward her every chance he'd gotten. And he had no explanation as to why. She knew what he did, and it didn't frighten her. But that didn't make it any less dangerous to invite her into his life.

Wincing, Kaz fought a painful groan, but only succeeded by half. Eyes blurring, he blinked. The bitter taste filled his mouth and he wobbled, unsure which direction was up or sideways. When the pain rumbled up in his throat, Kaz's tight moan prompted Zoë to scan her garden. When finally she met his gaze, he gave a little wave, then dropped to the ground on his knees, clinging to the gate as if that would keep him alert and conscious.

"Oh, goddess!" Zoë appeared by his side, her boots clicking the path stones, and knelt by him, touching his cheek with her palm. "What happened?"

Her touch spread warmth across his cheek. Damn, that felt good. Kaz winced and patted his hip. He didn't bleed much, which was the disturbing part.

"What is that?"

He drew away his hand to reveal the crazy weapon attached to his hip. "I was hoping you would know. Hurts like hell. I was minding my own business and got shot by someone I didn't even see. Probably a faery."

"Why would a faery— You must have pissed someone off."

"Always that possibility."

"This is a flechette. I've only seen these used by the sidhe. Get inside and take your shirt off. That thing will require some delicate surgery."

"Thanks, Zo—" Blackness toyed with his thoughts.

The witch smacked his cheek, shocking him to consciousness. "Stay with me. You're too big to toss over my shoulder."

Relief flooded his system with endorphins, and for the walk up the garden path and into her house, Kaz felt little pain. Or maybe it was following Zoë's sexy sashay that distracted his thoughts. Yeah, he could follow this chick anywhere. Into her house, into her arms, into her bed…

He trudged across the threshold and tugged off his shirt, which was bloodied at the hem, and it also sparkled. Wobbling like a drunk man trying to fight gravity, Kaz fingered the weird glitter. The cat swished about his ankles, nearly tripping him. He swung down an arm to pet him, but instead let out a groan and missed the feline entirely.

A beam of moonlight spotlighted Zoë, who stood before a window. A slim-fitted dress hugged her curves. Black, ankle-high boots and gray wool tights gave her an appropriately witchy look. Something bright glinted in her dark and light hair. A rhinestone barrette in the shape of a bow. And at her neck hung a diamond pendant he'd noticed yesterday, as well.

A dusted vamp would go crazy over those sparkly bits of decoration.

Her raspberry lips curved into a bow and she said, "Go

lie on the couch and pull down your jeans. I'll be right back with some tools."

"Tools?" Kaz winced, imagining the wicked torture devices with which the witch might return. Then he admonished himself for acting the sissy. He should rip the thing out, let out a good scream and be done with it. "Tools. Peachy."

Head spinning, he unzipped his jeans and shuffled them down to expose his hips. The weapon had chewed off some of the leather, so the pants did not stick. Then he collapsed on the couch, relieved to put up his feet and not worry some winged creature might be tailing him.

Wait.

"Kaz, what are you doing?"

He may have lured the faery to Zoë's house. This had not been a well-thought excursion. Sitting up, he thought to zip and leave, but Zoë's hand pushed him back down by the shoulder. He hissed at the pain of landing.

"I shouldn't have come here. I could have lured the faery who shot me to your door."

"Yes, you could have, but it's too late now, isn't it?"

He winced and shrugged guiltily. "Sorry."

"Despite my not believing in the fair folk, I do have faery wards on this house. As well as wards for vamps and weres."

"Probably should consider putting up a ward against hunters, eh?"

"Don't be silly. I wouldn't want to keep you away."

"Nicest thing a girl's ever said to me after 'pull down your pants and wait for me.'"

"And look how well you take orders." Her eyes skated over his hips and Kaz shyly swept his palm over his unzipped fly. Only his dark curls were visible, but still he felt the heat rise in his neck and behind his ears.

"You said you don't believe in faeries?" he asked.

"Course not. I'm not foolish," she said. "Didn't you stop believing in faeries when you were a kid?"

"Don't think I ever believed in them. That was girlie stuff. Uh, until now."

"You shouldn't."

"I don't. I mean—wait a second. You just confirmed this is a faery weapon stuck in my hip."

"It is."

"Then how can you not...?"

"Just because they exist doesn't mean I have to believe in them."

Kaz was having trouble following her logic.

"Belief grants them too much power," Zoë explained. "Stop believing in them, and they've little power over you. Now, let me take a look at the damage."

He yelped as she touched the flechette, tilting it side to side for inspection.

"It's embedded deep," she observed. "This weapon begins as a sort of ninja star when it's shot, but the arms of it hinge to secure a good hold. Barbed on the ends of the prongs, for sure. I'll have to pull away the skin and muscle and wiggle it out."

"Just yank it out quick," Kaz said through a tight jaw.

"And disperse the poison through your system?"

"Poison?"

"It's rare a faery weapon is not infused with poison. I suspect it's contained in a breakable tip. You wiggle it too much, you release the poison. Most likely it's a nerve agent that induces a slow and agonizing death. But if you want me to yank it—"

"No, that's cool." He slid a hand over hers, giving her wrist a gentle squeeze. "Slow and easy works for me."

"Mmm, yes, slow and easy." Zoë's eyelids closed and she licked those soft lips. Then she shook her head, rising from her wandering thoughts. "I'm going to numb the area with a spell, so relax and take in the words I speak without resistance."

Kaz nodded and closed his eyes. "Give it to me."

As Zoë spoke, he fell into the gentle recitation of magical words. He didn't understand them—they were probably Latin—but it didn't matter. Her focus was on him, and that felt all kinds of right. It wasn't often he got all the attention.

She didn't believe in faeries? Hell, he did. Unfortunately. But he also believed in this witch and the power of her healing magic.

He could feel her fingers moving about the flechette. Surrendering to the pain by allowing it to disperse and move through his body lessened its impact, and he was able to concentrate more on Zoë's sweet-smelling skin than the agonizing fire coursing through his muscles.

As she bent over him with what looked like long tweezers, her hair dusted his arm and he wanted to clutch the strands and press them against his mouth. Inhaling, he drew in her essence and imagined it filling his lungs like a white mist of magic. It was a sweet magic that would never choke him, and instead lulled him further into relaxation.

"Don't breathe," she muttered. "Ready?"

Before he could answer, fire exploded at his hip. Kaz tightened his jaw and his fists to keep from groaning loudly and from moving. Immediately after his induction into the Order, he'd taken a bullet while tracking a vampire tribe in Germany. It had burned through his marrow like molten lava. This was a similar pain, but it seemed to spread out from each of the weapon's prongs, prickling nerve endings all through his body.

"Is it out?" Kaz opened his eyes to see the weapon.

"I think this is Sidhe Cortège," she said, holding up the small five-pronged flechette to inspect. Blood and sparkly stuff oozed down the crazy ninja-star-like thing.

The woman was a miracle worker. She winked at him.

Kaz exhaled, melting with relief into the couch. Every muscle seemed to let go. Dodged a bullet, he did.

Make that a faery flechette.

"I've heard that before," he muttered. "Sidhe Cortège? Where have I heard that?"

She carefully set the weapon on the table. As the bloody metal landed on the wood surface, the metal prongs snapped back and resumed the original flat star shape. Kaz flinched, then checked his skittish reaction by sweeping a hand over his face. He didn't want to pick it up to inspect. It had a mind of its own.

Zoë moved her fingers over the wound on his hip, pressing together the serrated skin. That smarted, but at the same time, nothing in this world would make him ask her to stop. He wanted her touch.

"Sidhe Cortège operates out of FaeryTown," she said. "I think they are renegades from Faery, or they may even have been sent here by one of the sidhe courts. Not sure about their origins. Like I said—"

"You don't believe in them."

"Exactly. But for those who do believe, the Cortège is like, hmm…a faery mafia, if you will."

Ah yes, Vaillant had told him about them. "Great. A freakin' winged mafia. What? Will I find a unicorn head in my bed next?"

"Well, that little five-pronged present was your first strike."

"Three strikes and I'm out?" Kaz guessed.

"More like three strikes and you're dead." She beamed at him, and then blew something he could not see from her palm onto his hip. More magic, probably.

"Zoë, you just smiled when you said that I'd be a dead man come strike number three. Smiled."

She shrugged and dusted her hands together as if to signal the end of her operation. "In order to keep my magic pure and effective, I impart it with positive imagery. I was thinking about when we met that first night in the alley. You were so commanding, pulling me to you and kissing me silly."

He sat up on his elbows and met her dazzling gaze. "Silly?"

"Best first kiss I've ever had."

A smile twisted Kaz's lips. He had *known* that first night when she'd stood in his arms. And even though he didn't know how to define that knowing, the *feeling* of knowing was what kept the smile on his face.

Zoë picked up the flechette again and traced a finger along one of the prongs. "Oh, no. This is not good."

"Zoë, what are you—"

Suddenly dizzy, Kaz's head landed on the couch. The ceiling above him spun. Nausea curdled at the back of his throat and behind his eyes.

"One of the glass tips is cracked. The poison may have leaked out."

Chapter 8

"Are—are you sure?" Kaz's tongue tingled and felt three sizes too big.

"Shh. Close your eyes. Conserve your energy. You, uh...feeling okay?"

"Define okay."

"Shit. I'm going to have to bring in the big guns."

"You have...guns?"

"Don't speak. Just try to stay conscious. I'm going to spread healing magic over you. Big-time. This will take a lot out of me."

Kaz wanted to argue against her doing anything that would "take a lot out of her," but he wasn't in any position to argue. Feeling as if his head was filled with helium, he lay there, at her mercy.

A man didn't often find himself at the mercy of such a sexy woman. So why not go with it?

Zoë began to hum, not really a tune, but more a continuous vibration that he sensed birthed low in her throat. He cracked open one eye and saw she had closed her eyes. Her hands moved over his hip, not touching, but he could feel her heat permeate his body. So he closed his eyes and followed the movement of that warmth. As with the tone of her voice, it seemed to penetrate deeply, like some kind of focused massage combined with one of those mentholated heat wraps.

Except it didn't smell awful. Apples, cinnamon, herbs and even a trace of his aftershave scented the atmosphere. The air shimmered about his skin now, and he truly understood the power of her magic. It was as if particles of him—perhaps his very molecules—were sitting up and paying attention, because the command from the witch said such awareness was required for some super-duper healing.

That was how he imagined it, anyway. Drifting into the resonance of her melodious voice, Kaz floated up from his body, leaving behind the pain. Soaring, as if with wings, he didn't want to descend.

Zoë let out a gasp and her hair swept his bare stomach, tugging him back to reality with a scream of red pain. It was as if the poison had zapped his entire nervous system one last time, just for good measure, and then— complete relaxation.

"Whew!" Gathering her tools, she said, "Now you can rest."

Rest? He was no expert in witch magic, but he'd be damned if his body didn't hum with endorphins right now. He felt invigorated, no longer lightheaded and ready to jump up for action.

Had she just saved him from sure death by poison?

"Be careful. The skin at your hip sparkles, but I'm not sure if it's from the usual faery dust or the poison. Is this going to become a regular thing? You getting wounded and me fixing you up?"

"I hope not." Then again, what better excuse to return to her house for some one-on-one attention?

"Really?" Her head bowed, but then she looked up, sweeping the hair from her face and forcing a smile. She looked tired. "Because I don't mind the spell work. I like to practice my molecu—er, healing skills. And I certainly don't mind touching you."

"I don't mind you touching me at all. You wield a powerful touch."

"I should bandage that. Don't zip up your pants yet. No undies," she commented as she strolled from the room. "I like that."

Having forgotten that he normally went commando, Kaz felt his neck grow warm. Another part of him rose to attention, oblivious to the excruciating pain he'd just experienced. He tugged the zipper up most of the way, keeping the wound free from the jeans as best he could. He sat up. The wound didn't pain at all. Must have been a numbing spell. Whatever she'd done, he felt great, so he stood and gave his hips a testing wiggle.

"Good as new?" Zoë asked as she returned with a box of bandages. She stifled a yawn behind her hand.

Kaz looked at the box she set on the coffee table. He'd thought she was going to do the medical gauze and tape. But the Band-Aid she now wielded reduced his injury to a boo-boo. "Is that it?"

"You want me to cast it and put you on a stretcher?" she deadpanned.

He chuckled and spread his arms to give her access. "Make the boo-boo better, witch."

She placed two bandages over the wound and pronounced him slightly damaged but certainly capable. Kaz gave his hips another shimmy. "Thank you. I don't know how I can—"

"I'll take a kiss for the medical aid." She tilted up on her tiptoes, closing her eyes as she awaited her payment.

Kaz stroked her mouth with his thumb, thinking a kiss paltry payment for the kindness she had shown him. And there was that word again. Kindness. It occurred so little in his life. And yet, since he'd met Zoë it had become common. His thumb wandered up to the scar on her cheek, and he wondered if he could crack open his meager stores of kindness to make it better. Leaning down, he kissed the raised line of skin.

Zoë gasped as she pulled from him, a tear glinting in her eye. "Why did you do that?"

"Just wanted to make it better, I guess. Will you ever tell me how you got that?"

"What's done has been done." She stroked her cheek.

He kissed her cheek again, resolved to not press, but he would never let her off scot-free from an explanation. "Thank you, Zoë, for saving my life."

"I may have done just that. The spell countered the faery poison. It may also have given you a high when I transferred my vita to you."

"You transferred your—" He wasn't sure but he guessed that meant she'd given him her energy. She did look tired. "Sit down. You deserve a rest."

She sat on the couch and he knelt before her.

"I promise I'll pay more attention next time I'm in FaeryTown. I brought along an iron blade, but wasn't in a position to use it."

"You'll never see the Sidhe Cortège coming for you until it's too late. But keep the iron on you. If they show themselves to you, it could be a powerful weapon. Where did you get it?"

"Order arsenal."

Zoë's smile was tired at best. "The Order of the Stake fascinates me. Knights who take life-and-death vows. An arsenal of paranormal weapons. Bladed collars and secret brands. I don't suppose a witch could ever garner a tour?"

"Absolutely not. You already know too much."

"Hmm, then perhaps you should attempt to steal that knowledge from my brain with another kiss."

"Can I do that? Take away your memory with a kiss?"

She spread her hands up his bare chest and met his lips with hers, brushing softly. "You can certainly make it blurry. When you kiss me I forget everything except the joy of standing next to you. Your strong, hard chest." She stroked her palms over his chest. Kaz sucked in a breath. "The pulse of your heart against mine."

The press of her breasts against his skin cooled his fleeting desire to leave. What for? He'd just had surgery. Certainly he needed to rest a bit. He leaned forward, putting his hands on the back of the couch behind her.

Her lips parted, but inches from his. "Beguile me," she whispered.

Beguilement sounded too wondrous for a simple man like him to accomplish. So Kaz put aside that request and decided if he could kiss her breath away, that would do.

As their mouths joined, Zoë's body melded against his, seeking, finding, relaxing. He swept an arm around her back, supporting her weight, because he sensed she was really tired. Her kiss was lazy yet lingering, slow. She pulled back and yawned.

"Oh, I'm so sorry."

"If my kisses bore you—"

"I'm exhausted from the healing. I should—" She fainted.

Kaz caught her head and shoulders and laid her on the couch. "I'm the one who took all your energy from you. Vita," he recalled her saying.

She had given so much to heal him. And for what reason? He'd done nothing to earn her kindnesses. A few kisses meant little.

Hell, they meant a lot to him, but he didn't imagine a kiss meant much in the greater scheme of giving one's very life essence to save a man from death.

"I owe you a lot more than just the one kiss," he whispered.

Sid hugged his ankle, rubbing his tiny head against the leather of his boot.

Kaz tugged a blanket from a nearby chair and laid it over Sid's mistress. "Keep an eye on her, Sid. She's good stuff. Really good stuff."

Too good for him.

He kissed Zoë's lips, and suddenly odd images he'd once chased as a child invaded his thoughts. It was about the faery tale of the sleeping princess and her rescuing knight. He'd kissed her and brought her back to life.

Knight that he was, Kaz didn't know the first thing about chivalry. He couldn't give life, or even bring a person back from death, as she had done. His only skill was in taking life. Probably staying away from her would be best for them both.

"Can't do it," he muttered. "I like you too much, witch."

Kaz's phone rang to the tune of *Ride of the Valkyries*. He'd programmed each ringtone according to who was calling.

He answered, "Rook."

"I need you in the eighteenth right now," Rook said without preamble.

"I'm close." Kaz turned and started walking east. He hadn't gotten more than a quarter of a mile from Zoë's house. "What's up?"

"Another victim of Magic Dust madness. A human was attacked by a vamp. She's still alive. I've sent the location to your phone."

"Be there in five minutes." Kaz picked up into a run down a darkened residential street, while he brought up the address Rook had sent.

It must be after midnight. No one was out on this street but he could hear traffic and the nightlife two or three streets away. Remarkably, his hip didn't hurt. That spell had jacked him up like six cups of coffee.

He rounded the corner and entered a residential area populated with centuries-old houses stacked close and low. The coordinates Rook had given him led up a narrow path overgrown with long grass that was near to hay length. Likely an older resident lived within the limestone-fronted, two-story house.

Kaz rushed through the open front door, using caution as he entered. He stopped, pressed his back to the foyer wall and pulled out a stake. If the victim had just been attacked the vamp could still be in the area.

"Kaspar?"

He raced up the stairs toward his supervisor's voice. To the left of the landing, an open door revealed the bed sheets pulled to the floor and a scatter of jewels everywhere. Kaz avoided stepping on a tumble of diamond rings that glinted in the moonlight and snuck to the bedside where Rook stood over a woman. She was eighty, maybe ninety. Her long, gray hair strewn over a pink satin pillow was stained red, and her throat was drenched in blood. Her eyelids fluttered at the sight of the men standing over her, then closed and her jaw fell slack.

"Almost dead," Rook confirmed with no emotion. The Order leader was dressed casually in slacks and a sweater. He rarely went out on the hunt, though he did wield a stake in one hand. "I was strolling down the street when I heard her scream. Couldn't not investigate, right?"

"So this just happened." Alert, Kaz looked out the door. "The perp must have attacked her while she slept. There's too much jewelry lying around."

"The vamp must have been scamming for something that sparkles," Rook said, standing back from the old woman and looking over the floor.

"So why attack the woman? She couldn't have gone to bed wearing jewelry."

"Maybe." Rook inspected the woman's throat without touching her. "Some of them tend to wear their valuables if they have a lot of meaning to them. Madame may have worn her finest to bed."

"Okay, I can buy that. But the vamp didn't get what he came for, save some blood."

Rook nodded, confirming they should investigate the rest of the house. He bent to scoop up a diamond necklace from the floor. "Bait."

"I've got something even better." Kaz displayed the small glass vial of faery ointment he'd gotten from Zoe.

"What the hell?"

"Not Magic Dust, but something more alluring to a vampire than cold, hard diamonds, I'm betting. I'll take the lower level."

Knowing that if a vampire were still in the house he must be aware of the two hunters, Kaz decided he was a smart dust junkie. Most would not be able to remain so quiet or hide. Either that, or the attacker was gone. But he'd not risk letting down his guard without thoroughly checking out the place.

The woman would not survive the ambulance ride to the hospital. Unfortunate, but he'd seen lesser wounds and had watched the victim die.

Stepping into the foyer before the opened front door, Kaz silently closed it, then turned down a narrow, dark hallway that led toward the back of the house. Moonlight beamed through the far window. Reaching the window, he held up the glass vial. The black ointment caught the moonlight and sparkled madly.

"Got something for you," he called. "You like the spar-kly stuff?"

Kaz stepped into the kitchen, vial held high. A hand

grasped for the vial. Kaz snatched it away, and spun, slamming the vamp against the wall, his hand squeezing its throat and the stake finding its place against the vamp's thudding heart.

"Where do you get your dust?" Kaz demanded.

The vampire sputtered blood at him.

Rook rounded and entered the kitchen, stake at the ready.

Kaz tucked away the vial in a coat pocket while the vampire squirmed against his hold. He wasn't strong, very weak, in fact, and that made Kaz guess he was not high on the dust, but desperate to get more.

"You can have all the dust you can inhale if you tell me who sold you the Magic Dust," Kaz insisted.

Rook pressed a hand to the vampire's shoulder. He kept his stake down. This was Kaz's kill. "Answer the man," he prompted.

"Don't have a name!" he eked out. "Give me the magic!"

"Why'd you go after that woman upstairs?" Kaz asked. His anger forced a cocky stance. "She look like a dust dealer to you?"

"Just want the sparklies. Searching all the houses. Found some."

"You're not going to get anything from this one," Rook said.

With a heavy exhale, Kaz nodded agreement. "Hell's waiting, asshole." Squeezing the paddles pinioned out the stake into the vampire's heart. Within seconds, he began to ash.

Outside, police sirens sounded and flashing red lights glanced off the kitchen walls. A neighbor must have called after hearing the woman's screams.

"Back door," Rook said.

The men ran out the back as the police were entering the front. With luck, the emergency team would transport the woman to the hospital in time. But Kaz believed she was already dead.

Faeries and dead humans. He believed in too much, and none of it good.

"You touch anything?" Rook asked as they dashed through the dark alley away from the scene.

"Just the longtooth. No prints. Do you even have to ask?"

Slowing, Rook stopped in the middle of the cobbled alley, the darkness revealing his narrow face in shadows. "I'm not sure what I need to ask of you anymore, Rothstein. What the hell are you doing with faery ointment? Is that the same stuff under your eyes?"

He'd forgotten he still had the stuff on. He expected the man would know its use. Rook knew everything.

"You don't think it a necessary tool for investigating in FaeryTown? Why was I never told about this stuff during training?"

"The Order hunts vampires. We keep our distance from faeries. It's not wise to fuck with the sidhe."

"Yeah, but if you haven't noticed, this investigation is twisted all up in the faeries' business. I need all the help I can get, and if that means smearing some glitter under my eyes then I'm going to do it!"

As Kaz's words abruptly ended, the night fell heavily upon the men. Normally, he would never raise his voice to Rook. Call it a long day. Hell, he'd been shot by a faery and now had found yet another victim of Magic Dust.

"What's up with you, Kaspar?"

Rook laid a hand on Kaz's shoulder and he shook it off. The man had a way of looking into him with a touch. He didn't like it. It was creepier than a witch with a tattoo gun.

"What's wrong is I feel as if I'm chasing my tail trying to get a clue in this case. A one-fanged vampire? Don't they heal instantly? So if he lost a fang, it's probably already grown back."

"Possible. They can regenerate bone, but some of the research excludes the teeth."

"We can hope. And the faery angle. I'm out of my element with all things Faery. If the vamps are selling faery dust, they have to have a source, which, I'm guessing, is in FaeryTown. But someone is modifying the faery ichor, changing it chemically to this new drug, Magic Dust. Did you have the sample analyzed?"

"We're still looking at it. We don't have a forensics team to study the faery dust. We need a powerful witch or warlock, or maybe even a faery. I've got a witch looking at it now, but don't get your hopes up."

"With today's technology can't we reverse engineer the stuff?"

"It's sidhe, Kaspar. They are from a completely different realm. It's like analyzing Martian soil. They are not like us and we haven't the skills to analyze the unknown."

Yeah, but Zoë had some crazy skills. She'd counteracted faery poison. Kaz should have her take a look at the Magic Dust. But he'd keep that info from Rook for now.

"The best we can do is continue to track vampires and take them out, as our vows demand." Rook pulled out his cell phone and hit speed dial. "We left the vamp in a pile of ash. I'll have to bring Tor in for this one."

Tor would arrive on the scene and get to the reporters before they talked to the police and emergency crews. The woman's death would be reported as a burglar with a knife, no doubt. The ash pile? He wasn't sure what sort of double-talking Tor would finesse for that one.

Rook finished giving Tor the address and hung up. He slapped Kaz across the shoulder. "Thanks for coming so quickly. That was good work. You heading home?"

"Not sure. I need to clear my head, think this through. There's something I'm missing. I'm sure of it."

"Walk home, let the air settle you. It'll come to you."

"Will do. Uh, Rook?"

"Yes?"

He didn't know how to ask delicately, so Kaz just tossed what he was thinking out there. "Do you believe in faeries?"

Rook tilted his head and a tiny smirk curved the edge of his mouth. "How can you ask such a thing when you've apparently seen them, thanks to that ointment under your eyes?"

"Yeah, I did see them. But Zo—er, someone once told me that if you believe in them, you give them power. So if you don't believe in them, then..."

"It's an interesting theory. I don't know what to tell you, Kaspar. At all turns, you must focus on the vamps."

"I know. I will. I'll talk to you later, man."

Rook turned and jogged off.

Yeah, he needed to put his mind in a different place than stalking vampires and chasing sparkly faeries. Something unrelated that would allow his brain to wander. He couldn't sleep now, that was sure.

The one thing that always put his mind in a different place was sex. But he was pretty sure the only woman he was interested in wouldn't be receptive to a booty call. She was sleeping like a baby right now, under Sid's watchful care.

With a sigh, Kaz headed home. He spent the next hour before the city map, redefining the borders of FaeryTown to include the victim's home.

Odd thing? Zoë's house hugged an edge of FaeryTown.

Had she purposely chosen that location? She was in the know about faeries. He had to ask her to look at the dust. Nicely. If she didn't believe in them, could she possibly figure out what made them tick? Probably not, but she had shown him some amazing skills in counteracting the poison.

Perhaps he could wield seduction to soften Zoë's distrust for all things involved with faeries?

After a long day concocting the blend, Zoë was ready for a break. She'd missed supper, so reheated a bowl of stew. That hit the spot. Sid licked the bowl clean.

She'd woken close to noon on the couch, and realized Kaz had left her there. She must have fainted or literally fallen asleep when he'd been kissing her. Gotta be some bad sexual karma in that. But the molecular healing had really knocked the energy out of her.

All day her thoughts had vacillated between focus on the spell and Kaz.

"I need to explain to him so he doesn't feel rejected."

Just when she wished she had the hunter's phone number, he appeared at her doorstep. Kaz's smile beamed at her, and he bounced on his heels and rubbed his palms together.

Nervous? That was surprising.

"You like to dance?" he asked.

"Uh, yes?"

"Do you want to go dancing?"

"Right now?" Night hugged the front lawn and moonlight glinted in the neighbor's windows across the street. "You don't have slaying to do?"

"Later. I just want to spend some time with you. Get my mind off the job and maybe—"

"Maybe a little break from all the stabbing and killing?"

He shrugged sheepishly. "Yes?"

Kaz's clever smile rolled over her like warm rain. It made her shiver in anticipation. "Yes to dancing," she answered without thought. "But I need to change."

He nodded. "I can wait." He reached for her hair, but Zoë stepped back, clasping the thick clutch of white hair before he could. "Did you do something to your hair? I don't remember the white streak being so...wide."

She shrugged. "Must have parted it differently today." She didn't need to explain that with every healing that involved her bringing a person back from near-death, the universe extracted some of her life force as payment. "Let me go touch up my face and hair. Ten minutes!"

While the hunter busied himself in the living room chatting up Sid, Zoë pulled out dress after dress from her closet and laid them on the bed. A goofy giddiness scurried about her core and she felt as if it was prom season and she had but moments to prepare before the coach arrived with her handsome prince.

"No, that's not right," she muttered, touching the hem of the red silk number. "That's Cinderella, not prom. And I certainly can't talk to mice."

Not that she hadn't tried.

Zoë hadn't gone to prom, but only because her father had been teaching her that evening. As well, she hadn't been asked to the prom. So she'd been a wallflower attending mortal school. Quickly, she'd learned it wisest to keep her witchy eccentricities to herself if she had hoped to make it through the teenage experience in one piece.

The red dress she'd flung across the bed was too short and too low-cut. Made for a night of club dancing, which, she hoped Kaz hadn't in mind. She wasn't up for frenzied, sweaty stuff because she knew nothing about current dance steps.

She touched the floral chiffon gown that had once belonged to her mother. Tiny pink roses were embroidered about the empire waistline, and a tea-length underskirt of pink barely showed through the white overlayer dashed with pastel roses. It was filmy and romantic and…no doubt far too fancy for the dancing Kaz had in mind.

Surely he was thinking nightclub, not ballroom.

She held up the gown and admired it in the mirror and remembered how gorgeous her mother had looked in it.

"Why not?" she asked the imaginary damsel in the mirror. "Nowadays, most any style is acceptable."

Stunned by the vision that floated down the stairs, Kaz clasped a hand over his chest and gaped. Flowing fabric hugged Zoë in all the right places and billowed at the calves like some kind of angel garb. Her soft pink cheeks and lips pursed into a wondering smile.

"Uh…you look…" He didn't have the words for her kind of gorgeous. Yet he felt too much right now. Desire. Admiration. Hunger. Wonder. Want.

"It's too much," she decided, her smile falling.

"Uh…"

"Yes, it's too much. Oh!" She flung out her hands as she landed in the foyer. "I'm such a dork at dating and romance. I love this dress, and I started thinking how pretty my mother looked when she once wore it and then I put it on, but—we're going to a nightclub, right?"

"We were, but, uh—"

"I'll go change."

"No!" Kaz grabbed her hand, staying her, and with his other hand tugged out his cell phone. "Just hang on, gorgeous. I saw something about an event in the paper over my morning coffee…."

He searched the events calendar he had delivered to his phone each day. Yep, there it was. He wasn't exactly dressed for it in leather pants and a sweater, but he could work with it.

"It's going on right now at the Trocadéro," he said. And with a wink, he added, "Let's do this."

Chapter 9

The Place du Trocadéro glittered with lights strung across the esplanade between the two Palais de Chaillot buildings. Across the river, the Eiffel Tower twinkled. The air was filled with the lush sounds from a local orchestra playing a lilting waltz.

Zoë didn't know how to waltz, but Kaz led her up the stairs and into the crowd of elegantly dressed dancers who had come to enjoy an outdoor celebration of dancing and champagne. She didn't need to know how to dance because following Kaz made it effortless. He knew what he was doing and led her into the rhythm with a surprising confidence. So without allowing herself to think about cartoon princesses swishing across the screen in the arms of their heroes—okay, just a few minutes—she swished right along with him.

No man had ever taken her dancing, nor had any man she'd met at a bar even known how to move his body to a rhythm, let alone lead her in the dance. Kaz surprised her around every turn, and those surprises touched her very soul.

The next dance was a quick step, and he started in with a few short, sideways steps, and she ran along with him, not getting the steps, but not caring.

"Just follow me," he said. "It's more about keeping up."

His confident smile enchanted her, and she danced the entire song as if on a cloud.

Now Zoë stood crushed up against the gorgeous knight with the magic feet. The orchestra played a slower song. This was a dream she didn't want to end.

"I can't believe this night," she said. "It's magical."

"Coming from a witch, I'd say that's a pretty strong statement."

"It's beyond any magic I've ever touched." She laid her head on his shoulder and melted against his primal heat.

His thick biceps hugged her and he whispered, "Here with you is the best night. Puts my brain in a new place. I needed this."

"You come up with something to help you with your investigation?"

"Nope. And that's okay. I needed some breathing room, to not think."

Finding her place against him with an exhale, Zoë lost herself in the hard planes of his chest and abdomen, the sweet licorice-and-leather scent of him and the lulling strains of the orchestra enticing all to surrender to what love had to offer.

She wouldn't fool herself. Despite her aspirations for happily ever after, this *affaire de coeur* was not love. But it was exciting and made her toes curl. Any woman who ignored that was a fool.

Because love was harder and deeper. It took much longer to develop. Or at least, that's what she supposed. She'd never been in love. Blind adoration, surely. But Zoë had always gotten over her infatuations and moved on to the next guy, determined never to make the same mistakes, and to learn with each new lover.

It was stupid to blame her bad relationships on the scar marring her cheek, but, when her ex-lovers had been truthful, they'd confessed it bothered them. And as for those who hadn't confessed, she sensed it in the winces they had tried unsuccessfully to hide.

Kaz's hand glided down her back, mapping the curve above her hip until he landed on her derriere. Their bodies swaying to the music, she sighed against his chest and he hugged her closer and kissed the crown of her head.

It was odd, standing in the arms of a mortal man who had taken it upon himself to slay vampires. Zoë tended to walk a wide circle around those who believed problems were best solved with a cruel word, punch or an even viler act. She always sided on giving a person every chance possible, because everyone who walked this earth was just trying to survive and get along.

"You won't hurt me, will you, Kaz?" It just came out. She regretted it immediately.

He pulled back, his eyes searching hers. He shook his head, but couldn't hide the hurt darkening his eyes. "Why would you ask such a thing?" He stroked her cheek. "Oh."

"No, it's nothing to do with that." Clasping his hand, she pulled it from her cheek. "I was thinking about you." She nuzzled against his shoulder again. "Being a vampire hunter."

He rubbed a palm up her back, stirred up a giddy tingle that swam up her spine and embraced her surely. "I won't hurt you, Zoë. Not physically."

The added clarification startled her. Did that mean he might hurt her otherwise? Mentally? Emotionally?

Perhaps he couldn't promise such a thing. He didn't know where this new relationship was headed, nor did she. The best he could give her was a promise of safety from harm.

Best she accept that, and take whatever the future promised for their relationship with her head held high. This damsel would take the dance and be happy with it, no matter if she never saw the dashing knight again.

"I've never been good in relationships," he whispered at her ear. "I always seem to screw them up. I prefer to run rather than tough things out. Just so you know."

"You keep giving me that excuse," she said. She tugged him toward the edge of the dance floor where half the dancers lingered and clinked champagne glasses. They found a spot against the waist-high stone wall that looked over the Seine. "If I'm just a fling, Kaz, tell me, and I'll know how to work with what's going on between us."

He tapped the diamond pendant resting at the base of her neck. "It's not an excuse. It's just the same record playing over and over in my mental process. You challenge me to change it, though."

"Will you accept that challenge?"

"I will." He squeezed her hand to cement that acceptance. "I want to see what happens with us."

Such a hopeful gleam in his freckled brown eyes. He was ready to give the damsel a chance. Zoë touched his cheek and pressed her palm to his skin. "Yes, let's see what happens. Come what may."

"Cool." Bending, he delivered a sweet morsel to the tip of her nose. "Damn, you really put me in a better place, Zoë."

The conductor announced the final song would be a waltz.

"You want to get out of here?" he asked.

She nodded.

He slid a hand into hers and they strolled, arms swinging happily, toward the Metro.

They arrived just as the train took off, so Kaz and Zoë settled onto a bench to wait the five or ten minutes for the next train. They hadn't let go of each other's hands. Zoë clasped Kaz's hand to her chest and closed her eyes, taking a moment to imprint the magical dancing at the Trocadéro in memory. It was something a girl would never forget, but she trusted memory more when she reviewed it.

"Did you have a good time?" he asked softly.

"The best. How did you learn to dance so well? It's not something I'd expect…"

"From a guy who walks around with stakes and holy water in his pockets?"

"Well, yes. Did your parents make you dance when you were little? Did you have an eccentric aunt who whisked you onto the dance floor at family gatherings? Or does the Order train their knights in the seductive arts?"

Kaz chuckled. "You thought my dancing was seductive?"

"Yes. You won me tonight, Kaz. Holding me in your arms and swirling me about the dance floor, you just… Wow."

He pressed a kiss to her hand and clasped both of his around hers to hold on his lap. "You have a much higher opinion of my dancing skills than I've ever had."

"Trust me. You seduced the hell out of me. So it's an Order skill, huh?"

"Nope. The Order is all about militant skills and protecting the innocent. I actually learned to dance after I ran away from home. Spent a lot of time hanging out behind Madame du Monde's Dance Emporium. Best place to sleep on a cold February night was tucked behind the garbage bin and wedged against the wall of the dance studio."

"Oh, Kaz. You ran away? I had no idea. Were you very young?"

"Fourteen when I took off from my dad's house." He shrugged, sensing the further questions she didn't dare speak. "It is what it was."

"I wish you hadn't had such a hard life."

"Made me the man I am today. Dancing machine that I am."

She smiled at his light tone and laid her head on his shoulder. He'd volunteer information about him and his dad if he wanted to, so she wouldn't ask. Besides, she wanted this night to stay magical and not dip into the dark side.

"So you took dance lessons from Madame du Monde?"

"Yes and no. I was sort of forced into it with the lure of cookies and coffee. I knew Madame du Monde was aware I snuck about her building, but I never gave her any trouble, so she never gave me any. One night, though, she came out looking for me. Said she needed an extra man to dance with her students. I thought she'd slipped on some ice and cracked her noggin. But when I smelled the cookies, well... Wasn't often I got a hot meal, and the coffee was the perfect lure in the winter.

"So this stupid fifteen-year-old kid stumbled about the dance floor, forcing himself to hold the hands of the old ladies who smiled at me with their bright, painted lips and crooked wigs. I thought it was dumb. But my focus was aimed on the refreshments table. I was allowed to eat all the leftover cookies, and my stomach kept me coming back. Whenever Madame du Monde called, I was there. Eventually, I started paying attention, and—though I would never admit it to myself at the time—I enjoyed dancing. I was learning something new. Hell, I was warm and on a sugar high."

"I would have loved to have been one of those ladies," Zoë said.

"You just were." He kissed the top of her head.

"Can we dance again sometime?"

The next train pulled up with a squeal.

"I'm already plotting ways to get you onto the dance floor again," he said.

* * *

The subway train was quiet, and Kaz and Zoë were alone, save for an elderly woman who sat on one of the hard, red plastic seats, a tapestry tote clutched to her chest. She smiled at the twosome but didn't look interested in conversation.

Kaz grabbed a steel pole and pulled Zoë next to him. The pole between them, they stood face-to-face. She smiled up at him and he gave her a goofy wink. She was glad she'd seen his fun side tonight. There was more to this man than bladed collars and deadly stakes.

He was unsure of starting a relationship. She gave him points for being honest. Much as she would have loved to hear him profess his undying love for her, she realized she didn't want *the end* to come as quickly as she initially had. They needed more time to learn one another. A dozen more chapters, at the very least.

Tilting up on her toes, she kissed him, lingering on the softness of his mouth that gave so much. He always relaxed into her, as if she gave him permission to let go and not be the tough hunter all the time.

One arm wrapped about the pole, she slid the other around and under his shirt at the small of his back. The woman sat behind her, so that little move went unnoticed. She'd love to dash her tongue over his hot skin. Taste his danger and lose herself in the mystery of his licorice-and-leather essence.

The train stopped to let on three men at the opposite end of the car. Zoë gave them little notice, but Kaz's body suddenly stiffened against hers. The hand he rested at her hip jerked away and slapped to his chest. Then it slid down to his thigh where he unbuttoned the cargo pocket.

"What is it?" she asked. Turning a look over her shoulder she saw the men approach, menace in their eyes. Narrowing her vision, she spied the glint of white at the corner of the leader's mouth. "Oh, goddess."

Kaz twisted her around to stand behind him. "Vampires."

Chapter 10

They marked him immediately. But how? He wasn't wearing Order gear. The threesome looked like a gang of street hoodlums on the trail of trouble. All were slender and wore loose clothing, and had long hair. But Kaz did not miss the exposed fangs on the one in the front.

Vampires looking for a bite, or worse, mindless menace.

The old woman sitting before Kaz was unaware of the danger stalking down the narrow aisle between rows of red, plastic seats. Best to leave her oblivious and take care of the danger before it got too close.

He rushed the vamps, stake in hand. The first one swung a fist at him, missing. Kaz punched him in the gut. The vampire groaned and wobbled to his knees. Just because they were immortal didn't make them unbreakable. The guy behind the leader used Kaz's distraction to slash a blade across his biceps. That hurt, but it hadn't cut deep. Had he been wearing his coat, the Kevlar would have protected him.

The one at the rear of their trio jumped over the plastic chairs, his focus on the old woman. Kaz swung up his fist, catching the vampire midair; the stake entered his heart with little resistance. Ash formed in the shape of a man soaring through the air, burning clothing to embers, then dropped onto the seats in a dusty, smoking scatter.

The old woman didn't acknowledge anything unusual. With hope, she was hard of hearing.

A hand grabbed Kaz's ankle and he lost his balance, landing on the hard, rubber floor between two seats. He met eyes with the old woman, who leaned over, assessed him, then nodded reassuringly before looking up toward the front of the car.

As he pushed up onto his feet, Kaz craned his neck and spied Zoë looking like a fantasy princess in her long, airy dress and clinging to the steel pole—but vulnerable.

A vampire growled and grabbed him by the sweater, pulling him upright to face him. "Slayer, that was my best friend. Why did you do that?"

"He was going for the old lady."

"Don't you know the best vintages are the older ones? Franck!"

The vampire named Franck lunged over the seats toward Zoë. Kaz head-butted the vampire who held him. His brain jounced against the insides of his cranium and his eyeballs jittered, but the damned thing didn't even flinch, merely cracked a bloody grin and flicked out a switchblade.

Zoë screamed.

The sound of her fear heated the back of Kaz's neck and tightened his muscles like no witchy healing spell ever could. As the vampire's blade slashed toward his face, he gripped the attacker's wrist and twisted it toward him, breaking the fragile carpal bones. The vampire's scream didn't upset the old woman sitting to his right.

"Zoë, I'll be right there!"

Kaz heard Franck curse and knew Zoë must be fighting for all she was worth. If she could repel him with magic, he hoped she would do so. First, he needed to ash this annoying vamp that would not die. There was always one in every bunch. A knee to the man's jewels resulted in a creepy smile that dripped with blood.

"Want sparklies!" the vampire behind him growled.

Franck was on Magic Dust. And Kaz recalled the glint of the diamond pendant nestled at the base of Zoë's throat when they'd danced earlier.

He stabbed his attacker, but the stake landed at his throat. It wouldn't serve a death punch, but he compressed the paddles, anyway. The vamp croaked around the throat kabob. With blood dribbling out around the titanium stake, he shuffled his neck off the weapon, and jumped backward, clutching the gushing, yet not fatal, wound.

Kaz spun and kicked high, landing a boot to Franck's head. Zoë had sunk to the floor, curving herself inward into a ball. Why hadn't she used some magic and zapped the longtooth?

"Stay down," he directed as he turned to catch the other in a lunge.

Blood from the vampire's opened throat spattered Kaz's face. The stake was slippery with blood, and when he landed it against the vampire's chest, he gave it the death punch. The vampire gasped, swore and ashed.

The train car stopped, the doors sliding open. The old woman stood to disembark and stepped carefully over the pile of ash.

"Sorry," Kaz offered, feeling as if he'd made a mess all over granny's floor.

"I've seen worse," the old woman offered. And she scuttled off, tapestry bag in hand. Without a look back, as the doors closed, she called, "Watch out behind you!"

Gripping a pole with both hands, the stake clanging against the steel, Kaz swung up both legs and booted the vampire standing over Zoë. He saw blood on her neck.

"He's after the necklace!" he yelled. "Take it off and toss it."

"No!"

The vampire lunged for Zoë, and Kaz managed to jump onto his back. Trying to pull the manic fang-face off the witch was like trying to peel an octopus away from the side of a glass aquarium. He kept latching on, then detaching, then going back.

Zoë's arms were pinned. She couldn't reach the necklace.

Kaz reached over the vampire's shoulder, gripped the necklace at Zoë's throat and tore it away. He dangled the diamond before the vampire.

The dust freak followed, bloodied fingers clutching the air and eyes peeled on the sparkling bit. Behind them, Zoë scrambled upright, clutching her throat.

"Come on," Kaz beckoned. "You want it? Tell me where you go to get the Magic Dust."

"Want more sparklies."

The Magic Dust had reduced the idiot to lower than idiotic. It sickened Kaz. He should stake him to put him out of his misery. But he could use this one. He seemed to possess more self-control than the previous kill he'd made with Rook.

"You can have the sparkly. Just tell me who your dealer is."

"Don't know." He swung for the necklace, but Kaz jerked it away from his reach. "Sexy chick," the vampire added. "Pink hair."

Switch.

"Good boy."

"Gimmee!" The vampire swiped at the necklace.

Kaz swung his arm back, putting the prize out of reach, while seesawing around with his other arm. The stake entered the vampire's side, smoothly piercing between ribs and tearing through the thundering heart muscle. The vampire gasped, cast Kaz a how-could-you look, then ashed.

He didn't say it out loud—with Zoë watching—but another "Happy birthday" was due him.

The train squealed to a smooth stop. Kaz jumped over the piles of ash, grabbed Zoë about the waist and swept her into his arms. He leaped out onto the platform, and without another word, ran through the long concrete tunnel that angled upward. When they surfaced in the city, moonlight teased the sky with a silvery sheen

Zoë clung to his biceps. Her body shook against his chest. He sensed she'd been—or still was—crying. "Take me home."

Zoë didn't live far from the Clignancourt Metro stop, yet she didn't think to ask Kaz to let her down to walk. It felt too good cradled in his big, strong arms. She'd never thought a man capable of carrying a woman so far and for so long.

Her knight had rescued her.

He avoided the street before her home because she didn't want neighbors wondering what was up. It was well after midnight, but there were always lights on in the nearby houses.

For some reason she hadn't been upset over seeing the vampires staked, or even being attacked by one. It had been the old woman's nonchalant reaction that stung Zoë to the soul. As if she had seen so much in her lifetime that watching three creatures, who shouldn't exist, getting staked was nothing to her.

When had the world become so jaded?

Kaz stopped before the gate to her backyard. Night scents of primrose, heliotrope and moonflower greeted her. Only last night he had collapsed here in agony. They were both engaging in a lot of rescuing lately. Par for the course when manic vampires were involved.

Exhaustion toyed with her muscles in a way that reduced her to a melted bit of bones against her big, strong warrior. When finally he set her down on the cobbled path inside the wrought-iron gate, she didn't want to let him go. A vine of frothy honeysuckle dusted her shoulder with pollen. A cricket chirped along with a choir of frogs somewhere near the lilypad-dotted pond.

In the darkness, she felt his fingers move over her throat where earlier the vampire's fingernails had scratched her.

"How does it look?" she asked.

"Just a scratch."

"He didn't get his fangs anywhere near me. But why was he after my necklace?"

Kaz pulled out her diamond pendant from his coat pocket.

"I thought I had lost that. It was my mother's. I'm so thankful."

He placed it in her palm, then wrapped her fingers over it and kissed her knuckles. "It's a new kind of faery dust that's been circulating lately."

"A new kind…"

Like hers? Zoë's heartbeats thundered so suddenly she had to swallow to catch her heart from rising to her throat.

No, the blend she produced was designed to help the vampire kick the dust habit. It would never make them rage as the one in the Metro had.

"They're calling it Magic Dust," Kaz said. "It's regular faery dust times ten. Really amps up the vampire. Once in their system, it builds up and never dissipates. They'll grab for anything that sparkles. They just want more dust."

"That's why he wanted my diamond." Zoë suddenly felt lightheaded. Her knees bent and she wobbled.

Kaz caught her with an arm around her shoulder and walked her toward the back door. When they got to the step, she sat down and patted the step beside her for him to sit. He did so, taking a moment to sweep the hair from her cheek and kiss her.

"How do you know about this Magic Dust?" she asked. "Is it something the Order is investigating?"

"It's personal to me."

She studied his gaze, seeing the pain glinting in the freckled irises. "Personal?"

"I lost two friends recently," he offered. "Husband and wife. A vampire went after the wife's neck because she was wearing a rhinestone necklace. Ripped out her throat, then tore up the husband when he tried to protect her. I only managed to get to the husband in the hospital a few minutes before he died. He had a chance to tell me about the vamp who did it, though."

She heard Kaz swallow and clasped his hand in hers. She felt his pain and wished she could heal that, too. But mental scars were not something witches could ever heal.

"I'm so sorry, Kaz. Magic Dust sounds awful. I'm glad you're trying to stop it. I've many vampire friends, but I cannot tolerate senseless killing. A vampire doesn't need to kill for survival. Most need only drink blood once every week or two."

"Exactly. And they don't need to drink a lot. Just enough to take the edge off. This Magic Dust is creating real monsters. Someone has to stop them before another human dies. I wish you hadn't seen that on the train. I'm sorry." He drew her head onto his shoulder and kissed her hair. "That old lady was one tough cookie, eh?"

"It disturbs me that she wasn't horrified. Society has lost its repulsion toward violence. I hate violence."

"It's necessary sometimes." He stroked the scar on her cheek.

She melted against him, slipping an arm about his and clasping his biceps. Dire thoughts segued to more intimate feelings when she was close to him. Her focus zoned in on Kaz's calm, steady breathing and the heat of his hard, lean body. She felt safe with him.

"I want you to stay, but I'm so tired," she whispered. "You must be exhausted after fighting those vamps. Seems as if you can't set foot around the city without attracting either vamps or the Sidhe Cortège. Faeries and vampires hunting the hunter?"

"All in a day's work. Though faeries are a new challenge. You want me to come in and sit with you until you fall asleep? I'll lock the door and leave when you're snoozing."

"I'd like that."

Kaz sat listening to Zoë's soft breaths. She'd cuddled up in his lap like a kitten. He was tired, but not from fighting vamps. Lately, the world was piling all kinds of challenging situations upon him and he was having a hard time juggling them all. But he wouldn't change things for all the diamonds in the world.

They'd had a good time dancing, entwined together beneath the twinkling lights. It had felt like something he'd never had before. An intimacy he'd not thought possible. To stand and hold a woman and not think about having sex with her right then and there? What Zoë gave him was new and more erotic than a quick shag in the hallway. Because the wondering and waiting hummed in his bones and promised a satisfactory progression.

As well, she'd given him kindness and a certain trust he wasn't afraid to accept. He'd opened up to her about Madame du Monde. It had felt right to share his past with her. She respected his secrets as he respected hers.

He'd intended to take her out dancing to soften her up for when he asked her to analyze a sample of Magic Dust. Life had intervened. His life. Which was about as dangerous as it got.

He had blood crusted in his hair and behind his ear. He should go shower, but…

He brushed the hair from her face and wondered over the scar. It didn't bother him, nor did it make her ugly to him. But he wanted to know how she had been hurt, and maybe, somehow, erase the pain of that memory.

Not an easy thing to do, he knew. Some memories pained for a lifetime. Perhaps it was best he let her have that secret.

He decided to stay, to relax and think things through, while at the same time enjoy the woman cuddled in his arms. He stroked the black-and-white strands that spilled across his chest. That white streak had definitely gotten wider. Parting her hair differently? He didn't think so. She wore her hair long and loose with a part slightly off-center. The style hadn't changed.

"Thank you," he whispered as he stroked the white strands. "For everything you do."

His eyelids were heavy, so he closed them and focused on the softness of Zoë's hair under his fingertips. Something had begun between them. He'd felt it while holding her on the dance floor, his heart thundering not from dancing but from the feel of her body melded against his. In that moment, she had been his. And he would have surrendered willingly to anything she asked of him.

He'd known something had begun with that first kiss. And he wasn't eager to run away from it until he figured exactly what that something was.

Sighing heavily, he thought once about slipping out from under Zoë's arms—of running—and then…he began to snore.

Chapter 11

Kaz woke to spy a bowl of oatmeal in Zoë's hands. She wore a black robe edged in some kind of fluffy, feathery stuff—what did they call it?—marabou. She looked glamorous, and she wore no makeup. Her bright blue eyes held court against her pale skin and lips and drew attention from her hair.

He blinked and shook the sleep from his brain. "What time is it?"

"Noon. But I was in the breakfast mood, so…"

"More chia seeds?"

"I'll make you a believer sooner or later."

"The day you start believing in faeries is the day I'll start believing in the healthy stuff."

"Deal. I thought you were going to slip out after I fell asleep?"

He sat up and took the bowl with no intention of eating the stuff. "Couldn't bring myself to walk away from you." He cast her a glance, then looked away quickly. It was too early for emotional stuff, right?

Yet Zoë beamed at him. It was like standing in sunshine and his heart opened to suck up the warmth. Man, he was getting mushy in the brain. But he couldn't avoid the obvious: that he had stayed because he hadn't wanted to leave her.

"It was nice to wake in your arms," she said. "I didn't even mind your snoring. I've got pancakes for you in the kitchen. The chia was a tease. It's mine." She took the bowl from him and walked into the kitchen.

Kaz picked up the sweet smell of pancakes and followed his nose. Waiting for him on the kitchen table was a stack of fluffy pancakes topped with fresh blueberries and raspberries and oozing heavenly dribbles of butter and berry syrup.

Kaz dived for a fork and shoveled in a bite before he even sat on the chair. Zoë set a steaming cup of coffee near his plate and seated herself across from him.

He dragged his tongue across his lower lip as he considered what waking to such a gorgeous sight meant to him. It felt like...home. Something he hadn't known in well over a decade. The feeling planted itself in his core, and he didn't want to kick it out.

"What?" she asked.

"These pancakes are good, but you look even more appetizing."

"Is that so?" She blushed and tufted the feathers on her collar.

A black cat jumped onto the table and seated himself a paw's reach away from Kaz's plate.

"Kaz, meet Sid. I don't think the two of you have been properly introduced. Sid is my guy. He likes to chase mice, but never kills them. He's not a familiar. And he loves pancakes."

"I see. So just a plain ole alley cat, eh, Sid? No changing into a man? You don't know how relieved that makes me feel."

Not willing to give up any of his food for the cat, Kaz busied himself with plowing through the booty. Never had he tasted such fluffy pancakes, and they had little black seeds in them that crunched with each chew. More chia, no doubt.

Sid placed a polite paw on the back of Kaz's hand.

He looked to Zoë, but she gave him the big, sweet eyes. Two of a kind, the witch and her cat. Both wielded a soft touch to his hardened heart.

"Hell." Kaz broke off a piece of pancake and held it out for the cat. The feline snatched the whole thing and jumped to the floor. "Polite little bugger," he commented.

"Sid knows he's not supposed to eat at the table."

He sipped the coffee and—gasped. Eyes welling, Kaz tightened his lips and sucked down the dark brew.

"I hope you like it strong," Zoë commented sweetly.

"Hell, Zoë, this is like something a hillbilly would brew in a still!"

"Gets your day started, doesn't it?"

"Started? I'll have to run all the way home to work off this turbo-charged octane."

"You going vampire hunting today?"

"Uh, yes?"

"You can tell me, Kaz. I know it's your job."

"It's got to be done. You saw proof of that last night."

"Yes." She touched the diamond pendant at her neck. She must have fixed the clasp, because surely it had broken when he'd torn it off her.

Kaz wiped his mouth with the napkin and then, closing his eyes, downed the last of the coffee in one fast swallow. Octane, to the highest power. But he liked it. "I should have had some of this last night before we went out. Would have kept me dancing a lot longer. Might have avoided the vamps on the Metro."

"It's okay, Kaz. I can deal. Can you deal with the fact that I can deal?"

"I...uh..." He wasn't sure. He'd never dated anyone who

had a clue as to what he did or that an entire paranormal universe existed within the mortal realm. Should make things easier. So why wasn't he feeling kosher with it all? Dating? *Were* they dating? "Sure?"

"Wow. That was the least sure-sounding sure I've ever heard. Want to try again?"

"I can deal," he avowed. "It just surprises me that I can. You're new to me, Zoë."

"Strange kind of compliment."

"You know what exists in this world."

"Right. We all exist, even those things you might still believe are stuff of nightmares. Banshees and kelpies. Valkyries and dwarves. Demons and angels. All of them."

"But certainly not trolls."

She winced and nodded.

"Really? Ah, man." Kaz rubbed the back of his neck. "I had nightmares about those things after my mom read me a story about three billy goats."

"Trolls tend to stalk the Northern climes, but you'll find them abundant in Faery."

"Peachy. So, uh, have you been to Faery?"

"No, and I never intend to visit." She stood and set the breakfast dishes in the sink. "Bad things happen in Faery to those who don't belong there."

Kaz eased a hand over his hip. Yep, bad things came out of Faery, too. "But if you don't believe in them, then you couldn't possibly go there for a visit, anyway."

"Exactly. I shall make a nonbeliever of you somehow."

"I prefer to see when something is coming after me with a deadly weapon, so I'll stick with belief for now."

"Whatever makes you happy."

Kaz raised a brow. There was one sure thing that made him happy.

"Come over here," he said, pushing back on the chair and holding out his arms to invite her to sit on his lap.

"You know that robe hangs open just low enough so I can see the good stuff?"

She teased the tip of her finger between her lips and blushed. Man, he loved when her cheeks pinkened like that. Made him want to glide his tongue over the color to see if it tasted as sweet as it looked.

"I took a shower while you were sleeping, and was going to get dressed, but Sid insisted on being fed, so…" She fluffed the feathers that, unfortunately, covered her breasts and sat in his lap. "I've a thing for the American television show *Green Acres.*"

"You want to live out in the country and scamper about in sexy underthings while your husband drives a tractor nearby?"

"Doesn't that sound like a dream? Living off the land. Growing your own food, with chickens scampering about. But still living close enough to the city to buy pretty things that sparkle."

Pretty things that sparkle were exactly what he should be paying attention to right now instead of Zoë's soft mouth.

Kaz tapped the pendant at the base of her neck. Vampires going for the sparkle—and taking lives. *Focus, Kaz.*

He was almost there, prepared to stand and march off to work, utilizing the octane high of the coffee as muscle fuel, when Zoë put her arms around his neck.

The marabou tickled his chin as she leaned in to kiss him. "Come back later, pretty please?"

"I don't need to leave right this moment."

She wiggled on his lap, which brought things up and hardened them to a wincing tightness. "You want to fool around?"

"Is that a question or a challenge?"

"Both. I do have some spell work to tend to today, but I don't have to get to that immediately."

"What does a witch do, exactly, when she says spell work?"

"Oh, a little of this, a little of that. I'm always practicing and perfecting. A witch can study for centuries and still never master an element of magic."

"And what elements can you control?"

"Earth, air, water."

"No fire? I heard something about witches and fire."

"It's our death. We can be burned to death even after we obtain immortality."

"And immortality comes from the vampire heart thing, right?"

"You don't want to talk about such things, do you, my big, strong hero?"

Her eyes danced over his face and she trailed a finger along his hairline. The touch tickled one of those good shivers over his scalp that then skittered down his arms and coiled in his chest. He was beginning to associate the feeling in his core with home and rightness.

Zoë nuzzled aside his cheek and lashed out her tongue to tease his earlobe. And everything on him that was hard grew adamant.

Kaz slid a hand down the slippery fabric that covered her back, wanting to feel skin. Zoë twisted on his lap and straddled him. Her tickling ear tease glided lower, along his jaw and to the divot in his chin.

"This is cute," she said of the odd dent he'd once thought was because his father had punched him too hard. It hadn't become defined until he was a teenager and he knew better. It was a cleft. But blaming his father came naturally to him. "Why don't you have a girlfriend, Kaz? Don't tell me your job keeps them away or that you have to remain single because your life is too dangerous. You're a sexy man. I can't believe I'm not fighting off hordes right now to kiss you."

"If this is what a horde looks like—" he tapped her lips "—then bring it on."

The kiss was immediately dangerous and daringly deep. Zoë dived into him, passionate and bold. She crushed her chest against his and moaned into his mouth, and he answered with a rousing agreement. She grasped his hair and squeezed his hips with her thighs. Cleaving to him, melding herself against him.

"If I'm the only one," she said between kisses, "then I have to ask, what the hell is wrong with you?"

Kaz laughed because he wanted the answer to that one himself. "It is the job," he said. "Believe it or not. But it could be me, too."

"I don't think it is. But I'm one lucky girl if I'm the only one on your dance card."

"You don't think I keep returning to this place just because I like cerulean, do you?"

"Maybe it's my chia pudding?"

He lifted her, putting her legs about his hips, and walked her over to the counter where he set her down and kissed her again. "It's your kisses, and your sweet smile, and your pretty eyes and your mysterious hair, and you can even toss in the cat if you want to."

"I adore a man who likes cats."

"Only the polite ones," he said. "Can I make a confession?"

"Mmm, sounds intriguing."

"It's about you and...well, women in general."

"I'm not sure I like being lumped in with women in general."

"Oh, you're not. You stand all on your own, Zoë. And that's what I mean. I'm kind of a player. I love 'em and leave 'em. And I'm going to use the excuse of my job for that, even though you said I wasn't allowed. I just never want anyone to get too close, you know?"

"I can understand that. But still, that doesn't give a Lothario good reason to ditch out of bed before his lover even opens her eyes."

"I suppose not, but it's worked for me."

"So your confession is that I should set a trap on your side of the bed?"

Kaz chuckled. She was way ahead of him, but he liked that about her. Nothing about him seemed to put her off.

He caught her sigh in the next kiss and it felt like an angel had settled on earth and he held her in his arms. Though, from what he had heard about angels, perhaps he'd take a creepy witch over one of those malicious and deadly winged beings from Above.

"Your kisses are something to linger in," Zoë said. She tilted her forehead against his and trailed a finger down his chest. "Anything else you want to take your time with?"

He nuzzled his nose into her hair and kissed the edge of her jaw. Drawing his hands around and up her torso, he sought the softness beneath the robe, cupping her breasts. "How about this?"

Her back arched, lifting her breasts, and Kaz nuzzled against the fabric and mouthed her nipple. "I approve of your confession, hunter."

He chuckled against her breast and peeled aside the robe. With a dash of his tongue, he teased close to her nipple. She wrapped her legs about him. A glide of his fingers released the robe to fall to the crook of her elbows and expose her breasts.

She moved against him, daring him to suck hard and long and swirl his tongue about the rigid tip of her. She tasted fresh from the shower and a little salty, and her moans seasoned the treat.

Every part of him wanted to tear off the clothing and ram his cock inside her, satisfying need and desire. Yet never to satisfy that core swirl of emotion that he was beginning to tap into. Slow. Yes, slower and he would probably tap into that emotion he'd always put aside. Whether or not he'd know what to do with it when he got there, he wasn't sure, but he was determined to give it a go.

The magic of Zoë wasn't a white mist that soothed his wounds but rather the easy confidence she gave him to not be the one who demanded and took, and then ran off.

A musical ting sounded somewhere above their heads.

"Oh." Zoë pulled from Kaz's licking kisses. "That's my spell room. I've work to do."

"Seriously?"

She nodded, sucking in a corner of her lip in regret. "Terrible timing, but I'm working on something that demands a specific schedule."

She gripped him by the back of the head and pulled him in for a hard kiss. "I don't want you to go, but—"

"I have work to do, too. Besides, maybe this is the universe telling us to keep it slow."

"I'm beginning to have a change of heart regarding slow. We could skip entire chapters if you're willing."

"I have no idea what that means."

He bent to lash his tongue over her nipple and her entire body shuddered. Zoë drew up a leg and cooed sweetly. "You don't need to know what it means. You're already on the pages, and that's all that matters to me."

"You are most certainly made of magic," he commented as he watched goose flesh rise on her skin and recede. "I'm coming back."

"You'd better. Tonight?"

"Nothing can keep me away from you. I'll think about you all day."

"Don't do that. I'd hate to have you off your game when you need to be on the alert for fangs."

Crushing her in a hug, Kaz buried his face in her hair

and held on to her as he'd wanted to cling to someone for over a decade. Had he finally found home?

"You've bewitched me, Zoë. And I'm not sure if that's good, bad or crazy as hell."

"And here I thought you had bewitched me."

"Really?"

"From the first moment we touched, you began the bewitchment."

"Cool. I'll take credit for that one."

With one final kiss, he left her there, sitting on the counter, and retrieved his shirt from the laundry. Standing in the threshold of the witch's home he palmed the key in his pocket. *Safe.*

He stepped outside. Turning back to the cerulean door, Kaz couldn't stop a smile.

Chapter 12

Kaz jogged the quarter mile from the Metro station to his apartment. Since meeting Zoë, he'd been doing a lot of running home to shower and change. Tor had found the apartment for him in the fifteenth arrondissement. When Kaz had officially taken vows and joined the Order at seventeen—and being formally homeless—he hadn't the finances for inner-city living. Yet he did appreciate being away from the bustle and tourists.

The downside to his address was he risked luring dangerous vampires into a residential neighborhood. So he kept his head down, and always looked over his shoulder. He'd been a knight for ten years and hadn't any incidents, and intended to keep it that way. He could separate his home life from work.

But could he separate work from the pleasures of all that was Zoë? Business had mixed with pleasure when he was forced to slay vampires to keep her safe. Why had those vamps come at him in the subway, anyway? He hadn't been wearing the Order uniform and certainly hadn't been tracking them.

A few vampires did know him by name and appearance. Who had it out for him? Vaillant, he trusted. That vamp was good to the core, much as he looked like some kind of rock-star wannabe, and woe to the person who got in his way while that vamp was out for a drive.

Could it be Switch? He'd thought he'd lost in the scuffle against her and her henchmen. She had no reason to come after him, unless she felt the job wasn't finished until he stopped breathing.

The only other guess was that the vampires in the Metro had seen the diamond at Zoë's throat.

Kaz fisted the wall as he stepped into his apartment and strode toward the bedroom. He couldn't conceive of letting down the Order. All tasks to exterminate vampires must come first and foremost. But Zoë ranked right up there, too. And if that wasn't enough to worry about, he now had to wonder if some kind of faery mafia had it in for him.

Peeling away his clothes, he dropped them in a heap near the closet door then wandered into the bathroom. The wound on his hip from the faery flechette was scabbed and no longer sore. Zoë certainly did have the magic touch. Good thing, because if she hadn't been able to counteract the poison, he'd be pushing up daisies right now.

Flicking on the shower, he stepped into the hot stream and let out a shout as the water scalded him across the shoulders. Shaking his head and growling, he endured until his skin adjusted to the hot temperature. It was like Zoë's coffee, a "wake you up and get you going" kind of brew.

Soaping up, he stuck his face under the water. He hated to wash off Zoë's kisses, but he'd return later for more of the same. And her legs wrapped about his hips. And her breasts crushed up against him. He wanted to dive inside her and get lost. Forget that vampires existed. Forget the world, save for Zoë.

"You're thinking like a crazy man, Rothstein," he muttered.

For now, his focus must remain on finding the one-fanged vampire who had murdered his friends.

* * *

Zoë and Sid watched the last batch of the special blend settle in the alembics suspended by iron holders. The liquid ichor quickly dissolved into bright sparkling flakes and settled onto the bottom of the container.

"Pretty, isn't it, Sid?"

The cat rubbed his cheek along her hip, and Zoë scratched him at the base of his ear. When she hit the sweet spot, the feline's back leg started scratching the air, not quite committing to a full-on scratch, and happy to let her do the work.

"I really should think up a name for this stuff. Zoë's Fantastic Cure? Probably too pompous, eh?"

Sid agreed with a loud purr.

"The Blend is kind of boring. How about Fix-A-Vamp?" She chuckled and shook her head at the terrible names.

With a snap of her fingers the glass vials assembled on the table, lining up in military precision to await the sparkling contents. Zoë used her magic to lift the alembic and steady it over the vials to pour in measured amounts. Suddenly, Sid's body stiffened on the table, four paws stabilizing the feline against a powerful sneeze, but in the process, his tail whipped vigorously, knocking over all the vials.

Zoë grabbed for the vials, but upset the alembic, which toppled out of her magical spell and landed on the floor at her bare feet. Sid jumped from the table, paws outstretched before and behind his furry body.

"No, Sid! Be careful of the glass!"

The cat landed at the threshold, a safe distance from the shattered glass, and hightailed it out of the spell room.

Stuck in the center of a scatter of fine, broken glass and mounds of glinting purple faery dust, Zoë looked about for cleaning supplies. "Where's a broom when a witch really needs one?"

She didn't want to step aside and risk cutting her foot,

and she was no master of levitation. She could perform transprojectionary dislocation on objects, not herself.

"Bother. Now I'll have to get more ichor and start over on this batch. It's due tomorrow. I'll never obtain a large enough quantity of ichor on such short notice." Raking her fingers through her hair, she flung out her hands in defeat and sighed. "Well, they'll have to be short. Nothing I can do about it. What a mess. I sure hope this isn't an omen that the damsel's glass slippers have shattered. The knight will never be able to pick up all the pieces."

Closing her eyes and using mind mapping as a sort of magical GPS, she traveled downstairs to the kitchen closet and snatched the broom and dustpan with her mind and floated them upstairs. The broom zoomed into her palm, landing with a smart snap.

"Ouch!"

Realizing she was upset, Zoë breathed in and out, seeking calm. "It's not a problem. The courier will understand. And if she doesn't, what can she do about it? The place is warded so she can't enter. I'll provide the missing batch next week. No problem."

She hoped. She'd yet to meet Mauritius, and even though he was doing a good thing by distributing her blend, she suspected he preferred his employees to be punctual and keep their promises.

"I should head out to FaeryTown and see about getting more ichor."

She'd never gone shopping for ichor before, nor did she know the price it commanded. And dealing with creatures she chose not to believe in could prove a challenge. But how difficult could it be?

The vampire ashed before him. Kaz's fist, still wrapped about the stake, swung forward through the ash cloud. He closed his eyes to avoid getting dust in them. They stood in a dark alley. No mortal had witnessed this slaying. As it should be.

He retracted the killing point back into the titanium stake and fitted it at his hip in the loop beside another stake. Tonight he wore full slaying gear.

He'd gotten the call earlier from Rook that a series of burglaries had resulted in attacks to the necks of two citizens. They were not dead, but the perp was on the loose. Hadn't taken long for Kaz to track the odd trail of abandoned rhinestone jewelry right up to the vampire who had been shivering in a corner, moaning for more sparklies.

He tugged out his cell phone and called in a report. He didn't directly talk to Rook, but left a message. "Mark exterminated." He checked his watch. "11:45 p.m. Was unable to question him regarding current investigation. Manic and raging for Magic Dust."

That said it all. It said too much.

Another kill. Life was a party. Without the cake.

Tucking away his phone, Kaz kicked off the ash from his boot toe. The clothing had burned, as well. Looked as if a bum may have set a fire in the alley. Still, he gave Tor a call.

He'd tracked the vampire after seeing him climb out of a residential window, a trail of sparkling jewelry spilling from his pockets. Kaz had phoned the police and given them the address—he suspected there would be human casualties inside, thus the call to Tor—while he had pursued the predator.

One less drugged-up maniac to threaten the innocents now. But how many more were out there? He estimated, as the Magic Dust grew more popular, the incidents of vampires attacking mortals could increase tenfold.

The longer it took him to track the source, the faster the apocalypse would arrive. He hated thinking in such devastating terms, but he couldn't imagine anything less than all-out mayhem once the vampire population started hunting the humans in a mad quest for anything that sparkled.

He did need backup. He needed a whole team. At the moment, Rook was the only other available hunter in the city. The other local hunters, Lark and Dmitri, were away on a hunt in Spain, since that country was lacking a cadre of knights. If he asked Rook's help, he'd prove he wasn't up to the task. But seriously? This task could be too big for the Order within a few days.

He could handle this. Nothing fanged, clawed or even winged could defeat Kaspar Rothstein.

Kaz sensed he was walking in FaeryTown now for the minute tug at his skin, like a breeze, that he'd previously placed to walking in the other dimension overlaid upon the mortal realm. He wished he had brought along the ointment, and cursed himself for forgetting that small detail. He didn't need it to find Switch, but he certainly would like to have an eye on whatever winged creature watched him right now. Because someone did; if he believed anything otherwise, he'd be making a big mistake.

He did believe in faeries, damn his soul.

He should have asked Zoë if she'd known a method to fight back against faeries who fired poison-tipped flechettes at him.

A flash of pink caught his eye. The woman sporting the bright hair pushed through a group of young men, not reacting to their catcalls. She was dressed to offend with tight black leather on her legs and torso. Strategic rips below the ass and ribs exposed strips of flesh.

"Maybe there will be cake," he muttered.

Crossing the street, Kaz assumed the tail. He'd follow her at a distance. She must spend a lot of time in FaeryTown if she dealt dust. This was where her clientele could be found. But where was she getting the Magic Dust? From a faery? Had to be. Some faery that was altering the ichor in a manner that made it more deadly to mortals than anyone could imagine.

As he dodged a human couple walking hand in hand, in his peripheral vision he caught sight of a pretty, young woman with black-and-white hair. Zoë? Was she in Faery-Town or treading the mortal realm? He couldn't get a good enough look to see if she wore the dark ointment under her eyes.

"Damn it," he said, fighting the urge to call out to the witch.

Every part of his being wanted to rush to her and keep her safe. His arms twitched, wanting to wrap around her and pull her in close. And his trigger fingers flinched, preparing for defense in case a vampire attacked her.

On the other hand, maybe she was simply on a grocery run?

Deciding the best course was to stay on the vampiress's ass, Kaz forged onward with a glance back to confirm Zoë was still there. She was, but her attention was drawn to the shopfronts.

"She had better be shopping."

Because if Zoë was doing something else—and he wasn't sure what that could be—he wanted to know what it was, and if he had a reason to be jealous.

Jealous?

She wasn't his girl. Well, sort of. Kind of? They had been teasing dating the past few days, but he wouldn't call a quick lunch a date. Though the dancing the other night could be construed as a date.

Hell. He was dating a witch. Who'd've thought?

Smiling to himself, Kaz realized he'd let his gaze wander. *Focus.* He flicked his eyes left to right and said a thank-you for the vampiress's bold, pink hair.

Switch turned between two buildings. Kaz quickened

his pace, turning to follow her down the narrow pathway that could lead to a small courtyard, or exit to another street. She turned to spy him just as he grabbed her arm and shoved her against an old limestone wall littered with bright-blue-and-orange graffiti.

"Need to have a chat with you," he said, moving his hands down to grip her wrists and slam them up against the wall near her shoulders. He pressed his thighs against hers, preparing for defensive moves. She didn't have her henchmen to distract him now, and he could certainly hold his own against a woman, vampire or not.

The vampiress spit blood at him. Blinking, but not releasing her wrists, Kaz marked that one down as a new and annoying weapon. Good thing vampire blood did not harm humans.

"Classy," he said.

"What is it with you, hunter? You didn't like the beating I gave you the other night so you're back for round two? Oh, I get it. You like the rough stuff, eh?"

"Your henchmen are nowhere to be seen, so I figure we can talk real nicelike. I'm not here to hurt you, Switch. I have some questions."

"Fuck your questions."

"That's not very ladylike language."

She looked ready to spit again, so he slammed his elbow against her jaw. Not as hard as he could…

"Asshole." She tongued her front teeth and spat to the side. "What the hell do you want to ask me? And it better not be for a date, a bite or to narc on one of my fellow vamps."

"None of the above. A date? Seriously?"

She jutted up her chin and dragged her tongue across vivid red lips. "I've had a hunter or two in my time." Her eyes flashed with a creepily seductive challenge.

He didn't even want to know.

"I know you're dealing Magic Dust, Switch."

He waited for her reaction. Not a blink or a flinch marred the vampiress's pale complexion. Her dark eyes had dropped the tease of seduction and now stared through him, indifferent to his needs. A predator to the core.

"Since you're not denying it," he continued, "I need to know who you're getting the dust from."

She tilted her head and shook the tousle of pink-and-black strands. The silver rings trailing down her ear clacked. Not about to spill on that one.

"If you won't give me a name, then who manufactures it? Is it made here in FaeryTown? You're smart, but I doubt you've a chemistry background."

"Chemistry? Ha!" Obviously, that one had thrown her for a challenge. "I'm smart enough to not touch the stuff. It's nasty."

"Yet you have no problem selling it to your fellow vamps. You know Magic Dust drives them insane? It's not like regular faery dust."

"What do I care? Come on, hunter. Are we finished here? I got an appointment."

"With your supplier?"

"I am this close to ripping out your carotid and sucking you dry."

"Bite blade, bitch."

She smirked, warming up to his challenge as her eyes took in the shining blades at his collar. "You're too pretty for a hunter. I bet you've screwed vamps before you've slain them, yeah?"

"Wouldn't touch your kind if you were the last creatures on earth."

"Yeah, mortals aren't all that, either. Though they can be tasty midorgasm."

"Enough sharing."

Kaz twisted the vampiress's arm, swinging her around

and hooking a foot between her legs to hobble her into a stumble and land her knees against the wall. Cranking her arm backward and up to the point where he knew *he* would certainly let out a yelp, he then smashed her face against the wall with his other hand.

"Give me a name and I'll stop trying to turn you into a pretzel."

"She doesn't have a name."

She? That ruled out half the population.

Kaz pressed hard against her skull. The brick must surely be cutting through her cheek. A flash of Zoë's scar appeared in his mind and he almost relented.

Almost.

"I can do this all night," he tried. "I know you vamps heal fast, but do you really want me to make hamburger out of your pretty face?"

"You do and you will not live to see morning, hunter."

He pressed harder and the vampiress let out a yelp before confessing, "I know it's a witch!"

"A witch?" He did not relent the hold on her skull. "Who is a female?"

"Putting two and two together. Points for the human."

He pressed harder.

"A witch makes the dust," she provided in a sputter. "I pick it up once a week. That's it. I'm not saying any more."

Kaz shoved her away, far enough so that if she decided to turn and attack, he had room to defend himself. Reaching for the stake, he paused. Switch flipped him off, and then dashed away in the direction they'd come, cursing his mother and promising him death.

He'd heard it too many times before to let it bother him. Death threats were flung at him like confetti. And his mother, may she rest in peace, was in a better place now. But he wasn't sure what to do with the information he'd gained from the vampiress.

"A witch?"

There had to be hundreds of witches in Paris. Where to begin?

Surely Switch wouldn't lead him there tonight now that she knew he was on to her. He let her go. He didn't want her dead. And if she made pickups once a week, he'd track her to the source with the same ease he'd tracked her this evening.

He took out his cell phone and dialed Vail. He would owe the vampire if he could help him on this one. As he waited for the ring he remembered having seen Zoë. He scanned the streets for her black-and-white hair. What was that witch up to?

But more important, how many witches did she know, and could she help him track the one who was making the Magic Dust?

There was only one way to find out.

Kaz stood before the cerulean door, smiling. Funny how the bright color made him feel happy yet a little anxious. It was because of who lived behind the door. The witch did things to him. She stirred up his senses to high alert. A good kind of alert, at that.

He'd hung up with Vail after leaving FaeryTown. The vampire promised to ask around about the witch who manufactured Magic Dust. He did have a hunch which vampire was heading the operation, but wouldn't give Kaz a name until he'd checked out the suspicion.

Vail had a family to protect and was unaligned with any tribe, so Kaz allowed him the slack and respected his caution. Ultimately, the vampire would come through. He had to.

Now he was prepared to ask Zoë about what she had been doing in FaeryTown. He had a right to know.

Didn't he?

She could have been visiting a friend. In which case, if he asked, he'd sound jealous. She could have been shopping for supplies for witch spells. In that case, he'd sound nosey.

He wouldn't ask her.

Shoving his hands through his hair, he squeezed his eyelids tight. He didn't *need* to know about her personal life. He just…wanted to know as much about her as he could because he liked her. And yes, he was suspicious, especially with the current investigation, as to why a witch would be in FaeryTown, and whom she had gone to see.

On the other hand, she could prove a valuable asset if she knew of any witches who might have a hand in making Magic Dust. So to not question her would be less than professional.

But he couldn't let it sound as if it was personal. Don't sound jealous, he cautioned. Make it business. However, to ask would mix business with pleasure again.

"Damn it," he swore softly.

The cerulean color screamed at him all things not business. Things like kisses from a sexy witch and her warm, healing touch.

Don't mix business and pleasure. How difficult was it to obey that one rule?

The door swung open and inside stood a smiling witch with black-and-white hair that spilled over a sleek silk nightgown—sans robe. Kaz's eyes traveled from the thin straps that hugged her slender shoulders, down over gorgeously rounded breasts. He licked his lips, ending with a tooth-clutch on the corner of his lower lip. The black fabric hugged her hips and thighs, and… He didn't get to her feet because his focus zoomed back up to her breasts.

"I've been waiting for you," she said in that sweet tone that belied the vixen beneath the innocent facade. Stepping back, she invited him inside. "You have a busy night slaying?"

"Uh…" Kaz knew he had been planning to ask her something.

Something important.

Zoë exhaled, and when she did her breasts pressed against the fabric, emphasizing the hard nipples beneath. They were tight and perfect and…so in need of his tongue.

"Kaz?"

"Uh-huh," he muttered, and dismissed whatever he'd wanted to say as unimportant. If he wasn't able to remember it, it couldn't have been that important, right? "You trying to seduce me, witch?"

She trailed a finger up his chest and tapped his lips. "I never try. I always do."

Chapter 12

Zoë carefully slid off Kaz's coat. The twin rows of blades along the collar tabs always gave her caution. When it was placed across the back of the balding velvet easy chair, she stood aside and watched the hunter shed his armor. With a reverent inhale, she felt as if she were witnessing a sacred ritual, the knight setting aside his armaments.

Kaz's broad shoulders and muscles flexed as he took off the stakes he had hooked at his waist, and the garrote she had *borrowed* the other day and set them on top of the coat. He may have been on to something when he'd suggested she seek her thrills in other manners. Since indulging in the sensual pleasures with Kaz, she had felt little urge to nick anything from him.

He flashed her a sly smile and shrugged as he shoved a hand in his pocket and pulled out a vial of holy water and a silver cross. A brass key he studied for a moment, then shoved back in the pocket.

The palm-size silver cross clattered onto the coffee table and Zoë had to smile. "I thought vamps were immune to holy objects?"

"Only if they haven't been baptized. Most created vamps nowadays have been, so the blessed stuff comes in handy. It leaves a wound that will never heal."

"That sounds awful."

"It is." He stood there, palms together, looking over his abandoned arsenal. "But someone has to protect innocent humans from the vampires without a conscience."

"I'm glad you do what you do, Kaz. No wounds tonight?" she asked.

"Want to check?" He tugged off his shirt and turned to her, giving her a come-here gesture with his fingers.

She snuggled up against the hard warmth of him and ran her fingers down the delicious curves of muscles and skin. Yes, she was glad he did what he did, and that he even existed to stand here in her arms. So hot and hard. Her heartbeats stuttered and she sighed against his skin. He shivered minutely at that hushed breath.

"You feel so fine," she whispered, her eyes dancing over the brand and then down to his biceps. "I think you're wound free, but I haven't checked *all* places on you."

"The checking can commence, but…I want to know why you answered the door dressed for seduction. What if it hadn't been me?"

"I wasn't expecting anyone else." She walked backward, leading him by the hand toward the stairs. "I want to show you something."

The man waggled his eyebrows and followed her up to the second floor where her bedroom door opened to the soft glow of dozens of candles. Yes, she had been hoping upon hope he'd show up at her door tonight. A girl could dream, couldn't she?

Tonight her dreams would come true.

She led him inside and he stopped at the end of the bed, taking it all in. From the candles on the windowsill, to those along the gray-painted floorboards, they cast a golden shimmer across the simple gray wood furniture and white bedding and window sheers. Along the ceiling, Zoë had strung tiny white Christmas lights a few years ago, and couldn't bring herself to take them down because they added a touch of enchantment to the room. Didn't matter that she didn't celebrate the Christian holiday.

"Now I'm really hoping it was only me you were expecting," he said, with a tap to one of the dangling lights.

"Only my knight cloaked in mystery and darkness."

"Ah, come on. I'm not so mysterious to you, am I?"

"I have learned a lot about you. I love that you've trusted me to open up, Kaz. I feel safe with you."

He curled his fingers about the ends of her fingers and they dangled there between them. "What are the reasons you don't feel safe?"

She shrugged, brushing it off. "Let's focus on moving forward, shall we? I said I wanted to show you something."

She strolled to the table before the window where a gramophone sat, and set the needle onto a record that had been pressed early last century. Strains of a French love song quietly echoed out. A chanteuse who had been famous in the 1920s, according to Zoë's mother. Francine Guillebeaux had listened to this record often, late at night. Zoë had heard it creep softly into her room and she'd always envisioned her parents dancing arm in arm, and that thought had coaxed her into sweet dreams.

She turned to find a smile on Kaz's face. He held out a hand for her to take. "Dance with me?"

"I thought you'd never ask."

She took his hand and he tugged her against his bare chest and they swayed to the soft music beneath the glitter of Christmas lights. Nothing so spectacular as the Eiffel Tower twinkling in the background, but much more intimate. An exhale felt the rise of his breath against her chest and an inhale took in his licorice scent. The man was positively delicious.

"Are you not into new technology?" he asked with a

nod toward the gramophone. "Or is that something you've had for a while?"

"Monsieur Mortal, are you implying I'm old?"

He shrugged against her body and the feel of his muscles challenged her resolve to take things slowly. "I don't know. Witches can be centuries old, can't they?"

"They can, but I'm not. That belonged to my parents. And no, I'm not into technology. I prefer vinyl to MP3s. It sounds richer, and feels—" she snuggled up to him "—so romantic."

"I can dig the romance stuff."

"You strike me as a man who might be uncomfortable with soft sighs and tender *bon mots*."

"I can do tender." He trailed his fingers down her back, which sent shivers dancing up her neck and across her scalp. Her nipples tightened and she instinctively arched her back, pressing against his chest. "I can also do this." He gripped her hand and slid his other hand across her back, and suddenly bent her backward into a dip.

Giggles pealed from Zoë's mouth and she didn't ever want to come up for air. Oh, bewitchment. It was a marvelous thing.

When Kaz did pull her to her feet, she danced around him, and stroked her hands down his broad, bare back, admiring the flex of his muscles as he moved subtly. Kisses here and there marked the curve of a muscle or the pulse of skin. She carefully marked a trail along the back of his neck where he smelled sweet and dark. Behind his ear sat the witch's spell against vampire bites, but he wore no other tattoos that she could see. The masculine hard lines of him coaxed her fingers to glide and touch and feel. Everywhere.

He tilted his head back and she pushed her fingers up through his hair, then kissed him at the base of his neck where the shorter strands tickled her lips. "Want to have sex?"

It was bold of her, but she was ready, so ready, to know this man completely. She hoped he felt the same. And if he hadn't gotten all her hints, then he truly was a failure at romance.

Sid wandered in along the wall and sat before a flickering candle flame. The cat's green eyes observed without judgment.

Kaz turned and as he sat on the bed, he pulled her forward. Zoë straddled him, sitting on his lap. He nuzzled his face against her breasts, kissing, licking and tonguing along her nightgown.

"Is that a yes?" she asked.

He nodded. He was busy. She didn't mind.

With a flick of his fingers, he slid the spaghetti straps down her arms. Zoë thrust back her shoulders. He tugged the silk down to reveal her breasts, muttered, "Oh, witch," and growled in satisfaction as he dashed his tongue across a nipple.

She trusted he wouldn't hurt her, in the physical sense. She feared the emotional pain of getting close to a man, but only because it had been so long since she'd been in a relationship that had lasted more than three or four months. He didn't seem to be bothered by her scar. Something so superficial shouldn't be reason for anyone to duck out of a relationship, but it had happened to her over and over.

She wanted to toss all her hang-ups aside and enjoy this moment. So she would. And to do that, she had to take control.

Zoë pushed Kaz back to lie across the bed. He gave her a questioning look accompanied by a daring smirk. Hadn't she been enjoying his attentions?

"Me first," she simply said, and tugged open the button on his jeans. "I should do triage to ensure you've healed."

Sliding down the zipper on his leather pants, she winked at him. Kaz lifted his hips, which loosened the tight stretch of leather as the fly sprang open and released his hard shaft. Her fingers fit around the hot column, and she mentally compared it to the titanium stake he often wielded.

"My turn to play the hunter," she teased as she gripped him as he would a weapon.

"Best triage I've ever had."

"Oh, I almost forgot." She inspected his hip where the wound was fading, as expected. "You've a swell healer, hunter."

"She's the best. Oooh…"

Bending, she tickled her tongue across the head of him. Like salted fire, his taste, and smooth and so thick. Kaz rocked up his hips and moaned encouragement.

"Now that's some magic," he muttered.

She smiled against the length of him and licked him firmly, tracing the vein. Cupping his testicles, she squeezed gently, then enclosed them in both her hands.

"Zoë…"

Tension tugged his voice, yet she guessed it was a good tightness. Rising onto her knees, and still cupping him, she lashed his erection once more before he grabbed her by the arms and flipped her onto the bed.

"My turn," he growled, and pulled the nightie from her body in a sleek move. "You're so gorgeous, Zoë. Your skin—hell, it's like cream. Bet it tastes even better."

He bent his head to her stomach. The heat of his tongue scurried over her skin and spread throughout her system. Zoë exhaled and closed her eyes, dragging her fingers through his hair, but not tugging. Her arms relaxed and she flung them over her head, stretching out her legs and opening herself to his ministrations.

The hunter trailed his tongue down her belly, nipping gently here and there, which rocketed the sensation up exponentially. She grasped the sheets, fisting them as he spread her legs and kissed her mons.

Shivers spread across her stomach and thighs. The touch of his tongue at her apex made her gasp and reach out to clutch the pillow. He tasted, dashing out his tongue once, then again, and then he feasted on her, connecting to the very center of her being with his mouth.

He glided a hand along her thigh and hooked her leg over his shoulder. Zoë dug her toes into his back, and he growled, "Oh, yeah."

Teasing her, he slid his fingers inside her, growling again in pleasure, and then slipped them out and slicked them across her swollen bud again and again.

Zoë moaned and reached down to touch the scruff of his short hair. He quickly kissed her fingers, then went back to the sweet torture that stirred her system to a spinning, swirling dream of abandon.

"Move up here," she gasped. "Let me hold you, Kaz. Please. I need to…have you in my hand."

He slid alongside her, without losing his place, his tongue mimicking the movement of his fingers. Kneeling, he bent over her, but she was able to clutch his erection, so hard and unbelievably solid. How could any man transform to such rigidness? It was an alchemy she admired, and it had come from her hand, yet not a touch of magic had been required.

"Zoë. Sweet witch of mine," he gasped as her hand slicked up and down his length. He rubbed her quickly but not roughly, just skimming her wetness and activating that desire that would soon explode. "I'm going to come," he growled.

"Yes," she cried as the energy within her arrowed toward her core and her muscles released, then tightened, and then released again as the immense wave crashed against her soul. At the same time, Kaz spilled over her fingers and the two of them shuddered through the shared orgasm, their bodies united in the delicious triumph.

He pressed his cheek against her mons, and wrapped an arm over her stomach to hug her. "Oh, yeah."

"That was…there are no words." Kaz sighed heavily, and rolled back to lie beside her.

"Of course there are words," she said, gasping and smiling as she turned to face him. "Sensational."

"Amazing," he chimed in.

She stroked her fingers down his chest, glistening with sweat. "Magic."

"Tell me you didn't use magic on me, Zoë."

"Not at all. It was a natural magic. Two bodies coming together…" She sighed.

He took her hand and kissed it then pressed it to his hard abdomen. "We are magic together. I like the sound of that."

She reached for him again and found him already firm even after his fabulous climax. "I want you inside me, Kaz. Filling me." She leaned in to kiss his chest and teased her tongue about his nipple. "Claiming me."

His hand glided along her hip and waist and gripped her firmly to draw her against him. She couldn't get enough of this man.

If bewitchment involved losing all thoughts save for those of the skin, scent and sound of the beautiful woman lying beneath him, then he was in for the whole experience. Bewitched made him want and need and take and give and wish it would never end.

"Bewitched," Kaz muttered as he moved back and forth, in and out of Zoë's hot wetness.

He'd sheathed himself inside her, and she wrapped her legs about his hips and gripped his biceps, squeezing, moaning, now and then catching his gaze. He could stay inside her forever. This was good, almost too good for him, but he wasn't going to go there. Couldn't allow a negative thought to spoil it all.

He'd found something good, and he wouldn't let her go.

Dipping his head, he nuzzled one of her nipples, suckling, drawing up her pleasure in wanting, gasping moans. The sound of her erotic agony only tightened him more and made him pump faster, deeper, seeking the core of her. He would own her.

Because she had claimed him.

Somewhere on the bed, the black cat wandered over the sheets. Kaz felt the weird tickle of fur along his ankle, and out the corner of his eye he noticed the feline watching. It was unnerving, and not. He wasn't about to kick the thing off.

Zoë's fingernails dragged along his abdomen, up his ribs and around across his back. Kaz groaned at the sweet pain and slammed his hips to hers, holding there, deep within her.

He withdrew his cock almost completely out. She hugged him so tightly it was agonizing not to slam back inside, but he took it slow, and with every little bit he gave her, she responded with those sweet sounds that were music to his ears.

Orgasm snuck up on him, tightening his muscles, and then…the universe assumed the controls and shocked him with a pleasure like he'd never known. It shivered through his bones and escaped his throat in a hoarse shout. It was all good, and good for all. Like some kind of musketeer motto, he wanted to shout it out, but instead he growled and rode the wave.

He collapsed on Zoë's soft, full breasts, cupping them on each side, and nuzzled his face against her throat and tangled hair. "Magic."

Chapter 13

A knock on the door below stirred Zoë from her semi-awake rest beside the long, lean form of her sexy hunter. Ignoring the knock, she stroked his skin and snuggled even closer to his insane heat—when she remembered.

Hiking herself from the bed and grabbing her robe, she charged out of the bedroom, dashed up the stairs to her spell room, grabbed the Hello Kitty suitcase and then glided down the stairs as if the devil Himself were prodding her heels with his fiery pitchfork.

From the foyer she saw the person outside lift a hand to knock again. Zoë swung open the door, gasping to catch her breath, and caught the robe before it spilled open to expose her nudity to the entire neighborhood.

"Bonjour," she said between huffs.

Above and behind her, she heard a cell phone jangle to the tune of—Johnny Cash?

Please don't wake up, Kaz, until I get rid of this vampire. He would have questions about why a vampire was at her door, and probably wouldn't pause to talk, but instead whip out his stake and ash her.

"I woke you," the pink-haired vampiress said with a knowing smirk. Her eyes took a quick trip over Zoë's disarray, but she didn't comment. "You got the goods? Hand 'em over. I'm tired. I hate these early-morning pickups."

"Mauritius set them up," Zoë said as she handed the suitcase over the threshold, hoping the vampiress wouldn't weigh it because she hadn't an excuse for not having a complete batch. It was close, perhaps ninety percent complete.

She could tell the truth about the accident with Sid sneezing, but she didn't want the argument right now. Not when the phone call may have wakened Kaz and he could be thinking of searching her out.

The vampiress wheeled the suitcase around, but didn't have an empty to offer in return, as was the usual deal.

"Where's the other?" Zoë asked.

"I'm supposed to tell you Mauritius will be in touch later today. See ya." She spun and headed down the flower-lined path to the waiting car across the street.

Zoë stood before the open door, baffled at this new development. Did Mauritius not want more of her blend? Had he found someone else who could concoct the same for a cheaper price? She didn't ask for much, just enough to pay her bills and to buy some pretty things. She was doing this to help vampires and didn't want to make the product too expensive, but she did incur operating costs.

There had to be a reasonable explanation.

Closing the door, Zoë decided she would worry about it later. Because who could worry when a naked man smelling of warmth, sex and sweet dreams lay in her bed?

"Sorry to call you so early, man, but I'm up with the baby so…"

"That's fine."

Kaz sat up on Zoë's bed, surprised not to find her next to him. Her pillow still felt warm. The cotton sheets were rumpled where she had lain next to him. He'd felt the reassuring weight of her arm draped across his back all night. She must have just gotten up before the phone rang. Maybe she was making him some chia oatmeal. Yuck.

"What do you have, Va—er, Dark One?"

"I got you a name."

"Of the witch making the dust? Excellent. I owe you one, man. Who is it?"

"First, you have to know that a witch who can alter faery dust is a very powerful witch. In fact, my source seems to think the only one capable of such magic is a warlock."

"A warlock? Isn't that a male witch?"

"No, it's any witch who has been cast from the Light for crimes against their kind, like, for example, altering faery dust."

"Altering faery dust is a crime against witches? I don't get it."

"It's not against the witches, per se, but it uses such powerful magic that it actually changes the molecules of a living thing. That's what's warlock about it."

"I get it. I think. So who is it?"

"Some witch who lives in the eighteenth. Pretty little thing. I've never met her, but she was pointed out to me once at a Halloween party. Don't even ask, man."

Kaz would not ask why vampires and witches went to Halloween parties. All he wanted was the important details.

"I'm surprised she'd be involved with something like this," Vail continued. "Didn't think she was warlock material. But you can't judge a person by the outside, can you?"

"Vail—"

"Dude, no names!"

"It's the name I'm waiting for. Give me the witch's name. Or warlock, if that's the case."

"All right, all right. Chill, man. Witch's name is Zoë Guillebeaux."

Kaz dropped the phone by his leg as Zoë wandered into the bedroom. Casting him a sweet smile, she climbed onto the bed, shedding her robe to reveal rosy nipples and full breasts, and snuggled up next to him.

Zoë Guillebeaux? His throat instantly drying, Kaz tried to swallow, but instead he cleared his throat roughly. Zoë was a common French name for girls. He didn't know what her last name was. He certainly hoped it did not start with a G.

"That was no one at the front door," she offered, trailing a finger down his thigh.

Vail's voice could be heard through the phone. Kaz flipped the phone shut. But Vail had always been a reliable informant. The vampire wouldn't grab any old name out of the ether.

But a warlock?

"Lover?"

As well, Vail couldn't know Kaz had been seeing Zoë, and for some ulterior reason, may have decided to use that against him.

Zoë snuggled against him and wiggled sweetly. "Want a morning quickie? Or even a slow one—"

He stood abruptly from the bed, finding her touch suddenly chilled him. He had to ask. "This is weird but, what's your last name?"

She shrugged, unaware of his concern. "Guillebeaux. Now about that quickie…"

Suddenly, all thought of sex felt…creepy.

Grabbing his pants from the chair, he said, "We need to talk."

Zoë watched Kaz pace the floor, gathering up his jeans and shirt. He moved like a predatory feline, all sinuous and sleek. She couldn't figure why he was so determined to dress, especially when she lay nude on the bed, and had suggested they have sex again.

Was that it? They'd spent the night together, now on to the next witch?

He had claimed to be a love-'em-and-leave-'em sort. And what did she really know about him? He slayed vampires. He liked to dance. He had a habit of collecting injuries like she collected bits and bobs from the people she met.

He'd also said he liked to run away from things. Like… relationships?

She'd thought they'd taken it slowly but perhaps last night had been a fast race over a cliff? It had been so romantic dancing in the twinkle of the Eiffel Tower, and then sharing secrets while they had waited for the train. She'd thought they'd grown closer that night, so when he'd shown up last night at her door she had been so ready to take the next step to intimacy.

Was he getting cold feet? Skittish? She'd thought what they had shared last night had cemented the beginning of something great.

Kaz shoved his feet into his leather pants and pulled them up, buttoning them hastily. Zoë could feel anger waver throughout the room, and that disturbed her.

Had he overheard her conversation at the door? She hadn't said anything that should make him angry. And he couldn't have known she was talking to a vampire.

"What's wrong, Kaz? I go downstairs for three minutes, and when I return you've changed from sweet, loving sex god, to uptight and angry, and I'm having trouble figuring you out right now."

Glancing at her, he fisted the air, winced, then spread out his fingers, as if fighting some inner anger.

"It was the phone call," she guessed. "I heard your phone ring a few minutes ago. What was it about?"

"Zoë." He stopped pacing and eyed her with such a serious gaze, she flinched. The predator, indeed.

Spreading out his fingers again and clenching them, he then said, "You know I've been investigating vampires who are selling faery dust. Stuff that messes them up and makes them go after innocent humans?"

He paced before her, hands on his hips and face tight. His forehead wrinkled, and she decided his concerned look did not appeal if it had anything to do with her. But how could it?

She nodded. "Yes, you explained it all. I witnessed it on the Metro." The phone call. He must have gotten a lead on his investigation. "You need to leave for the hunt? I understand. You can return later and—"

He lunged toward her so suddenly, gripping her shoulders in a less than gentle squeeze that she let out a frightened gasp. She sat there completely naked, and his aggressive touch stirred up the hairs on her arms, and not in a sensual way.

"Zoë." He opened his mouth to continue, but snapped it shut. Shaking his head, he seemed as if he was trying to not say something. And then he did. "The vampire informant I work with, and trust implicitly, gave me the name of the witch who has been manufacturing Magic Dust."

"A witch?"

"Or possibly a warlock."

"Hmm, that makes sense. Someone would have to possess great skill to alter faery ichor in the manner you've described to me." And she knew that firsthand.

He squeezed her shoulders and she winced. "You're hurting me, Kaz. I can understand your anger, but don't take it out on me."

"Are you going to play innocent with me now? After everything we've shared?"

"What are you implying?"

"I know, Zoë. And I can't believe you could bring yourself down to such a level. It's despicable."

"What?" She breathed out. Her heartbeat thudded and her skin grew warm. She couldn't understand why he was blaming her—or what for, exactly. "I don't have anything to do with what you've been investigating. How could you think to accuse me of such a thing? I abhor violence. I've spent my life working against it. The work I do now is—"

"Is killing humans, Zoë!" He shoved her away, and she landed on her elbows on the bed.

Pulling the sheet up around her breasts didn't help to close her off from his anger. She felt as though he'd smacked her across the cheek and the sting burned.

Kaz paced. He fisted the air. Something that he believed was so wrong, and yet—

"Wait. You can't mean…" She wrapped the sheet around her torso as she slid off the bed. "You've got it all wrong. The dust I've been making is a cure, Kaz. It's not the Magic Dust you've told me about."

"So you admit you've been manufacturing dust?"

"Yes, but—"

Following a particularly harsh breakup with a vampiress he'd hoped to marry, her friend Luc had been imbibing in faery dust for about six months. He'd wanted to get off the stuff, but couldn't. So Zoë had set out to produce a form of dust that would not cause addiction, and perhaps, allow a vampire to slowly wean off the drug.

It had worked. Luc had called to report he was feeling much better, yet didn't want her to see him until he was completely clean. Give him a month. But he'd also mentioned her project to his tribe leader, Mauritius, and things had proceeded from there.

"Is that your lab up there?" Kaz swung a fist toward the third floor. "I need to take a look."

He ran out and onto the stairs before Zoë could sweep up the sheet to chase after him.

"That's my spell room," she called from the stairs. "You are not invited to enter it. It's sacred!"

He stood at the fuchsia door, hand twisting about the pink glass knob. "You're hiding a crime behind this door, Zoë."

"No, I— Kaz?" Shaking now, she slowly ascended the stairs. "Last night was so perfect. You and I— I thought…"

She thought he had fallen in love with her. Because she had fallen for him sometime between the waltz at the Trocadéro and slow dancing arm in arm with him to the chanteuse on the gramophone.

But now?

"I don't know what you've been told, or by whom," she said, "but you need to calm down and tell me everything. Then I'll tell you everything, and you'll realize this argument is silly and has nothing at all to do with vampires killing humans."

He remained stoic, determined to stick with his anger. "Give me permission to open this door."

"No. It's a blessed area. I never allow outsiders in, and would never dream to allow a mere—"

"Human? You don't want a human stumbling onto your vicious magical laboratory? You ever see that show on TV, Zoë? The one with the meth dealer who makes the vile drug? Is that what I'll find behind this door? Some kind of Magic Dust lab?"

Hot tears spilled down her cheeks. Zoë couldn't summon words to defend herself. She hadn't been prepared for this. It shocked her that he could believe she would be involved in such a vile enterprise. She sank to the top step and sat, turning away from him.

"Do whatever you want," she managed, sniffling back tears. A snap of her fingers unlocked the door. "You've made up your mind about me. It's apparent you don't want to discuss this."

She hoped the fun-loving and gentle Kaz would settle onto the step next to her, take her hand in his and kiss it, then offer a discussion. But her spine stiffened as the doorknob turned and the hunter intruded upon her sanctuary.

No one was allowed in her spell room. She had smudged it and consecrated the space and it remained pure because of that. Anyone, whether human or paranormal, touching things or walking the floor, would contaminate that purity. It was comparable to him spitting on her food.

Zoë dropped her head into her hands and fought against tears. She, a drug manufacturer? Never. His accusations tore at her heart. She didn't know how to feel beyond attacked and beaten. It was a similar feeling to the night she had been cut on the face by the vampire, the blade dragged slowly across her flesh in revenge.

Kaz shuffled about inside for only moments before coming out and showing her his fingers. On them glittered the faery ichor that her spell had reduced to purple dust. She'd left an open bowl of the blend on the spell room table, remnants she'd rescued after sweeping up the broken glass.

"It's reduced ichor," she offered flatly. "I designed it as a cure for the addiction to faery dust. The vampire who uses it can slowly wean himself from dust and be clean ever after."

Kaz squatted beside her and she sensed the noise he made in his throat was more a growl than a surprised agreement. "What kind of faery tale do you live in, witch? Or is it warlock?"

"No, I'm not—"

"This is Magic Dust."

"No, it's—"

Kaz swung around in front of her, stepping down onto

the staircase, and thrust his dust-coated fingers before her face. "This is the stuff I've seen on the necks of the victims. We found a vial full of it abandoned near my friend's dead wife. Vials like the ones you have lined along your table."

"No, that's impossible—"

"You are not curing vampires!"

"It's not a cure, but it seems to—"

"Zoë, you are turning them into dust-crazed monsters who destroy human lives in an insane quest for anything that sparkles."

She shook her head adamantly, refusing to believe his lies. She had helped Luc. He'd told her he was getting better. Though she'd yet to see him in person. Could he possibly have lied? But why? They'd come to terms over the years. They were true friends now. He had no reason to want to hurt her again.

"No," she said firmly, unwilling to distrust the loving friendship she had honed with Luc. She'd known him a decade. Kaz, she had known a week.

"My friend said it worked for him. Luc wouldn't lie to me. He's no reason to. But I don't know you at all right now, Kaz, and maybe it's you who is lying to me for some reason. I don't know. Do you need a scapegoat? Is that it? Someone to drag into your Order and claim as the villain?"

He gripped her chin between his fingers. "I cannot *believe* that you can be so ignorant of your actions." He splayed the dust-coated fingers before her. "Look at this! This is death! You are a fine actress, Zoë. It sickens me to stand here."

And he trundled down the stairs, turning into the living room, and moments later flying out with his stakes and Order jacket over an arm.

"Get your story straight," he announced as he shoved his feet into his boots. "I'll be back."

The front door slammed, and Zoë felt the creaking wood shatter her heart.

Seething, Kaz marched down the street from Zoë's house. That she'd had the audacity to deny what he'd so plainly discovered in her lab chipped at his heart. Yes, a lab, not some silly little spell room, as she would have him believe. There had been vials and glass beakers and measuring instruments and scales—all tools of the drug trade. The witch was manufacturing a dangerous drug up in her glass tower.

She'd really pulled a number on him. She'd seduced him into her bed, and then thought to lie to keep him. To think he would believe she was making a drug that would cure the vampires? Couldn't the woman come up with a better excuse than that?

He rubbed his fingers on his coat, attempting to wipe away the purple dust, but it clung tenaciously. He sniffed it and it gave off the sweet odor with which he was familiar from his visit to the ichor den.

Kaz stopped in the middle of the street. What was he doing walking away from the witch? She was the person he had been seeking. He needed to march back through the cerulean door and take her into custody for questioning.

A smart black limo cruised past, and Kaz twisted his head to watch as it slowed to a stop before Zoë's house. Switch got out, clad in a long, black leather dress slit up to her thigh. She strode up the sidewalk.

"Her contact," Kaz muttered.

He clasped the stake at his hip. *They* had been working together all this time? His fist squeezed the stake and the paddles compressed, ejecting the deadly tip.

"Chill, Rothstein," he coached, and watched as the vampiress stood waiting at the front door.

Zoë would have wards against vampires. If the vampiress could cross the threshold then Kaz's gut would really twist. As well, his chipped heart would shatter and break in two. But she didn't. The door opened and Switch and Zoë exchanged words. Zoë had thrown on black slacks and a white shirt and now shook her fist at the visitor. He'd never seen her act so aggressively. Anger was not her thing. She was always forgiving. Even to a fault.

Suddenly, the vampiress grabbed Zoë by the arm, tugging her onto the step, and punched her. Zoë dropped into the vampiress's arms.

Strange way to do business.

Switch shoved Zoë's limp body into the back of the vehicle and got in on the passenger side. He wasn't sure what he'd witnessed, but Kaz would not let the car out of his sight.

The vehicle turned the corner and Kaz took chase.

Chapter 14

Zoë woke from her forced unconsciousness and worked her jaw side to side, wincing at the aching muscles. The vampiress had wielded a terrific right hook.

After Kaz had stormed out, Zoë had felt she needed to get some answers about what she was really involved in—from the big man on top. Only she didn't know where Mauritius was, so she had intended to go looking for the pink-haired vampiress in FaeryTown.

She hadn't expected Pink to return to her doorstep. When they'd argued, Zoë had inadvertently leaned out across the wards, and that had been all her opponent had needed to make a move.

Now, she lay on a black velvet chaise in a sleek room that must be an office, judging by the black desk with the unopened silver laptop in the center. The walls were slate with silver accents and black fixtures. A lamp with dozens of silver globes suspended from steel poles hung in the center of the room.

She spied the pink-haired vampiress standing by the door across the vast room, arms crossed, head cocked to the side and casting her the evil eye. She looked pleased as pickled punch to see Zoë in such a position.

No time for playing the victim—she had to stay alert

and suss the situation. Zoë sat up quickly. To her left, a man in a dark, pin-striped business suit stood with hands in his front trouser pockets. Not so tall, with close-cropped brown hair that was tousled as much as short hair could tousle. He had an average face, but closely spaced blue eyes. Zoë always identified close-spaced eyes with those of a predator.

He offered a hand to shake and she took it as he said, "Nice to finally meet the mastermind behind Magic Dust. I apologize for Switch's unnecessary use of force to bring you here today."

"Mauritius?" Zoë guessed. His British accent was more pronounced in person. And he came off as polite. But then, she'd had no expectations beyond fangs.

He splayed his hands out at his sides. "Not what you were expecting?"

"Actually, I thought you'd be older. Taller." She eased a hand along her aching jaw and shot the vampiress a look. He'd called her Switch? Where had she heard that name?

Kaz had mentioned it.

Everything was so tied together with Kaz's investigation. She couldn't believe she hadn't picked up the clues earlier. But he'd never mentioned he'd been talking with a vampiress whose hair was half black and half shocking pink. If he had, could they have discussed this reasonably without him marching out of her life in a rage?

"Why did you bring me here?" Zoë asked Mauritius. "Wait. If it's about the missing supply, I can explain."

"Please do." Mauritius placed his hands behind his back. He may not have appeared imposing but the aura he gave off chilled Zoë to the bone. His eyes weren't right. They were too young.

"I work in batches. One a day," she started cautiously. For some reason she felt as if she was being weighed and measured. "I needed six batches to fulfill the large order you had recently requested. There was an accident, and half of the last batch was destroyed. I didn't have time to obtain more ichor, though I did go to FaeryTown to try and buy some. That was an unsuccessful trip. I didn't know who to talk to. Faeries aren't my thing. I'll make up for it next time."

Maybe. She wasn't sure anymore what she was actually creating. A blend that would cure vampires of their addiction to faery dust? Or a vicious, amped-up version of dust that drove vampires insane? Kaz had suggested she was warlock. The molecular magic she used was the only thing capable of altering faery dust. Indeed, warlock magic.

She was in over her head. Where was her father when she needed him?

"I didn't bring you here because of the shortage," Mauritius said. "I can overlook your little mistake. Though I will insist you not contact any in FaeryTown for the base product. I will provide you all the ichor you need, Mademoiselle Guillebeaux. Your work is in the lab, not out procuring supply or even hawking the goods."

Hawking the goods? That sounded so not like a man who was trying to help vampires with her blend, but rather like an entrepreneur who was trying to increase sales.

"The demand has increased," Mauritius continued. "You shouldn't be surprised. Your product is remarkable."

Yes, but, she wanted to argue, just what kind of product had she produced?

"Switch deduced you've been creating the goods in a tower room, yes?"

Zoë nodded.

"You need a bigger lab to work in. I am having my men create a suitable work space for you as we speak."

"No, I— I need my spell room. The space is fine for doing what I do. The best work is done in small batches. And I've all my accoutrements and supplies at hand." Zoë stood and wiped her clammy hands down her pant legs. "But I'm afraid you're mistaken. I'm not making Magic Dust. I would never knowingly create such a wicked blend."

Mauritius arched a single brow and held her gaze with a devilish smirk. His pale blue eyes faded and the pupils pinned hers as if by a dark laser. Too much spoken in that expression. Too terribly much.

Heartbeats stalling, Zoë shook her head, unwilling to believe such hideous truths. "No, I can't be. Luc said…" Her best friend would not lie to her. Not after everything they had been through together. "Where is Luc? I have to see him."

"He's having a bit of trouble controlling his impulses lately. I don't want to unleash him on society when he's intent on tearing out the throats of anyone wearing something that sparkles."

"No, that's not right. He's not— Oh, my goddess."

Hands shaking, Zoë looked away from Mauritius, out the window. They were four stories in the air and she could see rooftops and not far off the arched buttresses of Nôtre Dame. So she must be somewhere in the fifth district. Where, though?

Kaz had hated her when he'd stormed out this morning, accusing her of horrible things and making her feel lower than the lowest. But had his suspicions been based on truth?

A truth she sensed was more real than she wanted to accept.

Could she cycle the world backward a day to find herself lying in bed beside her lover without a care in the world? They had been so close, had shared themselves. She could imagine Kaz's shock to wake after such a night, only to learn the woman he'd had sex with had betrayed him. *No!*

"You're lying," she insisted. "Luc told me the blend I gave him was helping him."

"He lied to you."

"He would not lie to me," she insisted firmly.

Would he? The vampire had fallen victim to the destructive clutches of ichor. When high on faery dust Luc had been erratic and less than trustworthy. Yet he'd never been cruel to her. Never so cruel as he once had been.

Zoë touched her cheek, feeling the smooth scar beneath her fingertips. "Why would Luc lie to me?"

"I assume because I offered him much more than friendship with a witch had to offer. I gave him security, a home and lots of cash for the information he gave to me. Along with an endless supply of Magic Dust."

"You bribed him?"

"Initially? No. Luc came to me of his own volition and told me about your blend. How he thought it would blow the regular dust out of the air, so to speak, and be a real moneymaker for me. He was looking for status. A business hookup with me can prove quite profitable. But then when he knew I would need you to work closely with me, he started to relent. That's when we had to, uh, detain him."

"You're keeping him prisoner?"

Mauritius shrugged. Switch shifted her feet to stand at alert, hands at her hips.

"You've been selling my blend, knowing it's harming vampires and making them worse?"

"Hell, yes. What do I care, if they pay me?"

"But you made me believe you wanted to help vampires."

"Tut, mademoiselle, you're not that naive. You can't possibly believe that what you were putting in those glass vials wasn't fucking up the vampires something fierce."

Zoë clasped a hand over her chest. Heartbeats thundered.

"I believed the blend was a cure. I studied my grimoires for months, concocting a spell that should have dispelled the efficacy of the dust."

Add to that the molecular magic, and…oh, she had failed on an inconceivable level.

"Perhaps you are that naive." Mauritius nodded toward Switch, who strode toward Zoë. "And yet, I know only strong magic can alter faery dust. So strong it's not sanctioned by the Light. Isn't that so? Do your fellow witches know of what you are capable?"

She stared hard at him. He would not use that as blackmail. Could not. Oh, hell.

"I admire you," he said with a wink. "You've such a manner that conceals the strength you harbor within. Marvelous. Well, what's done is done. Easily overlooked, yes? I need you to begin work on the next batch. Switch will take you to the new lab. Don't give her trouble. She's liable to give you a bruise on the other side of your jaw. Wouldn't want to have my star cooker work while in pain."

"Cooker?"

"You cook the product for me, yes? Or what is it you call it? Conjure it? Alter the molecules—"

"I refuse!"

Mauritius stood before her and she hadn't even noticed him move. Vampires had a way of doing that. The man was a head taller than she was and he smelled like nothing. A nonentity. Yet the tips of his fangs lowered over his bottom lip, speaking when words were unnecessary.

Zoë swallowed and shook her head. "You won't bite me."

"Why not? Witches taste good. I could enslave you, steal your magic and you'd conjure Magic Dust for me endlessly after."

Another swallow got stuck in her throat. Zoë grasped

the air with a fist. "There's one problem with your evil plan."

"I don't see a problem. And your blood smells..." He inhaled, closing his eyes as if drawing in the aroma of a fine wine. "Innocent, yet so powerful."

"If you steal my magic, it'll weaken me. As you've said, I use a very powerful magic to create the blend. If that special magic is drained, you've no Magic Dust."

He tilted his head in thought. A fang glinted. She had him. But that didn't make her proud or relieved in any manner.

"Let me go," she said firmly.

"Well, if I can't bite you, I'm going to have to keep you. I would be a fool to let my moneymaker out of sight. The lab, remember?"

"You can't keep me here. That's kidnapping. I want to be taken home."

"Your home won't stand for much longer. After your spell room has been moved, we'll have to torch the place to remove evidence. You understand."

"No! All of my things—Sid."

Mauritius looked to Switch, but the vampiress merely shrugged.

"He's my cat," Zoë managed, defeat lowering her shoulders and making her legs shake. She tightened her fists at her sides, but when she wanted to speak forcefully her words only whispered out, "You can't burn the place." Zoë beat her fists against the vampire's chest as he wrangled her into his grasp. "You bastard!"

"Mademoiselle Guillebeaux." The vampire bracketed her face with his palms and she felt a sudden heat flood her skin and relax her tense muscles. Her fists spread open. Her eyelids fluttered. "You want to do this. You believe your blend is helping vampires." The man's voice eased into her brain on a warm hush. She liked it. A tiny smile curved her lips. "You will honor our agreement, and you will be pleased with your new lab. Yes?"

While her brain wanted to scream and rage at him, Zoë found herself nodding in agreement. His voice felt so good, seemed to wrap itself around her in a lilting cocoon. Maybe what she was doing helped vampires, after all. She didn't know anymore. She couldn't react the way she felt necessary. It was as if he were controlling her with vampiric persuasion.

She needed to wield her magic against him. Magic that was never reliable when she was under duress.

"You're going to do as I say, yes?"

She nodded in assent to the vampire's command.

"Run along, then."

"Of course," Zoë said, and walked toward Switch.

Kaz waited beside the limo parked behind the office building. It had taken him five minutes to catch up with the limo as it had driven through the streets, across the bridge and to this building in the fifth. He'd run as if the devil was on his heels, and he was only now catching his breath.

This was the car he'd seen Switch shove Zoë into. He wasn't sure if Zoë would return with Switch, but he had to take the chance that she would. Switch no longer mattered. Zoë was the key. He needed to get the witch alone and question her about her involvement in the Magic Dust operation.

As well, he sensed the least fight from the witch.

So when Switch swung around the building with Zoë's arm firmly in grasp and shoved her toward the vehicle, Kaz's brain cautiously warned, *Be calm and feel the situation out.* Yet his heart thudded at the sight of Zoë's rough treatment. No matter her intentions by creating the dangerous dust, he would not allow anyone to harm her.

"Kaz!" Zoë spied him as the vampiress opened the back door of the car. "Help me!"

Whether or not that plea was for real, or a trap to lure the hunter in closer so they could both take him out, Kaz didn't vacillate between the right and wrong of it overlong. Instinct screamed that Zoë was in genuine trouble.

He ran for the vampiress and punched her, only to receive a swipe of claws across his face. Fangs extended, the vampiress lunged toward his neck, but cringed back when she saw the bladed collar.

"Take a bite," he offered.

She hissed.

Stake still holstered, he kneed Switch in the gut and delivered an uppercut to her jaw, which snapped back her head and knocked her out. Vamps may be strong and immortal, but they could still be dropped by a fist to the mandible that pinched the rich collection of nerves at the base of the ear. She collapsed by the open car door. No stake necessary.

From out of the driver's side, another vampire charged Kaz. Big, male and wielding a knife. This time Kaz had no qualms to using the stake. He caught the vamp in the heart and the stake pinioned out. Ash rained over him. The knife dropped to the tarmac with a clatter.

Stepping back and jumping once to shake off the loose vamp ash, Kaz turned just as Zoë ran into his arms. She reached up around his neck, but he pushed her away.

"The blades," he warned of his coat collar. "You okay?"

"It's all wrong, Kaz. The blend isn't what I thought it was. I'm so sorry. Get me out of here before they lock me up and force me to do terrible things."

"How do I know I can trust you?"

"What?"

"You're working for the people I've been investigating, Zoë."

"Not by choice. I thought I was…doing a good thing. You can trust me. I need to get home. They're going to burn it!"

"Who's inside?" Kaz asked, casting his gaze up the glass-walled building.

"They went out the other way when Switch brought me down. Mauritius did."

"Mauritius?"

"He's the vampire behind it all. Please, Kaz, I have to get home. I understand you need to take care of this problem, but… Please," she said on a gasp that felt to Kaz as helpless as she looked.

If the man behind the plan, Mauritius, had already left, then there was nothing more he could do here. At the very least, he needed to keep the creator of Magic Dust in hand.

Did he trust Zoë?

Not for a moment.

Kaz was all business as he strode quickly toward her home. He didn't offer to take Zoë's hand, and she had to run to keep up with his urgent pace. She sensed his speed wasn't because he worried for her home, but rather, was fueled by his anger.

He hated her.

And it was all her fault. All this time, she was the person he had been looking for. It sickened her to realize that, and she had no idea how to make it better.

Everything was not as it should be, and she had made it so. That he could even stand to be near her proved his strength, or rather, his focus on doing his job.

When they got to the end of the block, Zoë saw the smoke curling up from her rooftop and flames dancing inside the tower windows.

"I have to get inside!"

Kaz caught her about the waist, and swung her off her

scrambling feet and into his arms. She beat against his shoulders, but he was intent on keeping her in hand. But he could not stop her. He didn't understand. "You're not going to run into a burning building. I've done that once before. Never again."

"Wh-what?" What was he talking about?

"We'll call the fire brigade."

"No! I don't care about my things. Everything is replaceable. But Sid is in there."

Kaz did not relent his tight clutch on her. And Zoë did not relent her struggles, kicking the air in an attempt to lever away from him, but with no success.

"Sid will find a way out, Zoë. Cats are smart."

"Not if the doors and windows are closed. It's been so cool lately, I've had the windows pulled down."

She wrestled away from his grasp and started running down the street, but Kaz caught her again, swinging her from her feet to hold her struggling against his body.

"Set me down!"

"Not if you're going to run into a burning building. Never again! Do you hear me?"

She wasn't sure what it was about fires that was making him say such nonsensical things. He slapped his hands about her wrists, holding her with an ease that proved his strength.

"Witches and fire, Zoë. Think about it." She stopped struggling and looked at him, finding his gaze wasn't so hard, perhaps even teary. "If I let you go, are you going to be smart?"

"Yes! I promise."

He set her on the cobbled street, and while Zoë's body jerked toward her home, she maintained a jittering stance before Kaz. He stared at the flames, tears now rolling down his cheeks. Lower lip sucked in and jaw tight, he was not in the present, she felt sure.

Kaz had experienced a fire before and, she guessed, he must have lost someone. How cruel of her to insist he allow her to go inside. And yet, her heart broke to imagine what Sid must be going through if the windows were all closed up.

"Please," she pleaded with the stoic slayer. "Sid is all I have."

Tears spilling down her cheeks, she blinked through them to find Kaz's expression was drawn, his mouth open in shock. "Zoë, you have me."

Those simple words struck her hard, right in the center of her heart. "I—I do? But…"

She'd thought to have lost his respect after the accusations he'd blasted at her. And earlier, finding her with Switch surely had confirmed all the truths he believed about her. Because, as much as she hated to admit it to herself, they were truths. She hadn't time to explain to him how wrong she had been.

"I may feel as if I want to hate you right now," he continued, "but part of me screams to trust my heart." He touched her cheek, stroking aside her hair. "You're good, Zoë. You didn't know what you were doing. At least, I hope you didn't know."

"I didn't! I swear it to you."

"Fine. But grant me some allowance of suspicion."

She nodded. "You have every right to suspect me. I'll have to earn your trust. I know that."

"So besides the cat, you have me. Do you understand that, Zoë?" He clasped her upper arms and squeezed. "I will do anything to protect you, which includes keeping you from rushing into a burning building."

He kissed her there in the middle of the street while her whole life went up in flames not three houses away. And for those few seconds of connection, Zoë surrendered to someone's need to do right by her. To keep her safe.

She had chosen the right guy this time.

Zoë pulled from her savior's kiss. "The fire scares you. Is that it? What happened to you with fire, Kaz?"

He shook his head. "Not now."

"I'll tell you everything," Zoë insisted. "How wrong I was. How this whole awful business has turned into a nightmare. But please, we have to go in for Sid."

Kaz's jaw tightened, the muscle pulsing.

"Please," she whispered.

Chapter 15

An hour later, Zoë sat across the row from Kaz on the Metro headed toward Kaz's home. Sid curled on her lap. The cat had been dusted with soot when he'd come flying through the broken kitchen window and had landed in her arms. His whiskers had been singed close to his maw and the tip of his tail had been burned, as well.

Kaz had quickly tugged her away from the building, and she'd felt as if he were carrying away, not her, but some past demon that had risen with the flames to torment him.

The fire brigade had arrived and Kaz suggested to Zoë she only explain she'd been away shopping, and had no idea how the blaze had been started. She couldn't confess that a gang of vampires had started the fire after removing equipment that would implicate her in the creation of dangerous recreational drugs. That would not have gone over at all with the authorities.

The fire brigade succeeded in getting the fire under control, but only after the roof and top floor had collapsed. The house was a complete loss. And witches did not have insurance. As well, if the Witches Council of the Light heard about the fire, they may ask questions Zoë didn't want to answer.

Zoë had a little money in savings, but no more than

enough to see her through a few years in a cheap apartment. But she could hardly feel devastated holding the shivering cat. What was most important to her had survived.

It had been one hell of a day. Kaz had woken this morning to learn the woman his heart had fallen for was the very reason he'd set out on a quest to track those dealing in Magic Dust. But now he wasn't so sure she had known what she was involved in. How was that possible?

He'd wait until she volunteered the information, because Zoë looked tired. She needed to decompress and clear her head.

He leaned over and kissed her aside the eye and smoothed away the hair that had fallen over her lashes. "We'll figure things out."

"Thank you."

Sid nudged his little black head against Kaz's chin. A cat thank-you? He smoothed a palm over the feline's body and gave it a pat.

Twenty minutes later, Kaz showed Zoë around his flat. The one-bedroom was large for the neighborhood, and most of it was empty because he only had a few pieces of comfy furniture, and nothing on the walls, save the map in the living room. He didn't do home decorating beyond the spray-painted wards against vampires on his door and near his windows.

He offered Zoë the first shower, and then ran downstairs to borrow some cat food. Madame Malone had been delighted to fill a plastic container with dry food and then directed him to the basement storage room where the building owner kept tubs of cat litter for the residents to use. He found an empty plastic tub and fashioned a litter box for Sid then placed it outside his door at the end of the hallway where a multipaned window looked over a small, leaf-strewn playground in the back courtyard.

He'd never seen kids playing out on the swings, and that was a good thing, in case a vampire had followed him home. None had done so yet. He hoped his luck held out.

Now he stripped away his shirt, unlaced and kicked off his boots and stood in the bedroom looking out the window. From here he could see the road that circled Paris's twenty arrondissements. Cars dashed madly to and from work. It wasn't as noisy as one would expect, living so close to a major freeway. He liked the industrial scenery for reasons he couldn't figure. Maybe because gardens were too fussy for him. The one plant he'd been gifted by Madame Malone as a moving-in present had promptly died two days later.

Out the corner of his eye he saw Sid jump onto his bed and before he could turn and give the critter a reassuring pat on the head, he felt the warm glide of Zoë's hand slide up his bare back. Her cheek rested against his shoulder. His licorice-scented shampoo scented her skin and wet hair.

"You hungry?" he asked, uncertain about their relationship now.

He would love more than anything to abandon good judgment, turn and lay her on the bed and have sex with her, but he was leery now. And after watching her house burn—well, they needed to talk. About everything.

"Starving."

"I'll order a pizza before I hop in the shower. You like mushrooms?"

"Anything but anchovies."

"My kind of woman. I put a litter box for Sid in the hallway outside the front door. It's near the garbage chute. Got some cat food, too."

"Aren't you the industrious host?"

"I do what I can. This building is filled with crazy cat ladies, so everything was at hand."

"Is it okay if I wear one of your shirts for a while? I want to put my clothes in the wash."

"Yep." Kaz walked to the door, avoiding the tempting heat of her scented skin. "Toss in the things I have piled on top of the washer, too, will you?"

"Sure. Kaz? I know you're angry with me. I'll make it better. I have to."

He nodded, and, not trusting his ability to hold back an angry accusation, he headed out to the kitchen to call for delivery. Was it even possible to make things better? Humans had died. More humans would continue to die if he didn't stop Zoë from making more Magic Dust.

But what caused the most worry? How to ransom the bits of his heart that he'd freely held out to Zoë on his open palms. She was everything he should hate. And yet sorting between right and wrong had never been more difficult.

Kaz chowed down the last slice of pizza as Zoë sat back on the sofa and stroked Sid's tail. It didn't appear as if his skin had been burned, just lost some fur. Yet he may have sacrificed one of his nine lives tonight.

As had Kaz. She could not erase the look of terror that had consumed him as they'd stood before her burning house. Fire would frighten anyone, but it had been the first time she'd seen real fear on the man's face. Not even vampires could bring up such raw emotion in him.

She hugged Sid and looked aside, catching Kaz's sidelong glance at her. He smiled and leaned forward, elbows to his knees.

"What did fire do to you?" she asked carefully.

He lifted his chin, his profile growing hard and pensive. She guessed his thoughts had just jettied away from this room and into a different time and place. Her heart pounded, and Sid rubbed his face against hers, sensing her apprehension.

Catching his face in his palms, and threading his fingers up through his hair, Kaz eased the heel of one palm against his forehead, then exhaled. "My mom died in the fire that destroyed our family home when I was twelve."

Zoë swallowed. Her heartbeats stuttered.

"It was a faulty heater. Old thing just up and exploded one summer night. I woke surrounded by flames, and heard my father's voice calling to me. I ran out into the hallway and his big, strong arms…"

He closed his hands over his face, and Zoë could feel the pain of memory tighten his every muscle.

"He grabbed me and carried me out," he finally managed. "I was choking and crying, and he was holding me and choking, as well. And then I called for my mother, and my father realized she was still inside. He left me there in the backyard and ran toward the house. I was so scared I called to him to come back to me. And when he paused before rushing back inside the burning house, the threshold collapsed and exploded, the force of it tossing him back into the yard."

He tilted his head back. His eyes closed; his lip wobbled.

"The whole house went down with my mother inside."

Zoë hugged Sid even closer, knowing that words could never heal such a wound, especially if the memory of it reduced him to a man who could barely contain the tears. Yet he did. "It must be difficult for one so young to comprehend such a tragedy."

He nodded, sniffed back a tear she hadn't noticed. "Yeah, well, it's in the past, right? Bad things happen to people all the time. I'm no one special. Nor was my mother. I just, uh… Watching your house burn brought back the stuff I hadn't thought about in a while."

"I shouldn't have insisted we go there."

"You couldn't have known. Besides…" He tugged gently on Sid's tail. "This little fellow was worth it."

She nodded against Sid's head and hugged him even closer, knowing she could never soothe the hurt that had been embedded in Kaz's very soul when losing his mother.

"Thank you for telling me about the fire," she offered. "I lost my mother, too, when I was thirteen."

He sat upright, turning to inspect her. "Really? I'm sorry, Zoë. I know how tough it is. Hell. You see? Everyone has bad stuff. Uh, how did you lose her?"

"Car accident. She didn't have good night vision, and drove into a ravine one night. To this day I don't like to drive or even ride in a car." She slid a hand along Kaz's thigh. "I'm glad you take the Metro everywhere."

"Paris is a bitch to drive in," he muttered, and then smiled.

The two shared soft laughter.

"We have things in common," Zoë said. "We both managed our teen years without a maternal presence. It's never easy."

"Nope. It's not."

"Did your mother's death have something to do with you running away a few years later?"

"Yep." He closed the cover of the empty pizza box, and Zoë took it as his signal that this conversational thread was closed. She'd give him that. Memory was a tough conversation, and it always tended to linger in one's soul, even after the words had been spoken.

This man was strong, and had been forged by his experiences, as had she. And her latest experience was nothing to be proud of.

"So I need to explain," she offered. "Will you listen?"

"You bet."

While Kaz cleaned up the pizza box and their plates and set them in the kitchen, Zoë explained everything to him.

How she'd been compelled to concoct a blend of faery dust that could help Luc kick the habit, and Luc telling her it had worked, and how a vampire he knew wanted more so he could spread the goodness around. She'd been thrilled.

Until the truth had crash-landed upon her naive little world.

."So why do you think Luc was compelled to lie to you?" he asked, strolling back around with a dishcloth to wipe off the coffee table. "You trust vampires?"

"Of course I do. Most of them. There are good and bad vampires, just as there are good and bad humans."

"Right, but you said you and Luc have been friends awhile?"

"Over a decade. We met—well, that's a long and even weirder tale." And as far as confessions went, they'd both shared their fill today. "The only thing that could have gotten into Luc was the dust. He began experimenting with faery dust after a tough breakup with a vampiress he'd been dating for two years. The guy was head over heels in love. I'd been giving him some space because of that, so I didn't realize how deeply he'd gotten into dust. And when he finally did confess his addiction, I knew I had to do something to help him. A vampire can't get clean of dust on his own."

"Just like any other drug. The addict needs help, a whole team of professionals who know how to facilitate healing."

"Yes, and I was determined to be his team." Zoë caught her chin in her hands and sighed. "I'm skilled in a special kind of magic. I can't talk about it, but my father taught it to me."

"The kind of stuff that only warlocks do?"

"Kaz, I'm not a warlock."

"Are you sure about that?"

No, she wasn't sure. In the sense that her magic had altered the molecules of a sidhe substance, then yes, she was, and that she had harmed humans inadvertently—oh, hell.

"Zoë?"

"Maybe I am," she said on a gasp. "Oh, Kaz, I never meant to cause harm. The magic I employed in the blend— the witches of the Light don't approve of its use. It's called molecular magic, and it alters the very molecules of a substance. Using it on faery ichor is tricky because the sidhe have a slightly different molecular structure than we creatures and the humans who exist in this mortal realm."

"I can believe that. Faeries sort of flicker."

"Exactly. They can never completely fit into this realm. I thought I'd mastered the ichor structure. But apparently, I had not. I can't believe I thought the blend was actually helping my friend. Luc's addiction must have stood up and cheered when he tested the dust I'd given him. And that same addiction wouldn't allow him to tell me the truth."

"Addiction can be rough," Kaz agreed as he sat on the couch on the other side of Sid.

"You say that as if you've firsthand knowledge."

He rubbed the heel of his palm over his stubble-dusted jaw, then finally confessed, "My father is an alcoholic."

"I'm sorry." An excellent reason for a teenager to run away, especially without a mother to shelter him. "It must have been tough for you as a child."

He shrugged, dismissing it as casually as he'd mentioned it. "He picked up the bottle after the fire. Blamed me for my mom's death. If I hadn't called out to him to come back, he wouldn't have stopped. The house wouldn't have caved in...."

"You may have saved his life by calling to him, Kaz."

"Yeah, maybe. You can't talk to a drunk, though. Anyway, I moved out when I was fourteen. Better that way. Dad can't help the way he was or is. The booze became him. I suspect the dust became your friend, as well. The dust lied to you, Zoë, not Luc."

That he brushed off his father's problem as if insignificant clued Zoë it was a much sorer spot with him than the fire that had killed his mother. She wouldn't touch those feelings. For now.

"Thank you for being so understanding," she said. "You could have pushed me away—"

He caught her hand and squeezed. "Part of me still wants to push, so don't get too excited. It's been a tough day. And this whole warlock thing, I'm not sure what to think about it."

He held her hand to his mouth and the warmth of his lips scurried up her wrist and tingled along her arm. Zoë exhaled softly. This knight was too good to her.

"But another part," he continued, "an even bigger part, knows you're too valuable to my heart—er, to me. I like you, Zoë."

He'd almost confessed that she was valuable to his heart. He *had* confessed as much, but he'd quickly changed his words. Still, it meant a lot to Zoë to know his heart. He had become an important part of her life, and she would do whatever she could to ensure she did not lose his trust. She had to gain it back. She wanted to defeat that part of him that needed to push her away.

He'd been on his own since he was fourteen so he must have had to grow up fast. No wonder he led such a hard life. Slaying was not for those who valued family and relationships.

"The dance studio," she suddenly remembered. "It was your one salvation."

"Probably. Like I said, Madame du Monde had great cookies."

"I'm glad you had her in your life. And when did you join the Order?"

"Couple years later. I was recruited on my sixteenth birthday. My life took a one-eighty that day. I'm thankful to the man who trained me, and a few others who I call friends. See? I'm not such a sorry case after all."

"Whether or not you realize it, you have risen from the ashes, Kaspar Rothstein."

"Maybe. And now look. I reduce others to ash. Sounds about right to me."

"Sounds as if the world is a better place, thanks to you." Zoë hugged Sid to her chest. "I have to get Luc away from Mauritius. That vampire is only concerned with making money. He'll let Luc die. I'm surprised he even takes care of him now. He's detained him against his will, I'm sure of it."

"He wants to control him, Zoë. Mauritius gave Luc something he values more than freedom. And in exchange, you know what Luc gave him."

She looked for the answer in his freckled eyes, and he finally offered, "You." The truth stabbed her in the gut. "And if Mauritius needs to control you, he'll use Luc to do so. He's not stupid."

She shook her head. "That hurts my heart to think about it. I have to go back. Luc was in the building somewhere. I know it. There was a residential floor in the building because I noticed a maid's cart with linens on it when I was riding the elevator down with Switch."

"You are not going anywhere near those vampires. Mauritius just lost his only supplier of Magic Dust. You can bet he'll have a team combing the streets for you."

"But I have to help Luc."

"The vampire means that much to you?"

Zoë looked up from her hands. "We had a rough start, Luc and I, but he's my best friend, Kaz. You must understand. Do you have a best friend?"

The man shook his head. "Not practical in my line of work. Doesn't matter. I'll go get him."

"You will? You won't stake him?"

He squeezed a fist tightly and shook his head. "But I'll have to detain him. He could prove a danger to others. You really want to deal with what your friend has become? Do you know a way to help him down from the addiction?"

"Apparently not. That's why I concocted the blend. Oh, I hate that it was something so evil and I didn't even know. I may have been responsible for human deaths. Oh, my goddess, I know I was. What you told me about your friends getting murdered by a vampire scamming for something that sparkled…"

"Don't think about it, Zoë. You can't." He sucked a breath through his nose and exhaled heavily. "What's been done is done. Now you move forward, yes?"

"Can you ever forgive me?"

"Forgiveness is important to you."

"It's everything. Without it, we become mired in the past and the things we can never change. I always forgive. It's unthinkable not to. But I wouldn't expect the same from you."

"I can forgive, Zoë, but I'll never forget. And my friends deserve retribution for their lost lives. Any information you can give me about Mauritius and Switch will be helpful."

"I didn't even know her name until we stood in Mauritius's office and he addressed her as Switch. I thought of her as Pink. I don't know where she lives, either."

"It doesn't matter. I've marked the location where Mauritius works on the left bank. And we'll find that lab he's set up for you."

"Thank you for believing me. I don't know what I'd do if I had fallen in your eyes."

"You would have moved on."

"No. Kaz, what you think of me means so much. I... I've—hell, I've fallen in love with you."

She met his gaze, seeking, hoping, pining for the same confession. The man slid the tip of his tongue along his lower lip and, with a shrug, patted the cat's head. "I've certainly fallen for you," he said, "but as for love..."

"It's okay. You don't have to love me. I needed you to know that's how I feel about you." She slumped against the couch back, the soft shirt she'd taken from one of his drawers reaching over her thighs. "I'm so tired. But I can't stop thinking about Luc."

"I'll go after him in the morning when the vamps usually sleep in." He looked around her at the sofa. "I can, uh...sleep here on the couch and give you the bed."

"You don't want to share the bed with me?"

"I need some space right now, Zoë. Please understand."

She nodded, not wanting to understand, but it was clear that she had forced him to act against his vows to protect humans from vampires when he had saved her. And now by agreeing to help her find Luc he would once again go against those vows.

"Sure. I'll see you in the morning?"

"I might be gone before you rise." He leaned over and kissed her on the forehead, then patted Sid's head. "I have to run out for a bit. Order business. Lock the door behind me."

He stood and, claiming his leather coat with the stakes and holy water and cross, he opened the door. Zoë watched him pull out a key from his pocket, then tuck it away as she'd seen him do before. Then he closed the door and his boots clunked down the staircase.

"He's running away, isn't he, Sid?"

The cat nudged his head up under her chin in agreement.

"Guess I shouldn't have expected him to want to share

a bed with me after the day we've had. Do you think we'll ever get back to the fun, new love we had?"

Sid offered no response, so Zoë stood and padded into the bedroom. Lying down on the bed, she spread her hand over the sheets and snuggled her face into the pillow. She couldn't smell Kaz in the fibers. So easily he had slipped from her life.

Rolling to her back, she allowed Sid to crawl onto her belly and snuggle. Her thoughts could not enjoy the quiet comfort of the softly purring cat.

What would the witches of the Light do to her if they discovered she had been using the same magic as her father? She cringed to recall the brand of the warlock her father had proudly shown her. Red and thick, it had been ugly, a symbol of the mistrust of others and ignorance.

She was not a bad person. She was just a little misdirected.

Kaz stood in the hallway before his front door. He'd checked his pockets for the key, feeling relief when the curved lines of it fit into his palm. He always made a key check before walking away from a closed door. It was an ingrained habit.

Damned past would never extract its claws from his shoulders. He'd been checking for a key ever since he was fourteen years old.

"Thanks for nothing, Dad," he muttered. "Except making me a freak."

A freak who couldn't even stay in the same room as his girlfriend and offer her comfort because he wasn't sure how to do that.

Talking. Man, they had talked. About things that still made him feel a little teary. But talking wasn't action, and action equaled trouble to him.

He always ran toward trouble. That compulsion had

been programmed into him by the Order. But now he was running away from conflict. A different beast than the trouble involved with stalking and staking vampires. This conflict required him to care enough to stand and meet Zoë's eyes and tell her exactly how he felt.

She'd confessed she loved him. He should have replied with his feelings.

"Can't do it," he muttered. "Don't know how."

Chapter 16

The vampiress with the ridiculous pink hair struggled against the magic that held her to the marble floor in the center of the huge sanctuary hidden in the depths of Faery-Town. Corinthian columns queued along both sides of the floor, and vines grew up from their bases as if they'd been planted in dirt, yet there was no sign of any growth medium. Overhead, the ceiling was nearly covered by a canopy of the thick vines, and long, white flowers hung, dripping their honeylike pollen onto the floor.

Faery glamour at its finest.

Coyote strolled before the pinned vampire, her bare feet silent on the warm marble. They'd found the idiot vamp lurking around an ichor den.

She smirked at Whim's antics. Her cohort danced about the vampire on his hooves, his velvet-antlered head bowed and tilted in glee as he spun and swept the tips of his wings over her face, not cutting, but imbuing his dust into her skin. The longtooth would get a contact high, but not enough to distort her thinking.

Off to the side, Never stood, expressing his usual feigned disinterest. The dark sidhe gave them his back, bared shoulders straight and proud. The arrows queued between his dark wings glinted with sunlight that beamed in from the stained-glass windows that encircled the room.

"If you don't tell me what I want, Whim will crush your bones," Coyote tossed out casually. She and Whim worked in tandem whenever they tortured; both played off the other, not having a predetermined tactic. "But you won't die. You'll feel the pain again and again. Until I have my dark one pierce you through the heart with his true weapons."

Switch spouted mortal curse words and told Coyote to do something to herself that she felt sure was impossible.

Whim pounced onto the vampiress's chest, squatting there and shouting louder than Switch's cries of pain. A sweep of his wings showered dust over the vampire's face and she spat at the substance.

"You've encroached upon our territory." Coyote continued pacing. "Selling product that has not been sanctioned. The Cortège will not suffer you to live."

"It wasn't me!" Switch yelled.

"Of course, you work for a vendor. But that vampire can't possibly make the product. Who manufactures the Magic Dust, Switch?"

The vampiress spat dust-glittered blood at Coyote's feet. Whim slashed a wingtip across her throat, spilling out blood. Unfortunately, the longtooth idiots had a tendency to heal rather quickly.

"Is it the hunter?" Coyote prompted.

She doubted a hunter, human or otherwise, would have reason to dally in dust manufacture, but crazier things had occurred. Never had recently marked the hunter as suspect.

Never switched his stance, which alerted Coyote. She stared at him, but he wouldn't gift her with a return glance. Annoying entitled bit of—

"Make her speak, Whim."

Whim jumped off the vampire and performed a jig near

her head. His clacking hooves tangled within the horrid pink and black hair and tugged out chunks. Howling like a banshee, the faery then danced a cruel storm upon the vampire's chest, sweeping his sharpened wingtips across cheeks, throat and mouth.

"The hunter is involved with the witch who is making the Magic Dust!" Switch cried out in a spatter of blood.

Coyote approached the vampiress, who groaned and cursed anything and everything. Whim stepped off her body, wings fluttering gaily. Vampire blood dripped from a wing tip and onto the pollen-spotted floor. "A witch is making the Magic Dust?"

"Her name is Zoë Guillebeaux and she's allied with the slayer Kaspar Rothstein. He's Order of the Stake."

"Ah, a knight on your ass?"

"He's too much of a wimp to take me out. Had the chance a couple times and only wanted to talk. What kind of hunter talks?"

"And yet, he's apparently taken the one person you need most away from you."

"I could care less about the witch. It's not my operation, it's Mauritius—"

Coyote seized the vampiress by a hank of bloody pink hair, lifting her head from the floor. "Mauritius of the Anière tribe?"

"Fuck."

Coyote slammed the vampiress's head against the marble, delighting when she heard the skull crack.

She had names now. Plenty of them. "Never!"

The dark sidhe lifted his chin, but still did not regard her. Yet she could sense his sinews tighten in preparation. How she did take delight in his sanguine methods to homicide.

"You bring the hunter to me. Alive," she directed Never. "I'll take care of Mauritius."

"What about the witch?" Whim asked.

"I hate witches," Coyote muttered. Witches had lured her mother to FaeryTown with the promise of prosperity. And then they'd drained her of ichor and used it in a strange ritual that Coyote had witnessed. It was the only time she had ever been literally sickened. "I'll save the witch for something special."

She strode away from the groaning vampiress, tilting Never a nod as she passed him by. Whim paralleled her.

Behind them, the dark sidhe introduced a flechette into the vampiress's chest. She yelled and spasmed and gave a good fight. Finally, she managed to pull the weapon out, but not so carefully that the glass tips did not shatter. When she ashed, the silence was cut by a giggle from Whim.

Her behooved cohort nudged his nose into Coyote's hair. "Pretty when they die."

Kaz hadn't gone home after leaving Zoë alone last night. He assumed she'd snuggled into his bed with Sid and had fallen asleep.

He'd slept in the Metro station on an aluminum bench. The station closest to his home was always quiet in the middle of the night. And no one ever bothered the sleeping bums. His neck ached and his back could use a good tug to get out the kinks, but he was standing upright and his head was clear.

More than he could say for the person he needed to find today.

"A vampire." Zoë's *friend.* "If Rook hears about this he'll kick me out of the Order."

Not that Kaz hadn't sympathy for a vampire who was under the influence of an addictive substance. The drug controlled the user, not the other way around. Luc may very well want to get clean, but could not. He was lucky he had a friend like Zoë, because had she not begged Kaz to find Luc, he may have staked the bastard had he run into him while investigating.

He wondered if Luc had ever attempted to achieve the Neverland Fix Vail had mentioned. A vampire never came back from that. Kaz was surprised he'd not run into one of those addicts. On the other hand, perhaps they were in no condition to move. Or maybe they were dead.

He couldn't help but feel sympathy toward them all.

When and how had he become such a softy? Had one night of sex with a pretty little witch screwed up his sense of right and wrong so wickedly?

Apparently, it had.

Which was why Kaz now stared at the red, metallic gleam on the facade of the steel business building where he'd rescued Zoë last evening. Inside he may or may not find the vampire Luc. Zoë had given him a brief description: tall, thin, dark loose hair and attractive. Hell, that covered just about all the vampires in Paris.

But the vampire would know Zoë, so he relied on that to ensure he nabbed the right one.

And if he ran into Mauritius while in there? Then he'd ash another with his stake. He did know what that vampire looked like, thanks to checking Order records earlier. He gave the sketch of Mauritius on his cell phone one last look, then turned off his phone and shoved it in a pocket. A sweep of clouds overhead cast shadow across the sunlit cobbles as Kaz crossed the street. He looked up, but noted the sky was actually cloudless.

"Hell of a big bird," he muttered, then entered the building.

The digital entry box detailed each floor and the business names. He guessed the third floor was the residential level because there was no label or business name on that one. Kicking the steel door loosened the dead-bolt locks at the top and the floor, and he managed to shoulder it open and pass into the parquet-floored lobby. No alarm went off. Hoping it wasn't a silent alarm, he veered toward the stairs.

Once on the third floor, he was surprised there were no guards. Odd, if they were keeping a vampire against his will. Or maybe they weren't and Zoë only believed Luc was a captive. He could very well be voluntarily involved with Mauritius, receiving payment in the form of Magic Dust to keep him appeased. Made the most sense.

Prepared to face the worst, and cursing the fact he'd made a promise to Zoë that he would not harm Luc, Kaz took out a half-inch-wide plastic zip tie that had been warded to withstand vampire strength from a pocket as he walked down the hallway. He stopped at the first door and listened. Silence. Sun beamed in from under the next door. Not the optimal place for a manic vampire to get some rest.

The door on the opposite side of the hall was also quiet, yet dark. At the next door he saw the movement of shadow at the doorjamb and then heard the crash inside. Sounded as if a piece of wood furniture had hit the wall. When he arrived at the door he saw it had been padlocked on the outside. Someone wanted to keep whatever was on the other side of this door behind it.

"Bingo."

Jamming the titanium stake end against the standard-issue padlock, Kaz pounded twice more. The cheap mechanism surrendered. He kicked the door inside and caught a raging vampire against his chest. Fangs gnashed across his coat sleeve and growls sounded more canine than human.

They both went down, Kaz landing on his back out in the main hallway, stake in one hand and zip tie in the other. The vampire had earned his freedom and stood, ready to dash away. Kaz tripped him, bringing him down. He couldn't let him out of the building or he'd never wrangle him.

Kicking at him with his bare feet, the vampire swore at him. "Who the hell are you? You're not one of Mauritius's thugs."

"Thank you for noticing my lacking evil."

Kaz dodged a lunging foot and snapped the vampire's arm behind his back. Rolling his body, he landed on the vamp's head with his back, smashing the longtooth's face against the floor.

"I'm trying to help you," Kaz said, but he kept his voice down. He didn't want to alert the cavalry, if there was one. "Zoë sent me."

The vampire stopped struggling, and in that moment, Kaz managed to wrap the zip tie around both his wrists and pull it tight.

"Did Zoë send more dust?" the downed vamp asked. "I need more Magic Dust, man. Gimmee!"

One punch to the vampire's jaw knocked him out cold. Kaz caught the vampire across his shoulders and hefted him up. Too light, he thought, and he felt a long, bony arm slap him across the back. He'd suffered for the drug. Poor guy.

Yeah, so falling for the witch really had screwed with his sympathies.

Taking the stairs down, he strode out into the lobby— and felt the *swoosh* of something pass by his cheek.

Dread curdled up Kaz's spine and he instinctually ducked back into the stairwell.

"Faeries," he muttered. "Has to be."

Cautious, Kaz snuck out into the main lobby, the unconscious vampire over a shoulder. He couldn't see the damn thing, but knew there was a faery in the building. The air stirred with a strange yet familiar vibration that he had remarked while passing through FaeryTown. The thing could be walking alongside him, for all he knew. He needed the ointment in his pocket but speed was of the essence right now.

When he made it to the front door, he began to slip through the broken frame and door when Luc let out a banshee cry.

"What the hell?" the vampire shouted.

The vampire jostled out of Kaz's grip, and he had no choice but to set him down and slam him up against the door. "Be quiet or I will stake you."

"What did you do to me?" Luc slapped his shoulder where a flechette like the one Kaz had taken to his hip sat implanted deep in the flesh.

"Don't touch it," Kaz warned. "It's faery. Poisonous if you remove it. Got that?"

Luc's lashes fluttered over his sunken eyes. "Faery stuff." He reached for the flechette with his bound hands.

Kaz punched him again, reducing him to a silent, but annoying lump of skin and bones that he preferred to stake. Zoë had better appreciate this sacrifice.

Opening the door deflected another of the flechettes that pinged the steel and dropped to the parquet, spinning once before defusing into a pouf of violet smoke and glittering ichor.

Kaz rushed outside and into a fine mist of rain, sure the faery would tail him. Yet he'd remembered reading something about faeries and rain. What was it? No matter. He had to keep moving. Heading down into the Metro system would prove a death wish, so he darted across the street and down an alleyway toward a more populated area. If the faery maintained glamour he wouldn't have to worry about innocent humans spying a creature flying overhead.

Another flechette tore the air above his head. "Damn."

On the other hand, the faery was invisible, so he couldn't see it, either.

Kaz fumbled in his coat for the vial of ointment and

managed, with one hand, to twist off the top. He stuck his finger into it, nearly losing his grasp on the vial, and smeared what little stuck to his finger under his eyes.

A glance over his shoulder spied a tall, dark faery still standing before the door to the business building, sheltered from the rain. One arm was thrust out, a weapon strapped to his wrist and hand. With a flick of his finger, he dispatched another deadly flechette.

Kaz slammed his body against the brick building, feeling the arrow skim the air, missing his nose by inches. A fine mist of faery dust trailed the weapon like a comet's tail. He spied a taxi cruising to a stop at the end of the alley and made a dash, hard-lining the right turn out of the alley just as another flechette cut the air beside him.

He shoved Luc into the back of the cab and the driver, thankfully, sped away when Kaz offered to double his fare if he got them out of this neighborhood immediately.

Luc grabbed the flechette on his shoulder, but Kaz smacked his hand away.

"That's not the good kind of dust. It'll kill you if you pull it out. You want to die?"

The vampire shook his head, but then snarled at him.

Out the back window, Kaz spied the faery, who did not attempt another shot at the car, but instead unfurled vicious black wings that looked demonic. The faery lifted into the air and soared backward into the alley through which Kaz had passed. He didn't suspect the faery was turning tail and running, only following discreetly.

"Holy hell, I have never seen anything like that. Not sure if this seeing-eye stuff is good, bad or plain stupid."

And yet, the thing appeared to be struggling with flight. Was it the rain?

Luc moaned and pulled up his knees to his chest. Kaz eyed the flechette, sitting against his bare skin, surrounded by seeping blood. Could the poison already be coursing through the vampire's system?

No skin off him. But Zoë would be devastated should anything happen to her friend.

"Keep your hands off that thing," he reminded Luc, then tugged out his cell phone and dialed Rook.

After three rings, his supervisor answered. "What's up, Rothstein?"

"I need a safe house," Kaz said, playing it by ear. This was so wrong, and yet, he was out of options for the moment with the faery on his ass. "Had a scuffle with some faeries and need a hideaway to think through my game plan."

The pause on the other end of the line told Kaz that Rook did not approve. So it was a surprise when Rook offered an address to an Order safe house.

"You've got it for the afternoon," Rook said. "You need my help?"

"Not unless you know how to kill faeries."

"Hell."

"I'm fine. I'll report in later."

"I rely on you, Rothstein."

Clicking off, Kaz glanced aside. The vampire stared at him from his crouched position on the backseat. The rain had increased, pounding against the window.

"I hope you're worth it, man," Kaz said. "I'd do anything for Zoë, but if you look at me the wrong way…"

The vampire snarled and flipped him the bird. And in that toothy snarl, Kaz noticed something missing.

Kaz's heart rocketed to hyper speed. He lunged for the vampire, gripping him by the throat, unwary of the flechette, and shook him.

"What happened to your other fang?"

Chapter 17

Kaz slammed the sneering vampire against the car window, well aware the wrong move could tear the flechette from his shoulder and it would be "goodbye, bloodsucker." The vampire deserved the agony, if his suspicions were true.

Kaz's fist bumped the flechette. Luc gritted his jaws and growled. He considered ripping the thing from the vampire's flesh and bone. It would be so easy. But he needed the truth first.

"How did you lose that fang?" he insisted.

"Hell if I know."

"How can you not remember losing a fang?"

The vampire's smile was slippery and gross. Of course he wouldn't remember if he'd been high on Magic Dust.

"What are you, man?" Luc slurred. "Zoë did not send you."

"I'm Order of the Stake, and this is your last ride if you don't spit up some truths right now, longtooth."

"When did Zoë hook up with the Order? Go fuck yourself, man."

A fist to the vampire's gut felt ribs crack. The creature yelped and screamed for more dust.

The cabbie yelled back that they had better settle down or he was pulling over.

"Did the man whose wife you murdered for her diamond necklace knock out that fang before you fatally wounded him?"

"Maybe." The vampire flicked his tongue through the gap in his teeth. "I need more sparklies. You got some?"

Disgusted, Kaz shoved the vampire so hard the creature's skull cracked the side window. The cab swerved sharply and pulled over to the curb.

"Out!" the cabbie insisted. "You're a block away. You walk from here."

Kaz dug in his coat pocket and thumbed a roll of Euro bills. He peeled off three hundreds and tossed them into the front seat. "Sorry about the window."

He shoved Luc out onto the wet pavement, the vampire landing on his shoulder, his wrists bleeding beneath the zip tie. The rain had picked up.

Kaz stepped on Luc's ankle as he got out. He hefted the vampire by the hair and slammed his head against the cement bollard used to keep cars from parking on the sidewalk.

"You are going to die, longtooth."

"Fuck you."

Kaz dug in his coat pocket and produced the fang he'd carried with him since watching his friend die. "Recognize this?"

Luc's hazy gaze landed on the tooth for a moment before he smiled and grabbed for the thing. Kaz snapped it away.

"Hey! That's mine!"

"I should stake you right now." Standing and jamming his boot onto the vamp's chest, Kaz tugged out the stake. "Ask for it."

"You said Zoë sent you! She wouldn't like it if you staked me."

No, she wouldn't. But what if he'd had no option but to stake the crazy vamp in self-defense? Kaz stood over the vampire he'd been looking for, the one responsible for Robert and Ellen's deaths. As far as he was concerned, the dust freak was already ash.

Zoë would never forgive him for it. But he'd get over her rejection.

No, he wouldn't. For the same reason he hadn't been able to remain angry with her after learning she had created the Magic Dust.

Because he loved her.

Kaz swore. Using the stake as a baton, he dashed it aside the vamp's jaw, knocking him out, and hopefully, loosening the one remaining fang. Tossing the unconscious vamp over a shoulder, he cursed his decision not to stake him then and there. He hoped he wouldn't regret this.

He feared he already did.

A pan of brownies sat cooling on the counter while Zoë took the phone call from Kaz. He sounded aggravated, but he'd found Luc. He wanted her to meet him at a safe house. He spoke so quickly, and she could hear Luc groaning in the background.

After scribbling down the address, she cut up some brownies and wrapped them in tin foil to bring along. Telling Sid she'd return soon, she slipped on her shoes, then ran out into the rain and caught the Metro to the seventh arrondissement. A safe house? Must be an Order thing. They actually took vampires into their care? Didn't make sense.

Spying the building, a nondescript limestone number that boasted three stories topped by a slate mansard roof, Zoë took the stairs up, expecting to hear shouting and a tormented vampire yelling at the hunter, but all was silent.

The door slammed open before she could even knock. Kaz grabbed her by the arm and tugged her inside, locking the door behind her. Stunned at his abrupt reception, she looked about the sparely furnished living room/kitchen. All was beige with no decoration and modern-styled furniture. A man pad, surely.

She set the brownies on the kitchen table beside her.

Kaz paced behind her. The tension strung through his body was palpable, and before she could ask him what was wrong, Zoë cautioned misplaced curiosity. He'd rescued her best friend.

Kaz was supposed to slay vampires, and he was dedicated to snuffing out those who used Magic Dust. Luc was everything Kaz most hated. And *she* had asked him to keep him alive.

He'd sacrificed for her in ways she couldn't begin to comprehend. Or rather, she could comprehend, but she had been too selfish to weigh the pros against the cons and to give a moment's thought to who would be most affected.

"Thank you," she said softly.

He still paced behind her.

"Where is he?"

"There's a soundproofed room in the back. I've got him chained up."

"Chains? I need to see him." She rushed down the hallway, but Kaz followed and slammed her against the wall. "What's wrong? I didn't do anything to you. Kaz?"

He fisted a hand beside his face, his expression tightening. His thigh muscles pulsed against her leg as he fought against—what?

"Zoë." Now he put his hands firmly against her collarbone. One twist of his wrists and his hands would be placed to choke her. "When I watched my friend die—the one I told you had fought the vampire to save his wife…"

"Because the vampire went after her necklace." She realized she was wearing her mother's pendant. How it must dig into his pain even deeper. "Yes."

"Why does everything about you hurt me so much?"

She sucked in her lower lip, but the tears were unstoppable. Indeed, she had done nothing but stir up his pain and anger. When she'd thought they were a perfect pair, dashing across the written page, she could not have imagined the tale would turn into a nightmare.

Kaz shook his head, as if dismissing something he'd wanted to say. "I just need you to be careful when you go in there. He's manic."

Her body quivered. Tears spilled freely. Zoë didn't want to step away from him. She felt every muscle in her body tighten—as did Kaz's fists—and then they twanged to a loose, shivering shudder.

"Oh goddess, this is all my fault."

She beat her fists against his chest, once, twice, then he pulled her against him and held her there tightly.

"No, it's not," he said and held her tighter, keeping her from struggling free to run down the hallway and look upon the monster that she had created.

"I've hurt you. You should not want to stand here like this, holding me. Kaz, I'm so sorry."

He hugged her and his fingers tangled in her hair as he kissed the crown of her head. "Hell, life isn't worth it without the struggle, right?"

"Don't do that. You hate me. Don't try to make it better."

"I don't hate you. I…think I might hate that I love you."

Zoë exhaled. Her chest rose and fell as she met his eyes. He loved her? And yet, it seemed to tear him apart that he did.

"I love you," he said again, and this time he kissed her on the forehead. "I can't help it. It is what it is."

She shook her head but he bracketed her face to stop her silent protest. "We'll figure this out. But right now, there's that." He nodded down the hallway. "He's contained. But…"

But hung there, and Zoë could feel Kaz's unspoken words. *He has to die.*

And she wondered if Luc should die. The Magic Dust had changed him, made him something not so different— she hoped—just more vicious. She knew Luc was capable of doing great harm when pushed to his limit. Yet he was also capable of forgiveness.

Tears spilling freely, she melted against Kaz's hard frame and let him lift her and carry her to the sofa out in the living room. The rain had picked up, the dark sky shadowing the room. She spilled her regrets out in tears against Kaz's chest until she had no more tears left to shed.

"I've the safe house only for today," he said after her sniffles had grown further apart. "We've got to move him, or do something with him."

"You think he should die."

"I don't know what to think anymore, Zoë. He's— When I was in Mauritius's lair I was followed by a faery. Didn't see the guy, but I'm sure he was the same one who was tracking me before. The rain slowed him down, but not before he fired a couple of those flechettes. He got Luc in the shoulder. The thing is still in him. I chained his wrists so he couldn't pull it out. You'll have to remove it."

Zoë nodded.

"Check the bathroom for what you might need to get the flechette out."

Hands shaking as she sorted through the few items in the medicine cabinet, Zoë claimed tweezers and some towels. Despite Luc's predicament, she couldn't help think of what Kaz had said. He loved her. And he hated himself for loving her.

What woman wanted to hear that? And yet, the confession had been honest. He genuinely loved her, and she wanted to give him good reason for that love.

"I will," she whispered. "If it's the last thing I do."

She followed Kaz down the hallway and stopped before the bedroom door. She looked up his broad, bare chest, and realized he wasn't wearing a shirt. Hadn't been since she'd arrived. He was so beautiful, both outside and in. And she didn't know how to make him not hate her.

"Kiss me," he said, his hand poised on the doorknob. "Make me remember why I just did the most foolish thing a knight in the Order could ever do."

"Confessing that you love a witch?"

"No, taking a vampire into an Order safe house."

She nodded. "A kiss won't change anything."

"A kiss in the alley, with four vampires lying at our feet, stole my heart."

"I don't think it can take away the hate," she said, looking away.

He touched her chin, tilting her gaze up to his. "You bring up strong emotions in me, Zoë. Love. Hate. Anger. Fear. That's powerful magic right there. I'm not in the middle about you. I'm right here. Whatever happens, I want it to be with you."

And he kissed her with urgency and insistence. The kiss was at once angry and then forgiving, and then so tender Zoë felt tears again spill down her cheeks. Kaz rubbed his thumbs through the tear trails, and finished the kiss with a simple press of his mouth to hers.

"It's not enough," she said. "What you've done can never be repaid. I'll take Luc and get him out of here as quickly as possible. I don't want you to get in trouble with the Order."

"Might be too late for that." He kissed her again. "I'd do it again in a heartbeat to know it was for you."

Zoë swallowed.

He touched the base of her throat and lifted the pendant. She nodded, and took off the necklace. Kaz pocketed it. He opened the door and Zoë walked inside.

As soon as he saw her, Luc moaned and twisted against the chains that bound him by ankle, wrists and across the neck.

"Zoë! You've brought me more magic. Need you so bad, Zoë. Oh, sweetie."

Luc was too thin. The torn jeans he wore hung on his frame. His chestnut hair, once his pride and object of at least an hour of grooming before going out, was now greasy and tangled. His bare chest and arms sparkled. He was full of faery dust.

As she moved closer he twisted and contorted within the chains. "More, yes, come on, Zoë. Hurry! Need more!"

The flechette hugged his shoulder and blood drooled from the serrated skin. Kaz had been careful to ensure the chain would not fall against it. Zoë wasn't sure how she was going to extract it with Luc gyrating and pleading for more of the drug.

She glanced over her shoulder, seeking Kaz's reassurance.

He gestured to the whining vampire. "You should get that thing out while he's chained down."

"More dust!"

"I can't do it when he's struggling like that," she told Kaz. Then she turned to her friend. "Oh, Luc, please. I'm so sorry."

"Give me!"

Kaz stepped around and as he approached the vampire, Luc lunged and gnashed his fangs at the slayer.

"Goddess," Zoë swore as she noted her friend's teeth.

Just one fang. He was the vampire Kaz had been searching for.

Luc had killed his friends. He'd taken lives in a quest to find more Magic Dust, to feed the ravenous craving within. And Kaz hadn't said a thing to her.

She searched Kaz's shadowed eyes. "He's the one."

Kaz nodded, bowing his head. Words weren't necessary.

"Why didn't you stake him the moment you realized he'd killed your friends?"

He stroked her cheek, the scar beneath his fingertips. There was so much he still did not know. And if he did? Zoë wasn't sure how to reveal all.

"He's your friend and you asked me to rescue him. I've done my part. Now it's up to you."

He didn't want to say he should stake the vampire. He wanted her to say it. She couldn't. Not ever.

But she had to make it stop. Right now.

"I'll get that thing out of him and then we'll figure things out. Can you silence him?"

Kaz punched Luc in the jaw, knocking him out cold. The thin vampire dropped, his arms wrenched back, his collarbone catching against the taut chain. It hurt Zoë's heart to look at how he'd changed from someone she called friend to a murderer.

Because of the Magic Dust.

That she had created.

"Hurry," Kaz said over her shoulder. "He's like the Energizer Bunny. Doesn't stay out for long. The Magic Dust burns in his system like some kind of manic fuel."

Forcing herself to study the flechette, Zoë glanced her fingers over the faery metal, moving it carefully from side to side. "I think it's embedded in the bone. I'm not sure I can remove it. Kaz, maybe you should pull it out."

They both knew such a move would release the poison, resulting in a dead vampire. Zoë had been able to bring Kaz back from near poisoning but only because a small amount had dispersed into his system. If she were to sacrifice her life energy to save Luc from so much poison, surely that would bring her death.

"You don't want death for your friend," he said calmly over her shoulder. "I know you don't."

"Neither do I want to set him free to kill again."

He embraced her from behind. The reassurance of his strong arms felt too rich, and she, so undeserving. Yet she wouldn't refuse the comforting offer, couldn't. Closing her eyes, she shut herself away from the horror chained before her and tried to step into what she had with Kaz. A new and exciting love. With a man who was willing to go against his very code of honor to help her. Her knight.

"You'll find a way to help him," he said quietly. "I know you will."

His confidence in her banished her fears and gave her hope.

Luc shook his head, coming to with a grin. "Zoë, love you." And he smiled that innocent smile that had won her heart so many times before. That apologetic smile that said, "I was wrong, and now that I understand, I want to make amends."

The single fang was down and Zoë wondered if he were even aware of losing the other. He must remember his cruel acts.

They'd talk about it later. After the dust worked through his system. Kaz had told her the dust built up, and unlike regular drugs, it never dissipated, only raged within the body, forcing the vampire to heinous acts against innocents.

Hands shaking, she reached for her friend's shoulder. "Luc, I need to get the flechette out of your shoulder."

"Pull it out!"

"No. It's embedded in bone, and if I break the glass tips, a faery poison will be released into your bloodstream."

"Do it!" He wriggled, attempting to twist his head to bang against the flechette, but could not. "Please." He caught her gaze and in those moments, his eyes said *forgive me* and *sorry* and *love you* again and again. "It's your turn to hurt me, Zoë. You have to."

"Don't say that."

"Then give me peace. Please?"

She shook her head. "No." She gripped the flechette, holding it steady against his struggles. "There's got to be a way to get it out. If you'll hold still."

"If I do, will you give me more dust?"

"It's killing you, Luc."

"Exactly. Slowly. Painfully. I've…killed, Zoë." Tears spilled down his cheeks. "I hate myself. You know I can't abide the kill. Do it!"

And Luc wrenched back his shoulder, tearing the flechette out of his bone and skin while Zoë was still holding it. She dropped the faery weapon and stumbled back, landing in Kaz's arms.

"No," she whispered. "He pulled away. I wasn't ready—"

Her friend's body began to spasm.

"No, Luc!"

Kaz pulled her toward the door.

"No, I can't leave him to die alone!"

"I'm not going to let you watch whatever happens next."

Kaz dragged her out into the hallway and slammed the door behind him. He drew her against his chest and they waited for the dying yell.

Chapter 18

The woman clinging to his chest and arms shivered so intensely, Kaz's bones shook in response. He identified this unfamiliar feeling as sympathy, an unusual emotion that he had been experiencing more and more. Thanks to the witch that he hated to love.

Even more, he hated that Zoë had to experience pain or heartache. But knowing her friend was probably now dead on the other side of the door had to be the worst.

And who was he to comfort her? He didn't know how to do this kind of stuff. He was solid and unshakable, sure, but so solid that he didn't have a clue how to soften and make it all better. He couldn't remember how his mother had done it for him when he was a child, and he sure as hell had never gotten comfort from his father.

He needed to let Zoë in, no matter how much it hurt him. He suspected it wouldn't hurt to give her access to his heart. He'd already done that, and it had felt damned good. But to simply open himself and give everything he had to her?

Kaz bent his head to nuzzle against the black-and-white strands of hair that dusted his lips, his cheeks and nose. She gave him softness in a manner he'd not expected or asked for. And, hell yes, he'd selfishly take it. He needed it to temper his hard edges. They did have much in common, as she'd said. They needed one another. And since everything in life happened for a reason, he could accept that.

Wrapping his arms about her shoulders, Kaz hugged Zoë until he felt her heartbeats thunder. Her body melted against his, her bones still shivering yet calming as he squeezed her closer. He could not remember ever being held like this, like a precious object one should not think to release. For to do so would shatter worlds and destroy hopes and dreams.

Yet to do so meant the person giving the hug loved the one in their arms and would do anything to make her world right.

"I'm sorry, Zoë," he whispered. And then, he said what he'd always wanted to hear from his father. "For all of it."

She nodded. "I am, too."

She blamed herself. Kaz knew how easy it was to blame oneself for things he didn't understand. Zoë could have had no idea the blend of faery dust she had made could have produced such devastating effects. If the vampire Luc had lied to her about it helping him, as opposed to granting a greater high, he had perpetuated the lie that Zoë had grown to believe.

He hated what he had to say next, but it was necessary. "I can't stay here overnight. I need to vacate the safe house. Can you go ahead to my place, and I'll meet you there? After I…"

"Oh." Releasing a heavy sigh, she shivered wickedly against his arm. "I understand." Nodding too quickly, she inhaled a deep breath and exhaled another shivering sigh. "Let me help you clean up."

"Not a chance. What's on the other side of that door is not for your eyes."

She peered up at him, a lost innocent fallen into darkness and shadows. Kaz stroked the scar on her cheek. Not so innocent, but nevertheless forced to tread the darkness.

"I'll wait out here," she finally said, "and then walk home with you. Yes?"

He nodded. "Go wait in the living room."

Twisting the doorknob, Kaz slipped inside the safe room. But what he saw took the horror from his heart and replaced it with a strange wonder. Really? But… How?

"Uh, Zoë?" he called. "Why don't you, uh…come in here."

She quietly joined his side. He grasped her hand and pulled her around to stand before him, placing his hands reassuringly on her shoulders.

She gasped. "Goddess."

The vampire smiled up at them. A whole vampire, not a pile of ash and faery dust. He was alive, and amazingly, smiling. His skin glittered with so much dust Kaz thought he might have been bombed by a bunch of mad faeries. But he decided it was instead the dust Luc had imbibed, bleeding out through his pores.

"Luc?" Zoë cautiously approached the vampire and knelt before him. She stroked aside a strand of dark hair from the man's eyes. "The poison?"

"I feel—" the vampire inhaled and exhaled deeply "—as if I am rising, Zoë."

"From the drug?"

He nodded eagerly.

She glanced to Kaz. He could but shrug and swipe a hand across his mouth in wonder. If he hadn't seen it with his own eyes… Who the hell knew anymore what creatures could survive what calamities? This whole business with faeries challenged his knowledge of the paranormal realms.

"Oh my goddess, you're alive." Zoë lunged forward and hugged the vampire, who smiled over her shoulder at Kaz.

Not the vindictive sneer he'd cast him earlier, but one of utter relief and salvation.

Yet as stunned as Kaz was, he remained stoic. The vampire had killed his friends. Just because he'd gotten a pass didn't mean he didn't still deserve the stake.

"The poison," Zoë said as she pulled back and dashed a finger through the dust on Luc's forearm. "It's faery derived. I wonder if it's acting as a counteragent to the Magic Dust?"

"I feel clear, Zoë. I think it's pushing out all that nasty dust. I'm so sorry. The things I did… I didn't want to lie to you, but Mauritius—"

"Shh…" She pulled him to her shoulder and hugged his head. "We'll talk later. We need to leave now and find a safer place to keep you. You shouldn't even be here."

"Where is here?"

"None of your business," Kaz tossed out quickly before Zoë could give away too much info about the Order.

"Will you unchain him, Kaz?"

Kaz drew out the handcuff key from his pocket, yet rattled it in his cupped palm. Keys meant safety to him. He wasn't stupid. They were never safe around a vampire. And the man's skin was covered with dust. Their kind got a contact high from the sparkly stuff.

"Please?" Zoë softly implored. "He won't harm me."

"I won't," Luc offered. "I swear it."

Going against every ounce of training that he'd lived, breathed and killed by for the past decade, Kaz unlocked the chain across Luc's neck and his ankles, but before he freed his wrists, he retrieved a zip tie from the closet in the bedroom—stocked with Order gear—and secured the vampire's wrists behind his back.

"Kaz, really?" Zoë asked.

"It's okay," Luc said. "As much as I feel no compelling desire to lick the dust off my skin, I don't trust myself. Let him do what he needs to do. I'm just thankful he hasn't staked me yet."

"Don't ever get comfortable," Kaz said as he pulled up the vampire and gave him a shove to start walking out of the room. He glanced over the floor, littered with faery dust, and wondered how he was going to clean this up.

He should be thankful. It was going to prove easier than cleaning up an exploded vampire.

Zoë spoke some Latin words and with a snap of her fingers, the dust lifted from the floor. A sweep of her hand sent it toward the ventilation grate. Within a few minutes, the room looked as clean as it had been before he'd chained up the vampire.

"Well, all right then. Let's go home," Kaz said, and took the witch's hand.

Initially, the plan was to go to Zoë's house, until they remembered her house no longer stood. She suggested Luc's apartment, but Kaz figured Mauritius would have dispersed scouts to keep an eye on the place. One option remained.

Sid snuggled up to Zoë on the couch in Kaz's living room. Luc slept in the back room where Kaz kept his weapons, his wrists zip-tied to an iron plumbing pole. She hated treating her friend like that, but even Luc had confessed he wasn't sure what he would do if left free.

With Luc resting, Zoë had washed most of the faery dust from his arms, but the stuff clung. Only time would tell if Luc could get clean or would perhaps grow worse because of the faery poison coursing through his system.

"I wish I could change it all," she said as Kaz wandered into the living room, bare feet padding across the dark wood floor. He'd showered after freaking over all the faery dust that had clung to his skin.

She shook her head. "Maybe it would have been kinder to stake him."

"I can make that happen. A guy really has to be in love to carry a vampire across his warded threshold." An act possible only because Kaz had carried the vampire in, granting his permission to enter.

Kaz kissed her, and then settled onto the couch next to her and pulled her onto his lap. Sid joined them, climbing onto Zoë's lap for a big ole family snuggle.

She knew he would like nothing better than to stake the vampire. And by rights he should, to take vengeance for his friends. She didn't believe in an eye for an eye, though.

"Thank you." She kissed him. "For always helping me. And never asking for help in return."

"I don't need any help."

"You do. You're just not willing to voice it. I can wait. But Kaz, please know how much this means to me. I understand it's difficult for you to have the vampire who killed your friends in your home."

"Beyond difficult. Like I said, it must be love."

She tucked her head against his shoulder, taking that declaration for its worth. Invaluable. And she felt it in her very soul. Misplaced, as her neighbor Lillian had alluded? Perhaps. But more and more she felt as if her soul were moving toward home, a place it belonged. And Kaz stood upon the threshold of that home.

"Will Luc be secure back there while he sleeps it off?"

"Yes. No more zip ties. Those chains will keep a werewolf down."

"You've all your weapons in the same room as the vampire. It is quite the arsenal."

"I've been collecting weapons for years. Come in handy in my line of work." Kaz rose and studied the map on the wall. "We need to find the new lab Mauritius set up." He tapped the map where the steel office building stood.

"If he was telling the truth," Zoë said, "he had his people take the things from my spell room before burning my house. I may be able to claim some of my most precious belongings like my grimoire."

"Yes, but then we're going to destroy anything that could be used to make Magic Dust. Deal?"

Zoë nodded. "I've the recipe up here." She tapped her head. "No one could figure out the transmutation spell to alter the faery dust the way I did it."

"What if they took some of the Magic Dust and reverse engineered it?"

"I don't think that's possible with a spoken spell, but I'm not sure. But Kaz, I have an idea!"

He returned to the couch and kissed her deeply. His warm licorice scent encompassed their embrace. "Lay it on me."

"The faery poison may be curing Luc."

"It's possible."

"So, that's all I've ever wanted to do—help cure those vampires addicted to dust. I need to find out what's in that poison."

"Huh. It might work. But if it means you have to ask the faery who was trying to kill me what he put in the poison, then no deal. I'm not letting you anywhere near that psycho. Dude had big black wings. Looked demonic."

"He only wants to kill *you*. I haven't had faeries after me."

"Yet."

"Remember, I don't believe in them."

He stroked her cheek. "You think when they discover you are the one behind the drug that may be dipping into their sales they're not going to want to change that?"

"I hadn't thought of that. But this could be a cure, Kaz."

He hugged her. His hugs were the best, so giving, and always taking a little, as well. "We'll look for the lab in the morning, and any talking to faeries you need to do will be done with me along."

She snuggled against his chest. "How did I get so lucky to find someone like you?"

"You know that first time we saw one another, right after I kissed you, I looked into your eyes, and I knew."

"What did you know?"

"I knew that you loved me," he said.

"Is that so?"

Kaz's kiss was true, seeking, melting against her mouth in a confirmation of all the questions that were tittering about inside her but she daren't ask.

Do you still love me? Can you love me? Do I offend you? Can you overlook the things I have done?

But most important: Can you still see that I love you?

"You were very perceptive," she said, and continued the kiss. "And very kind not to do too much damage to those men."

"You thought they were human?"

She blinked.

"They were vamps, sweetie. You stumbled onto a slaying, so I had to wing it until you left."

"You mean—after I...?"

"Ashed 'em."

"And here I thought I had a knack for recognizing vampires. Huh. I did love you that first night I saw you. I have a tendency to rush to happily ever after. You rescued me, pulling me into your arms and kissing me like I've never been kissed before."

"There was a reason behind that kiss."

"And that reason was?"

He shrugged. "Not sure, even now. Kind of like not knowing the why but just accepting the now, eh? I'm beginning to think, if anyone has done any rescuing in this relationship, that it was you who rescued me. You've made me see the world differently, Zoë. I've put up a lot of walls. They'll never all fall down, but you've added some windows."

"I like that. Can you see me through those windows?"

"You're the only sight I can or want to see."

"Do you still hate me?"

"I've never hated you. I just…"

"I know. It's the idea of loving me you are having a tough time with."

"It's getting easier every minute I hold you in my arms."

"Really?"

He nodded.

"Do you want to make love to me, Kaz?"

"Is that a trick question?"

"No, but so much has changed since we made love the other night."

"This hasn't changed." He pressed a hand over his heart. "Think Sid will mind?"

Zoë nudged Sid off her lap and turned to straddle Kaz. "He's a sex cat. He likes to watch."

"I did feel him snuggle against my back in the middle of the night. It was…"

"Nice, isn't it, to have a warm kitty pressed against your skin?"

"Sure, but I prefer a warm witch."

He glided his hands up under her shirt and cupped her breasts. Zoë hadn't taken the time to put on a bra this morning. His fingers found her nipples and toggled them softly. The touch shot through her system and traveled to her toes, which curled in delight.

She leaned in and whispered, "Let's make some magic."

He smiled against her mouth and kissed her deeply. "Should we be doing this with the vampire down the hallway?"

"Yes, we should. He's sleeping. And how can I not touch

you? You give me life, Kaz. Kind of like how my life energy is put forth when I heal. I can feel your energy gush into me whenever you hold me. I want to bathe in it. Drown."

He unzipped his jeans and lifted his hips so she could shrug them down. His erection sprang free. Unzipping her pants and sliding them to the floor, Zoë stepped out of them, and sat upon her lover's lap, grinding her mons against his steel cock.

He nuzzled her breasts, and bit through the fabric. Zoë pulled up her shirt, allowing him easy access. The lash of his tongue across her tightened nipple undid her. All the tension that had built up this day rushed from her in a sigh that spilled through the air. She felt her soul tingle in response. No longer misplaced.

Kaz positioned her over him and slid inside her. They assumed each other's rhythm, and the harmony they created sparked a new and divine magic that she would never master but would forever cherish.

Chapter 19

Kaz trusted that Zoë would be well enough on her own to visit Ian Grim this afternoon without accompanying her as a bodyguard. Grim's place was not far away, and after Zoë explained to Kaz that Ian was a warlock and had every ward imaginable on his home, he almost didn't let her go.

A warlock? Weren't those the bad witches, he'd wondered sternly. And wasn't she sort of, kind of, maybe one, as well?

Yes, but…

Zoë's father was warlock and she didn't consider him bad. But she had decided to keep that bit of information a secret for now. They would have to face the warlock talk soon. They'd been honest with one another about everything else; it wouldn't be right to keep that from Kaz. But she'd held on to that detail because unless the Light declared her warlock, she was not.

Expecting Dasha—Ian's longtime lover—to answer the door, Zoë was disappointed when the door opened to reveal a short blond man with a broad smile and tousled hair.

"Ian."

"Wow. That sounded absolutely dismal. You really know how to make a man feel special, Zoë. Come in.

You're letting in daylight. I need the house dark for a spell I'm working on."

She entered the dark foyer, lit only by candles, and it took her eyes a moment to adjust to the dull, yellow glow. How people had lived centuries earlier utilizing only candlelight at night was beyond her.

"I'm sorry. I haven't seen Dasha for years. I was looking forward to her greeting me. How is she?"

"As well as ever. She'll be home soon. Just ran out for some groceries. And to get away from the smell."

That's when Zoë noticed the sulfur that tickled into her nostrils and made her sneeze. "What are you working with? Rotten eggs or—"

"Demons."

Hands laced behind his back, Ian strode down the hallway. Dressed in a dapper black vest, maroon silk shirt and leather pants, he strode casually.

They passed a room with the door partially open. "Pay no mind," he said over his shoulder. "The less you know, the better."

Zoë glimpsed a cage. Inside lurked a short, dark thing with red eyes. It hissed at her. She immediately focused on following Ian. Indeed, the less she knew.

Up a spiraling, dark staircase two stories, they stepped into Ian's lab, which sported a glass ceiling much like Zoë's spell room. Here, though, the majority of the windows were grown over with vines, though some sunlight did breach the well-worn, wooden worktable and rows of books and magical accoutrements.

"The only place the sun can shine today," Ian offered with a gesture toward the windows. "Cinnamon tea?"

"Sure." Zoë glided her fingertips along a polished brass duck's-foot pistol that sported four barrels and the impression of the Christian cross on the wood grip. "This looks old."

"Picked that up for a kiss in the seventeenth century."

"Does Dasha mind the kiss?"

"She wasn't born until a hundred years later. And then she died twenty-six years following. So! What have you brought me today, my fine witch?"

Zoë always blushed at that title. After she'd been cut on the cheek, Ian had offered to help heal it, but she had refused. If anyone were going to heal this scar it would be herself.

"Wait," he said, and gestured to her hair. "More white than last I saw you. You've healed someone close to death."

She nodded. "A man I love."

"Ah, love. Fine stuff, that. He treats you well?"

"Yes. He's human."

Ian gasped out a hacking noise of disgust.

"Oh, please, Ian, Kaz is a fine man. He's a knight actually, in the Order of the Stake."

Now Grim grasped his chest and feigned a heart attack. "Zoë, what in all of Hecate's great kingdom?"

"Is my falling in love with a human any more shocking than your falling in love with a woman who lost her head in the Revolution?"

"She did find a new body," he corrected. "Fine. I shall not throw stones. But do be careful, Zoë. Promise me."

"I will and I am."

"So you want to show me something?" He rubbed his palms together expectantly. "Please let it be one of those fancy stakes the Order uses to ash vampires."

"Sorry to disappoint, but it is perhaps more intriguing."

Carefully, she extracted the faery flechette from her pocket, wrapped in newspaper, and laid it on the table. A fine scatter of faery dust sifted out as she unwrapped it.

"Lovely. Sidhe in nature, yes? Did you handle it without gloves?" Ian laid aside the paper to get to the weapon.

"Yes, but I think the poison has all leaked out."

The six-pronged weapon sported blunt ends where once had been sharp glass tips. The ineffable metal gleamed iridescently, and there were traces of what Zoë guessed to be faery poison on the ends.

"You say it *helped* the vampire?" Ian asked.

"Luc is this close to being clean of faery dust," she said, pinching her fingers together in display. After talking with him this morning, she'd found him lucid, smiling and complaining about the zip tie—yet he hadn't asked her to remove it. "I want you to take a look at the poison and tell me if it can be used as an antidote to faery dust on vampires."

"You've big dreams, Zoë. Trying to save all the dust freaks in the city?"

She shrugged. "Someone has to do it. I like to know I've made a difference. And I think I can with this stuff." And if it would counteract the harm she had already caused, then she had to try it.

"Even if I could break it down to the smallest elements of composition, I suspect there's faery magic involved. That's not something I have access to."

"Maybe."

"You've been practicing your father's molecular magic, haven't you?" he guessed.

"It's how I made the dust blend in the first place. But it wasn't the cure I thought it would be."

"That's some powerful magic. You shouldn't let word of it get out."

"The only ones who know are you, Kaz, Luc and Mauritius."

"Four people too many."

"There's nothing I can do about keeping Mauritius quiet. If the Light deems to cast me out as warlock, then so be it."

"Don't say that, Zoë. You're not cut out for life on the run like your father."

"You handle it well. I don't see you running away from anyone."

"Because I dabble in malefic magic, sweetie. The idiots of the Light don't dare mess with me." He sighed and tapped the flechette. "You sure about this endeavor to save vampires? What have the longtooths ever done for you?"

"I don't require reciprocation. You know I like to make changes in the world."

"Yes, you're just so…kind." Ian shuddered.

"Just look, will you, Ian?"

With a heavy sigh, and a wink, he nodded.

Below, the front door opened and closed.

"That'll be Dasha. You run down and say hello. I'll need some time with this."

Zoë kissed him on the cheek. "Thanks, Ian."

"Your kisses are so warm," he said wistfully. "I've forgotten the touch of living flesh."

Kaz returned home and only then remembered the vampire he had zip-tied in his back room. Just thinking about him there made him wince. A week ago this situation would have been impossible because he wouldn't have known Zoë, or cared to see the smile on her face.

Life had changed.

Actually, life had changed him. And it felt better than the first winter snowfall and wearing brand-new mittens. Good times, when he'd been a kid and his only worries were where to find the highest hill to go sledding, and how fast he could clean up his room so his mom would make him hot chocolate as a reward.

He'd not thought about his mother, or the fire, in a long time. But telling Zoë about it had opened something inside him. He wasn't sure if that something was good, though. His job demanded he keep a certain distance from emotion, yet more and more, he was opening his heart for Zoë to peer into.

Shucking off his coat and tossing it across the back of the couch, he strode down the hallway to look in on the longtooth. Luc stood up against the wall and offered him a nod as he entered.

"How's it going?" Kaz asked, hooking his thumbs on his pockets. He could be nice to a vampire. He did it with Vail all the time.

"Boring. But man, I feel so clear."

"That's a good sign. Do you trust yourself?"

"I think so."

"Not exactly the answer I'm looking for, man."

"I do and I don't. I mean, if you could just take the zip tie off, I promise I won't lunge for you."

Kaz slapped the stake holstered at his hip.

"I'm not stupid," Luc offered. "At least, I'm not now that the dust is out of my system."

Kaz fished a knife out of his back pocket and held it before him, eyeing the zip tie about the vampire's wrists even as he spoke to himself. *I'm not going to do it. No way. No how.*

He placed the blade against the plastic strip and locked eyes with Luc. He didn't want to stare too long, but was compelled to seek...something. Trust? Hell, no. He'd never trust a vampire. Or an addict. Humanity? Vampires were creatures. Some of them had once been human, but consuming blood had changed them, made them monsters.

"I care about her," Luc offered. "I would never hurt her."

For some reason, Kaz chose to believe the vampire with the missing fang, and slid the blade through the plastic strips. Yet he slammed the blade tip up under Luc's chin.

"I will not take my eyes off you, longtooth."

"You going to watch me shower?" Luc swept a palm

down his arm, which glinted with faery dust. "This stuff is impossible to wash away, but—"

"There's a rain barrel up on the roof. I know there's something about rainwater removing faery dust. I'll go take a look. Shower's down the hall."

"Thanks, man."

Luc strolled past Kaz toward the bathroom and he didn't even feel the urge to stake him.

Changes, indeed.

After retrieving a five-gallon bucket of the rainwater and leaving it at the bathroom door, Kaz tugged out his cell phone. Zoë should have returned by now.

"Why doesn't she have a cell phone?" He shoved it back in a pocket. "She's into all the old stuff, no technology. Would she be upset if I got her a phone?"

The urge to know where she was, to be able to check in with her, was strong.

"I am so whipped."

He sat on the couch, spreading his arms across the back. Sid jumped onto his lap and put his front paws up around his neck and met his nose with a kitty kiss.

"I love you, too, Sid. Even if you do have a weird habit of watching me have sex with your owner." He stroked the cat's sleek black fur and hugged him onto his lap. "I think I'm in love with your owner, as well. And I'm hating that idea less and less. What do you think of that?"

The cat meowed softly, as if he approved.

"Hey, Sid, haven't seen you in a while," Luc said as he strolled into the living room, wiping his hair with a towel. He'd put on his jeans, which glinted with dust in places.

With a hiss, the cat sprang from Kaz's lap and hightailed it down the hallway to hide in the bedroom.

"Cats don't like me," Luc said as he sat on the easy chair opposite the couch. He hadn't put on his shirt, and Kaz couldn't see a glint or flicker of faery dust on his chest. On the other hand, it was in his best interest of staying alive to give the vampire a dressing down, so he studied his exposed skin closely. He didn't see a single glint.

"So tell me about you and Zoë," he said.

The vampire propped an ankle across one knee and leaned back in the chair. His eyes were dark and shadowed, as if he'd been on a three-day bender. Kaz was surprised he didn't look worse for the addiction that had been riding him for months.

"What has she told you?" Luc asked.

He didn't like that answer. It implied that the vampire wasn't going to tell him anything he didn't get approved by Zoë, and that, indeed, he had things he didn't want to tell.

"How long have you two been friends?"

"About a decade. We go way back. She didn't tell you how we met?"

"Nope. Wasn't witch's blood poisonous to vampires until recently?"

"Yeah. So? You think I bit Zoë?" The vampire scoffed. "Never have. Never will. I love her, man. She means the world to me."

"Interesting."

"Being friends with a vamp does not require giving blood."

Unease climbed up the back of Kaz's neck. It was strange to notice. Had he let down his guard around this vampire too easily? The breed was dangerous. He would never be completely safe around one of them.

Kaz's gaze traveled to the end of the couch where his Order coat hung over the arm. There were two more stakes inside the pockets.

"You drink blood lately, buddy?"

"Why? You think I'm jonesing for your neck right now?"

"Are you?"

"I could use a bite, but I wouldn't bite any of Zoë's friends. You *are* her friend, aren't you?"

"Wouldn't have allowed a vamp in my home if I was anything but."

"Are you two…involved?"

"Yes."

Luc nodded and leaned forward, eyeing the cat down the hallway, who peeked out of Kaz's bedroom. "She's special. You'd better not hurt her like…"

"Like what? Like that insane vampire who gave her that scar hurt her?"

Luc's head shot up, meeting Kaz's eyes directly. Something in his pupils, growing so large and then instantly small, alerted Kaz. And he knew.

"Did you…" Kaz began. "No. She would never…"

The witch did have a weird tendency to forgive. But no, she could never forgive the vampire who had scarred her for life.

Luc nodded, splaying his hands. "It's a long story, man. One she apparently hasn't told you."

He *had* given her the scar.

Kaz lunged across the room, gripped the vampire by the throat and slammed him against the back of the chair. Ripping the stake from its holster at his hip, he held it against Luc's chest, his fingers squeezing the paddles.

"Kaz!"

Zoë's voice sounded at the same time the stake pinioned out from the titanium column.

Chapter 20

Zoë rushed toward Kaz and Luc. Kaz turned, saw her and thrust the stake across the room. He heaved out a frustrated grunt and fisted the air.

A bead of blood dribbled from Luc's chest.

"He hurt you!" Kaz yelled accusingly at her.

"I forgave him," she said, but it sounded so stupid right now.

"What? How the hell can you—?" Kaz swung toward Luc and shouted at him, "You enthralled her to forget!"

"I didn't! At the time I didn't want her to forget."

"So you did it later, when you decided you wanted to be friends with her."

"No, Kaz...." Zoë caught her breath.

The man she had fallen in love with had discovered the cruel secret behind her horrible scar. She should have trusted to tell him about it earlier.

"Why didn't you tell him?" Luc asked her as he inspected the blood on his chest. The stake hadn't punctured more than skin. "He could have killed me!"

"Two more seconds, man," Kaz muttered. "Just two freakin' seconds."

If she had been two seconds later... Her world would have shattered because of her inability to speak her truths.

Having spent an amazing afternoon with Dasha and Ian, Zoë had not been prepared to return to find her boyfriend trying to kill her best friend. A vampire, who had, indeed, hurt her badly. For reasons that had been so wrong at the time.

Kaz gripped her arm and forced her to turn and look at him.

"He did this to you?"

She stroked her cheek and nodded. She wanted to go to Luc and give him a hug to show him she still forgave him, but Kaz tightened his grip.

"You are not going near him," he warned. "Not until I hear the whole story. And it had better be damned good, or that vampire will leave this place as a pile of ash."

"Tough hunter," Luc said as he stood.

"Luc, he's every right to be angry. I should have told him. We've been through so much lately. Just—could you leave us?"

Luc looked to the door.

"No, you can't leave the apartment," she corrected.

"You don't trust me out there?"

Kaz slapped his arms across his chest, defying her to answer the vampire truthfully.

"I don't," Zoë said honestly. "Do you trust yourself?"

The vampire backed toward the hallway and headed to the room with the chains. And Zoë twisted her arm from Kaz's tight grip. "You could ask me how it went with Ian."

"I don't care what two warlocks do when they get together."

"Kaz!"

He met her shock with a stoic defiance. "I want to know how a woman could befriend a man who did that to her."

She stroked her cheek. "It's so horrible to you? Ghastly? Makes you want to look away from me?"

"Zoë, you know what I mean. It hurt, didn't it?"

"It hurt like hell. But the pain is long gone, and I've learned to live with it."

"Why did he do it to you?" He studied her eyes. The heat of him was too cruel right now. She wanted his gentility and his arms around her. Not his painful distrust. "And why, in all God's creation, could you forgive him for something so heinous?"

He deserved the truth. So Zoë sat on the sofa, because her legs wanted to buckle.

"I'll tell you all. But I can't do this with you standing over me like some kind of vicious guard dog. Please, Kaz, I need you to have an open mind right now."

"Oh, it's wide-open."

"No, it's not. You're riding anger as if it's your bitch."

Kaz sat on the sofa, exhibiting a less than open manner as he slammed his arms across his chest. She understood he could never accept anything she was going to tell him. He had been trained to destroy that which had almost destroyed her.

She reached for his hand, and, thankfully, he took hers and held it firmly. She wanted him to accept her and not stop loving her. But this was only going to give him one more reason to hate himself for that love.

"It was about ten years ago," she started, "when the Great Protection Spell was still active and witches' blood was poisonous to vampires. One evening, while walking home from the grocery, I was attacked by a vampire. She had no idea I was a witch, and I was so utterly taken by surprise, that I couldn't blurt out a warning. She bit my neck."

Kaz wrapped his other hand about hers and held it to his mouth. His leg jittered, a nervous reaction.

"Within moments she started to *sizzle* from the inside. It's what happened when a vamp bit a witch during the Great Protection. Another vampire came running out of the shadows—who I quickly learned was her brother—

and witnessed her death. She literally…exploded," Zoë said on a whisper.

"Let me guess," Kaz said. "The brother was Luc?"

Zoë nodded. "He cursed me for luring his sister to bite me. I tried to explain, but he was so aggressive, spitting at me and swiping punches, and at the same time his sister was this awful mess on the ground, so I ran off. But two days later he found me, and brought along his friends. They held me down while Luc cut my face with a poisoned blade. He wore gloves so my blood couldn't harm him. Said he didn't want to kill me but wanted to watch me suffer for killing his sister. And to always wear his mark."

"It wasn't your fault," Kaz protested with a hiss.

"No, but it felt like murder to me. And Luc was grieving. He couldn't think straight at the time. They left me there, bleeding and in pain. The blade had been dipped in hemlock, a poison that can't kill witches but it does irreparable harm. It felt like needles piercing my soul. I went home and tried some healing spells, but as I've said, a witch can't heal herself. I think I cried for two days. My father, who is also a warlock, had just gone under, so I had no one to turn to. The wound scarred. I decided it was a badge I must wear to forever remind me to be kind to others."

"But you didn't provoke the vampire in the first place." Kaz hugged her and swore softly as he rubbed her back. "That bastard—"

"Was acting out of grief," Zoë quickly interjected.

"Oh, Zoë, you are too forgiving."

"Forgiveness is good for the soul, Kaz. And if I intend to live many centuries… Forgiveness is crucial for me."

"Says the chick who was responsible for— Sorry. I'm so sorry. I shouldn't have said that."

He'd been about to lay the blame on her for killing innocent humans. And it wasn't a lie. Her soul had been muddied, and now Zoë wasn't sure how it could ever come clean. Had she thought to find a home for such a dark and cruel soul?

"Hell," he muttered.

"What?"

"I just remembered what it is about witches that creeps me out. You plan to live for centuries?"

She nodded, sniffing back a tear.

"You going to eat a vampire heart to achieve that?"

Again, she nodded. Once a century, a witch must consume a live, beating vampire heart to maintain immortality. It wasn't a pretty act, but necessary. It was something she had yet to face, but she would have to in another decade or so.

Kaz winced and caught his forehead against a palm. "What if...someone you loved asked you not to do such a heinous thing?"

Zoë sucked in her breath. He wasn't asking her right now. Or was he? "I suppose I'll have to deal with that challenge if and when it is presented."

He nodded. Not the answer he had wanted to hear, but really? They had worse things to deal with right now.

"My soul is tainted," Zoë said. "I've harmed so many. Perhaps I should go to the Light and accept the status of warlock."

"Don't say that, Zoë. Everyone makes mistakes."

"My mistake took the lives of others."

"That is between you and your god when you die."

"You mean my goddess?"

He swallowed and nodded. Even if he could accept them as a scarred and imperfect couple, could he ever really accept a witch into his heart? And should it ever come to the point where they were still together and he asked her not to perform the immortality spell, could she refuse?

Much as they were physically alike, their beliefs were so different.

And it was all about belief, wasn't it? What you believed in made you stronger. What you did not could never harm you.

Kaz hugged her and melting into him, she was able to release some of the angst, but never the doubt. He genuinely cared for her, but he struggled between hunter and lover. And human and witch.

"Years later, Luc and I ran into one another again. I was in a nightclub and some vampires were bothering me. The Protection Spell had been dropped, so they didn't fear witches anymore. Luc punched one and told me to get out of there. I took it as a rescue. He didn't say anything more to me.

"Until a few months later, when I was sitting outside a coffee shop. He walked up to me and apologized, and explained how he knew now it was wrong what he had done because his sister had attacked me.

"I forgave him, easily."

Zoë buried her head against Kaz's chest and the soft trace of his thumb across her scar brought up tears. "Of course you did. God, I love you, Zoë. But I wonder if sometimes you need to be a little tougher. Is there anything you would find unforgivable?"

"Of course there is. I cannot begin to understand those who take pleasure in giving others pain or harming children. They are the lowest of the low, and do not deserve forgiveness."

"We agree on that. But sometimes it's the drug or booze doing the harm." Kaz's voice was distant, as if his thoughts were a thousand miles away. Or, most likely, years.

"You're thinking about your father. Have you ever forgiven him for blaming you for your mother's death?"

"I think so. Maybe. I don't know. But I've not forgotten. Me and the old man will never be friends. That's for sure."

He dug in his pocket and pulled out a key. It was an old brass key that Zoë had seen him pull out many times before.

"Tell me about that. Why do you always pull it out before you leave a building?"

He smirked and jiggled the key in his cupped palm. "It's nothing."

"Must be something if you do it every time you walk through a door."

Kaz hugged her and kissed the top of her head. "He used to lock me out after he started drinking. First time, I was twelve. He was wasted, and probably didn't even realize he had a kid and that the cries out on the front step should be tended to. It happened a few more times before I got smart and found an extra key. After that, I never left the house without checking to be sure I had this key. It means safety to me. Weird, isn't it?"

Zoë touched the key, warmed by his hand, and he let her take it and look it over. It was shiny, worn over the years by fingers stroking it, hoping upon hope it would always turn the lock to shelter.

"I can feel your strength in this," she said and pressed the key to his palm, holding hers over it. "You should never stop carrying this with you."

"Never will." He shoved it back in his pocket, and with an abrupt, "So!" he changed the subject deftly. "You forgave Luc and the two of you became best friends, just like that," he said flatly.

"Not so quickly as that. It took years. Without his sister, he was suddenly alone and without a tribe, frightened to be facing the world on his own. We earned one another's trust. He's good, Kaz. He's had a tough life. He wasn't born vampire, but rather created by his father after he got involved with a nasty tribe. His father forced him to this life when he was—well, the same age as when you ran away."

"Still doesn't excuse him hurting a woman out of revenge."

"You don't have to forgive him," Zoë said. "You just have to accept that I have. Can you do that?"

"I'm not sure. It might be easier if he weren't around me right now. I really want to stake him, Zoë. It's an impulse. It is what I am. I protect others from his breed. And I wasn't able to protect you."

His last words were uttered on a gasp, and Zoë turned to kiss him, to tender softness and let him know it was okay. "You've protected so many. And you've saved me many times. I think he's good to leave and go home. But I was thinking we could use him to track Mauritius. And we need to find that lab."

"You may have an idea there. Just tell me one thing, Zoë."

"Anything."

"Do you trust Luc completely? To never go back on dust? And to always have your safety first and foremost?"

She bowed her head and closed her eyes, but not for long, because she didn't have to think about it overmuch. "I trust him to always have my back, but I don't trust him not to be lured back to dust."

"And on dust, you can't trust him to have your back. Right?"

She nodded.

"He's dangerous to you."

"You want to stake him? Go stake him."

"Don't do that, Zoë. Don't make me choose between you and a vampire."

"Maybe that's what needs to happen."

"No, it doesn't. I will always choose you. But that includes seeing to your safety, so that choice may also include staking the vamp."

"A wicked dilemma."

He fisted the air and paced before her, his anxiety apparent in his inability to stand still.

"I need some air," he said. "Can we go out and walk? Maybe look for the lab? I...can't be here with the guy so close."

"I'll go anywhere with you, anytime, for whatever reason."

"I like the sound of that."

"Kiss me first. But only if you love me."

Kaz swept her into an immediate and dizzying kiss. He stole her breath but she didn't need it. He filled her with life, vitality and hope. This knight had truly come to rescue the damsel from herself.

"You really do love me," she said on a gasp.

"He does." Luc stood in the hallway.

Kaz's entire body tensed against Zoë.

"I have to leave," Luc said. He rapped the wall with his knuckles. "I have to find a bite, if you know what I mean. And I don't want to intrude on the hunter's life any longer. Thanks, hunter, for not killing me."

"I still have the stake."

"I'm aware. And if you come at me again, then I'll know it's because you're doing your job. But know I appreciate how kind you've been to Zoë. You're good for her. She needs you."

"To protect her from you?"

Luc shrugged. "I hope not. But I can't know what another day will bring."

"Yeah, I think you need to leave. It's safer for both of you."

Zoë stood and only reluctantly did Kaz release her hand.

She walked Luc to the door. "You can't go near FaeryTown, Luc. Nor any of your dealers."

"I won't."

"Can't go home, either," Kaz said. "Mauritius will be on the lookout for you."

Luc nodded. "If I can get some hot blood in my system, I'll feel one hundred percent."

"Isn't there like an AA for dust addicts?" Zoë wondered.

On the couch, Kaz scoffed, and Zoë allowed him that disdain. But then he offered, "Check with Vaillant."

Luc looked at the hunter. "You know him?"

"He's a...friend."

Even Zoë raised an eyebrow at that confession.

"The vampire was addicted to dust, and fights it every day," Kaz explained. "He's been clean for a long time. If anyone can help you, he can. I'll give him a call—"

"No, I know how to get hold of him," Luc said. "Thanks, man."

"Tell him I sent you. And if he wants to complain, he knows my number."

Luc nodded, then hugged Zoë and kissed her on the forehead. "Can I come to your house tomorrow?"

"I don't have a house anymore. Mauritius had his henchmen burn it down."

"Zoë, I'm so sorry. Did you get your things? What about your mother's necklace?"

She grasped her throat. "Kaz took it off last night when you..."

"I'm sorry, Zoë. I was jonesing for the sparkle," Luc said. "By going to Mauritius, I really betrayed you. Can you ever forgive me?"

"You know I can. But we've a big mess to clean up now."

"I'll do whatever you ask. But I have to leave. Hunger pangs."

"You can find me here," she called after him. When she closed the door, Zoë said to Kaz, "I know you won't let him back in."

"Damn right."

"I should probably look into finding a cheap rental to stay in until I can get a new place. I've taken advantage of your kindness."

"You are welcome here as long as you like. Sid, too."

From behind them, Sid meowed heartily. And that confirmed it: Zoë had found home.

Chapter 21

Zoë had to be strong if she were going to help Kaz find the new lab. No more shirking in fear and allowing her magic to take a hike. It was only when she was calm and confident that she could actually wield her powerful magic in public.

"Stay calm, stay strong, keep a hand on the magic," she muttered as she and Kaz got off the Metro in the eighteenth in the heart of FaeryTown.

They both wore the black ointment beneath their eyes—a gift from Ian Grim—but they weren't looking for a winged being. Zoë wasn't, anyway. Kaz, on the other hand, had been followed by a mysterious faery who harbored a death wish for him, so they decided that seeing what may soar toward them was the best option.

"You feeling good about this?" He winked. "Pretty little witch."

That he used a term of endearment meant he'd been able to get beyond the stupid thing she had done by concocting the blend. Even though it had created a big problem for him—and ultimately caused the death of his friends—she trusted he did not hold it against her.

She had to trust that because right now, she had nothing else in this world to cling to. She'd lost her home, everything she owned and all her magical accoutrements. Yet she didn't feel lacking, for she had saved Sid, and Kaz had rescued Luc. And with all hope, Luc may recover and leave his addiction to dust behind.

"Zoë?"

She chuckled softly. "Yes, I do feel good about this. So much so, I was counting my blessings. And one of them was you."

She kissed him, and only when tourists walking by on the street nudged them did Kaz pull away with a smile on his face.

"You're my blessing, too."

"Sort of a forced blessing, I'd say," Zoë said. She didn't want him dwelling on the bad, though. "You smell so good."

"Save the flirting for later. It's hard enough trying to divide my focus between work and you."

"On to the vampires, it is."

"And I'll keep an eye out for armed faeries. Watch the wings coming this way." Kaz dodged a faery's blue wings, but they fluttered right over his head as if the creature were a figment. "I forget we're in a different dimension."

"Yes, the faery can allow you to feel them only if they wish it. There are a couple vamps across the street sitting by that café table. They don't look threatening."

"They are always a threat," Kaz growled. With a sweep of his gaze over the next passing faery, he then decided, "Not a threat."

They strolled down the sidewalk through the depths of FaeryTown. Zoë pointed out the vampires coming in and out from the ichor dens, and the occasional vampire walking down the street seemingly unaware he tread through such multidimensional territory. She trusted Kaz would know which one he wanted to approach, if any at all.

Just when she sensed they neared the edge of Faery-

Town, Zoë spied a familiar face in a passing black vehicle. She squeezed Kaz's hand.

"I saw the fangs," he verified. "Is he someone you recognize?"

"I'm pretty sure he was one of Switch's cohorts. Wasn't he the guy who drove the car?"

"I staked that one."

"Right. But he's familiar. I must have seen him at some point while I was being held by Mauritius."

"I trust your hunch. I'm going after the car. Stay close if you can."

They raced down a street and when the male vampire got out of the vehicle and spied Kaz rushing toward him, he darted inside a pastry shop.

Zoë inhaled the sweet, greasy scents as she trailed the men, passing behind the counter with apologies to the human cashiers, and headed through the back baking room.

The back door swung open, and the vamp managed to swing out and jump over a wooden delivery crate to curl around a corner. Moving deeper into the block and away from the touristy area, they turned many corners and ventured into narrower alleys, until the vampire leaped for an iron staircase hugging a brick wall. Kaz grabbed him by an ankle and brought him to the ground. Stake in hand, he held it over the vamp's heart.

The vampire shifted his gaze to Zoë as she arrived huffing and glad the chase was over. "Mauritius wants your head, witch."

"I'm not his slave and I'll never make the Magic Dust again."

"Stupid witch. And you! You took out Switch!"

Kaz slapped a hand over the vampire's jaw. "Wasn't allowed that pleasure. You telling me Switch is dead?"

The vampire nodded from behind Kaz's hand.

"Sounds as if I missed that party. That means you're going to have to do some talking. Where did Mauritius move Zoë's lab?"

The vampire tried to bite Kaz's hand so he twisted his palm over his mouth.

"He won't be able to tell us where it is if you do that."

"Zoë, let me handle this, okay? Stay back and out of danger."

She stepped back. At the end of the alleyway, she spied a flicker of dark wings and focused on the motion down there. A faery? Her concern level for the winged creatures was so low she had difficulty seeing them even with the ointment.

"I will stake you," Kaz warned the squirming vamp. "Is the lab near the building where Mauritius does business?"

The vampire shook his head. Kaz took away his hand from his mouth and the vamp spat at him. Slashing out his arm, he managed to cut Kaz's jaw with his sharp fingernails.

"Stop that!" Zoë yelled and thrust out her hand, focusing her magic. Seeing the vampire hurt Kaz stirred up her energy and forced it out in a wave of anger. The air swooshed over Kaz's body and slammed the vampire, pinning his arms flat on the ground. It was obvious he tried to lift his head, but could not. "I did it!"

"So you did. Thanks, Zoë." Kaz sat up, taking his hands from the vampire, but keeping the stake firmly placed over his heart. "Now talk, or I'll have to use the big gun."

"Screw you, hunter."

"Big gun, it is." Kaz pulled a silver cross from his pocket. "I'm guessing you are baptized, yes?"

"So what?"

Kaz held the cross over the vampire's face, putting it but inches from his eye. "Dare me, longtooth."

"Get that thing away from me."

"If this cross touches you it'll burn a wound incapable of healing into your skin. It'll eat through your eye and your skull and into your brain. You won't die today, probably not even tomorrow. It'll slowly gnaw away at your gray matter until you've no brain left. Hell of a way to die."

"You've not the courage! You don't want your girlfriend to see you commit such a vile act."

Kaz turned to Zoë. He quirked a brow at her in question.

He was asking her permission to harm another being. In principle it went against her values, yet in that moment, she could think of no reason not to induce such harm. The knight was doing his job. The vampire was not rational, and was involved with an organization that ultimately harmed humans.

She nodded her approval of anything he needed to do to make the vampire talk.

"Wait!" the vampire yelled as the cross traced his lashes. "It's in the fourteenth. Near the catacombs. I'm not sure of the address because I've only been there once."

"Liar." Kaz brought the cross closer to the vampire's eyeball.

"All right, all right! It's behind the train station. But the building doesn't have a number on it. You have to look for the symbol."

"What symbol?" Zoë asked over Kaz's shoulder.

"Mauritius's family crest. Just stake me now, hunter, because I don't want my boss to know I narced on him."

"Nope." Kaz stood, tucking away the cross and the stake. "That's your problem to deal with now. Let's go, Zoë. Can you keep him pinned for a bit? We don't need him running to Mauritius and tipping him off we're on our way."

"I think I can handle that."

Pleased she'd controlled her magic while normally she wouldn't have been able to access it under stress, Zoë spoke a few Latin words to lengthen the spell, then blew a kiss to the vampire, who struggled against nothing more than the air spell.

"Voila!" she announced.

"Good going," Kaz said. He wrapped an arm across her back and led her down the alley. "What made you able to access your magic now?"

"I think because of my connection to you. You give me confidence."

"Works for me."

They exited the alleyway, and Zoë tugged Kaz in protectively. "Earlier, I think I saw something with dark wings. But it wasn't clear or even solid. It felt menacing."

"Sounds like my stalker. Where was it?"

"I haven't seen it since, but we'd best keep our eyes peeled."

Feeling newly revitalized over her magical skills by the time they reached the fourteenth, Zoë followed Kaz's hasty footsteps up the Metro station stairs to street level. She sensed he was in some kind of hunter mode, fierce and focused, and wasn't about to spoil it with conversation.

Kaz drew her close as he slowed his pace over a sidewalk that stretched before older business establishments. "You see anything move, even a flicker, let me know."

Zoë scanned in all directions, standing tall and ready. Like a hunter. It helped to think in those terms. Put her in action mode. "You think that vampire told the truth about this location?"

"I can only hope. If not, we'll search building by building for that symbol."

"It'll be small," Zoë said, "and most likely marked in blood."

"Nice," Kaz added with no appreciation whatsoever.

Zoë scanned the people they passed but all were human, and the tourists stood out with their tennis shoes and cameras. Kaz wore the Order gear, and that coat was a dead giveaway to any vampire who was in the know.

A fleeting shadow passed over them, drawing their attention to the sky. Zoë gripped Kaz's hand and he squeezed.

"Faery," he muttered.

"I think so. But not in attack mode. Just keeping an eye on us."

"Peachy. The Order doesn't train their knights for this kind of combat. Wait." He dropped her hand and shuffled out of his coat, tugging the sleeves inside and reversing it.

"What are you doing?"

"I read something in the research about wearing my coat inside out."

"Oh, yes, it should make you invisible to the sidhe. If you believe, of course."

"Worth a try, eh?" He tucked the collar down so the blades would not cut his neck. "What about you? You want to turn your shirt inside out?"

"I'll be fine. Nonbeliever, remember?"

"Zoë, they believe in you."

"But more so you. So you'll be the one they take out first. That'll give me time to run. Yes?"

His smirk ended in a chuckle. "Your logic is strangely sexy, you know that?"

"Well, I am a little strange. And I'll take sexy."

He squeezed her hand and as they turned to continue the search, something caught Zoë's eye. "There." She stopped at the curb before crossing the street. "That building with the metal-studded door. Do you see that small red mark? Looks like an *M*."

"Obvious much?"

"And I think that was a vampire that walked away."

"You think or you know?"

"Think. But it's the closest to knowing I've felt since we arrived. Trust me."

"I will. We have no idea how many are inside, so I need you to stay close to me."

That he hadn't asked her to stay outside lifted her confidence even more. "I'll have my magic at the ready."

"If you can do more of that trick where you hold them down with nothing more than air, then yes. But don't get fancy. We're going to play this cool and smart. All right?"

She nodded in agreement. "I'll wait for your signal. Promise."

"Follow my lead. If we're lucky, the place will be empty. Unless they are busy setting things up."

"Mauritius made me believe they'd be doing just that."

"And he'd like nothing more than for his star witch to wander inside and allow herself to be captured." He grabbed her by the shoulders. "You should stay outside."

"But if I'm out here you'll not see if some vampire grabs me."

He mentally wrestled with the two bad choices.

Zoë touched his chest and spread her fingers over his frantic heartbeats. "I'll be fine. I'll duck when there's trouble, and fling some magic when you need it. I won't get in your way, nor will I let a gang of vampires grab me from behind."

"Those are skills not even we knights of the Order have completely mastered. But there's no other way to play this right now."

"Exactly. So lead on, hunter. I'll have your back."

"I know you will."

His confidence filled her with a burst of elation, and with a nod to confirm to one another they were ready, they crossed the street toward the warehouse.

As far as warehouses went, it was small, but ten times the size of the lab Zoë had in her home. Former home. A twinge of loss snagged her stalwart posture and her shoulders deflated as she walked down the aisle between two lab tables set up with pristine glass containers, alembics, burners and other accoutrements of the trade. Everything was stainless steel and sterile. No magical resonance could survive in this cold atmosphere, let alone harmonize to a workable frequency.

A drug lab, she decided. It sickened her.

"See anything that belongs to you?" Kaz asked as he inspected a sealed container of what looked like liquid ichor. A gallon, easily. Just waiting to be reduced and transmuted into Magic Dust.

Zoë averted her eyes from the substance that had been taken from a faery's veins—she hoped not all at once— and then she knew it probably had been. Forcing herself to remain calm and not freak out over something that she had unknowingly masterminded, she let her eyes skim over a stack of papers and books at the end of the table.

Rushing over, she picked up the leather-bound book that was over five centuries old. "My family's grimoire." She'd been adding to it since her father had handed it down to her. He had thought it best to remain in her hands when he'd left to go into hiding.

Beside where the grimoire had lain were assorted papers, some with hand-drawn diagrams and notes. Had someone been trying to figure the chemical composition of the faery ichor? Zoë hadn't a clue when it came to formulas and chemicals. It was all in the magic. And in her head.

"They won't be able to reproduce it," she said, confident the Magic Dust blend would remain her secret.

"Is that all you want?" Kaz tapped a delicate glass vial with the end of a long steel bar he'd claimed from near the doorway.

Zoë nodded, and then rushed over to the door, clutching the grimoire to her chest, as she knew what would happen next.

Kaz swung the metal pipe, knocking over the glass alembics and vials in a clatter of fine, sharp particles. Meanwhile, Zoë worked her magic to contain the shards in a vortex to keep them from flying everywhere. The tornado of debris grew larger with everything he smashed or knocked over. And when it was done, he gave Zoë a signal and she clapped her hands, dropping the vortex to the floor in a gentle crash.

She stepped carefully to his side, recalling how she'd initially imagined him her knight and she the princess who would never wear glass slippers. And for good reason, she thought now, as the glass crunched beneath her heels.

"No one will be able to manufacture Magic Dust here. Ever," she said.

"Unfortunate!"

Both turned at the sound of a man's voice. Kaz gestured to Zoë, who joined his side. He wrapped an arm about her waist.

"You've been a naughty witch," Mauritius said. Pulling out a gun, he took aim and fired.

Kaz only had time to react by jumping in front of Zoë.

Chapter 22

As Kaz jumped, his gaze averted upward and he glimpsed the faery landing on the rafters above. The sweep of his black wings cast an ominous shadow in the air. Then Kaz's eyelids shuttered as he felt the bullet pierce his shoulder. It burned through his flesh and felt as if lava pored into his bone. Not a fatal hit, but he might have wished for it, to stop the excruciating pain.

Zoë's scream was the only thing that kept him in the present moment. Focusing on that horrible sound enabled him to twist, grab her by the waist and shove her back so she stumbled, landing on the glass-littered floor. The grimoire fell from her hands and slid across the glass. A second bullet whizzed over their heads.

Gripping a holstered stake with his good hand, Kaz squeezed the paddles, deploying the business end, and thrust it toward the vampire—whom he knew was Mauritius—like a throwing blade. It was counterweighted for such use.

The vampire caught the stake in his hand, mere inches from entering his chest. Tucking the gun under an arm, he made show of studying the deadly stake tip, drawing a finger along the length of it.

"She can't give you the formula," Kaz said. If he could

talk to the vampire, he might win Zoë a chance to escape. "It's in her head."

"Then I'll have to extract it with persuasion," Mauritius said. He tested the paddles and the stake pinioned back into the column. "Handy thing, this. A nice addition to my collection. Give the Order my thanks, will you? Oh, wait. You won't live to report on today's adventures. Such a pity."

Kaz wavered on his feet. He wasn't sure how long he could stay conscious with the incredible pain searing his arm. And there was that damned faery perched above he needed to keep an eye on. If the vampire didn't shoot him, the faery would fire one of those nasty, poisoned flechettes directly into his skull. *If* the thing could see him wearing the coat he'd turned inside out.

"I'll spare your hunter," Mauritius said to Zoë, "if you come along with me. You've only to demonstrate how you concoct the Magic Dust, and then you are free to go, as well."

"That's a lie," Kaz barked when he sensed Zoë step forward.

"He's right," she said from behind him. "You lied to me about Luc getting better. You've lied to me about selling my blend. You just want to make money."

"Money is very useful. And with that blend I can rule FaeryTown." Mauritius laughed loudly.

Kaz noticed the faery above aimed his weapon at the vampire. Interesting. If he could just keep the longtooth rambling about his evil plans...

"Won't the faeries have something to say about that?" Kaz called to the vampire. "You ruling them, and all?"

"They are idiots. Stupid creatures who would sell themselves to make a few bucks so they can live in this realm. Bunch of outcasts and ne'er-do-wells. I'll make it easy for them. I'll buy their ichor—by the body—and end their miserable lives before they can comprehend the futility of an insignificant mortal lifestyle."

"Is that so?"

Both Kaz and Mauritius watched as a female faery alit from above and landed on the cement floor beside them in a predatory crouch. Dressed in strips of leather that barely covered the important bits, and sporting white body tattoos, she looked a warrior. The weapon she held in a hand resembled a pistol made of copper, but…not.

Kaz noted the dark faery remained en pointe with his weapon, high in the rafters.

Standing, the female drew in her pink wings with a snap. Crossing her arms over her chest to display the weapon warningly, she cast her violet gaze at the vampire. "The Sidhe Cortège will have a say regarding your grand plans, longtooth."

"The Cortège?" Mauritius gestured dismissively. "Bloody faery mafia. Riské—the idiot with wings who runs the group of glitter freaks—is a fool."

"He is my lover," the woman pronounced. "And the Cortège ruler, le Grand Sidhe."

Kaz felt Zoë slip her hand into his, and he leaned against her, only now realizing she already supported most of his weight. It felt as if sandbags weighted his eyelids. But he battled to keep one eye open, on the dark-winged faery lurking overhead. A battle he was losing.

Using every ounce of her strength, Zoe braced herself to hold up Kaz, but he slumped to his knees. She held his arm, though her eyes never left the vampire and faery before her.

"Tell your lover I've a deal for him," Mauritius said to the winged creature.

"No deals." The warrior faery slashed a wing across

Mauritius's cheek, leaving in its wake a thin, red cut. "You're dead, vampire."

Before Mauritius could protest his death, his arms flailed outward and his head jerked back. In succession, half a dozen of the flechettes attached to his shoulders, back and skull. Induced by a high-pitched banshee scream from the dark-winged shooter, the flechettes snapped and sprang free from the vampire's back in a plume of iridescent dust. Mauritius dropped to his knees, his limbs shaking violently as the poison coursed through his system.

"The poison doesn't kill vampires," Zoë said to the female. "It—well, maybe. If he's not a dust addict and doesn't have any in his system, it could prove lethal."

"Never!" the female faery called for her cohort.

The dark faery in the rafters lighted down with impeccable grace and stood beside her. Wings extended regally, he imbued a tethered menace into the cold, sterile warehouse that touched Zoë's very soul. His eyes raked Kaz. The inside-out coat apparently served no efficacy.

"Kill the hunter," the female faery commanded.

"No!" Zoë dropped Kaz's arm, and he slumped to the ground, sprawling before the vampire, who now shuddered manically. "He's no harm to you. He was after the vampires selling the Magic Dust. He wants to end it as much as you do."

"And yet you are the very witch who put the product out there. Wait, Never," Coyote said to the dark faery who reloaded his crossbow. "The hunter will die from blood loss soon enough. I do prefer a slow death. As for witches, I believe—"

"I don't believe in you," Zoë said with as much fury as her shaking voice could manage. "You are nothing to me."

"Your lack of belief is apparent. How else could you manufacture such a vile substance without a care for those who gave their ichor?"

Zoë couldn't reply to that one. When she'd received the ichor it had been detached from the faery who had given it, making it easy enough to overlook the heinous act that must have occurred to actually obtain it.

She swallowed, feeling her stomach revolt. The things she had done... But Kaz had encouraged her to accept it because she'd not known better. And now that she did? She would do better.

She mustn't allow the sidhe the upper hand, or she would again be unable to utilize her magic. By all means, she must remain strong with Kaz fighting to survive beside her.

"Begone with the both of you," Zoë commanded.

With a cry to rend the very stones from their plastered walls, Mauritius suddenly ashed in a wicked dusting of blood, ash and glittering ichor.

Zoë turned her head to avoid getting the stuff in her eyes. In her peripheral vision she saw the female faery approach, and something inside her clicked. Yes, she had committed grave acts against many, both sidhe and human, but she would redeem herself. Somehow.

Thrusting out an arm, she recited a repulsion spell, *"Suivre repulsus!"*

The faery's body was tugged backward away from Zoë, slamming her into the dark one, and thrusting them across the room. She did not land, however, and instead, gained control midair. She flew up and away before the dark one landed against the wall.

Gliding overhead, the faery chuckled. "I hate witches."

"I'm not so keen on faeries, either," Zoë offered.

"But you believe in me now, yes?"

"Hell, no. You're just a bit of dust and wing. A faery tale."

The faery swooped overhead, dashing a wingtip close to Zoë's cheek.

"It doesn't have to be like this," Zoë called. "I didn't realize I had created such a powerfully addictive blend. I'll never make another drop. But that's a promise I make to myself, not you."

"Insolent witch."

"I want to learn how to craft the poison your dark warrior puts in his flechettes," Zoë said. "That poison seems to get dust junkies clean."

"We will never help the vampires," the faery said as she landed on a rafter and sat there, her legs dangling. "Nor an ugly, old witch."

Zoë stroked the scar on her cheek, momentarily put off by the accusation. But really? What did she care what a homicidal faery thought of her?

Not one iota.

This time she summoned resonance from her soul and enforced its strength by humming deep in her throat. Forging it from all she had learned from her father, Zoë thrust out the molecular magic. It caught the faery around the feet and tugged. Flailing, the faery fell through the air, and couldn't catch herself before hitting the cement floor. Hard. Magic crept along her skin and lighted in her wings, glowing and smoking, changing the composition of her wings until they began to melt.

The dark faery picked himself up and walked over to his mistress. Zoë kept a keen eye on his trigger hand. The one called Never looked to Zoë…and winked.

"Soon," was all he said, and then he flew off and exited the building through the open door.

The female faery groaned, slapped a hand over her shoulder where her wings oozed through her fingers, and grumbled at the grossness of it all.

Meanwhile, Zoë nudged Kaz upright. He suddenly gripped her by the hand and pulled her forward. Zoë fell, her palms hitting the glass-littered floor as the faery's clawed hand missed cutting her throat.

Kaz yelped. The claw had cut his forehead and one eye.

"No!" Zoë tried for her magic but before she could summon a spell, one of Kaz's stakes pierced the faery in the heart.

The sidhe laughed and clutched the weapon. Mortal metal would not keep her down.

Kaz charged the faery, who tugged out the stake just as their bodies collided. Zoë couldn't throw magic at them and risk harming Kaz. While the faery's wing literally dripped from her back, Kaz struggled to pin her flailing arms.

Another banshee cry pierced the air as the faery fell, lifeless, at Kaz's feet.

That was when Zoe saw the stake. In the struggle, the faery had managed to turn it on Kaz. He tugged it from his gut and faltered, but not before winking at Zoë.

In the faery's chest, a rough, old blade had been hilted.

"Iron?"

"Oh, yeah," Kaz said before he dropped.

Two blocks away from the ER entrance, Zoë stood with Kaz's arm across her shoulder to brace his weak stance. He refused to go inside.

"Order rules," he insisted.

"Yeah? Does the Order offer emergency care? Kaz, you've a bullet in your shoulder."

"Take it out!"

"No, I— You've been stabbed in the gut. You haven't stopped bleeding. And your eye—"

"It's just a scratch."

Zoë gasped as she pulled her hand away from his gut and his blood trickled down to her wrist.

"Please, Kaz, don't be foolish."

"A knight lives to serve and dies fighting," he said with a growl. He was talking incoherently.

"Don't recite some stupid macho rules."

"I'm off the grid. Can't go into a public place like a hospital without a lot of questions I can't answer. I took a vow, Zoë."

She managed to shove him against the brick wall and pressed her chest against his to keep him from toppling forward. Bracketing his face with her bloody palms, she pleaded, "What about the vow you made when you won my heart?"

He peered at her, blood blurring his wounded eye. "I... vows. Yes..."

"You can't die, lover. After all we've been through, is that what you want for us?"

"No, I...love you, Zoë." His eyelids fluttered.

She kissed him, knowing now was not the time or the place to infuse him with her molecular healing magic, but wishing it was so easy as this kiss to save him.

"All I have is the Order," he managed. Bowing his head to hers, he whispered, "And you."

Much against her better judgment, Zoë helped him onto the Metro and managed to get him home. She wasn't so keen on mortal institutions of medical care herself. And if she couldn't save him, then no one could.

Kaz woke to the burning of a thousand bees stinging his shoulder and burrowing under his skin with a precision that focused the pain and made him yowl through his tight jaw.

A hand pressed upon his chest, beckoning him to lie down. Soft hair dusted his face. Smelled liked the witch with whom he had fallen in love. Yes, Zoë, of the strange hair, and the scar she'd gotten from a vampire whom she called friend. A witch who had saved his ass after he'd saved hers.

His thoughts blurred and he passed out.

When awareness next teased, he saw a white mist being moved about by the witch's hands, directing it above his face and toward his shoulder. Felt like ice droplets kissing his skin, cooling the burning wound.

God, he loved the witch.

The third time he touched consciousness Kaz looked into heaven. Bright blue eyes held his gaze. Angels had eyes like that. And she even smelled heavenly.

She kissed his mouth and whispered, "I love you. But you almost died."

"Died?"

"I would never let that happen." She sighed and Kaz felt her exhaustion in the strain of her voice.

"Zoë?" He touched the hair on the side of her head. Where once it had been streaked with white, now it was more a swath, four times as wide as before. "What happened?"

"Takes a bit out of me when I have to bring someone back from death. If I stick around you for any amount of time, my hair may grow completely white." She yawned and smiled sweetly before laying her head on his chest. "I'm tired. Do you mind if I snuggle?"

Her body melded against his and he wrapped an arm about her and together they slept through the night and beyond noon the next day.

Zoë woke against a warm, hard surface that smelled like the best night she'd ever had. Turning her face to nuzzle Kaz's bare chest, she kissed him below the curve of his pectoral muscle. It flexed and he murmured something low and deep that sounded like, "I love you."

Healing him had drained her. It was well after noon to judge the bright sun that beamed across the hardwood floor. She'd needed that rest.

"Love you," he said again.

No magic in the world felt as good as those words.

Zoë went up on an elbow to inspect his shoulder, upon which she had not laid a bandage, wanting the wound to scab and heal. The skin was pink and rough. She kissed his shoulder.

"How's it look?" he asked. "It feels...like nothing."

"Nothing?"

"I mean, I don't feel any pain. You have the magic touch. Literally."

"Anything for you, lover."

He stroked aside her hair from her face, wincing. "So every time you save someone from death your hair grows whiter? Weird kind of payment for using redeeming magic."

"It's because the life is literally sucked out of me. It's a small price to pay, don't you think?"

"You could work the white hair. Did I tell you I love you?"

"You did, but you can say it as many times as you wish and I'll never tire of hearing it."

Nuzzling his chest, she breathed in the sweet, masculine scent of him. He was hers. She was his. They belonged together in a strange clash of human and paranormal, and... they worked.

She reached down and unsnapped the button on his jeans and slid her hand inside his pants.

"Whoa. You always wake up so horny?"

"I woke up on top of the most handsome man I've ever known. You think I'm *not* a little horny?" She found his erection, which was as hard as one of his stakes, and squeezed it. "You did say you were invigorated."

"That I am."

"Any objections to a little fooling around?"

"Besides the fact my breath might kill you? Uh, no."

"We'll save kisses for after the shower." Zoë glided down to kiss him below the belly button. "Mmm, I've found something to play with."

"Oh, you witch." He raked his fingers through her hair. "Great way to start the day."

Chapter 23

The shower pattered over their skin, washing away the kisses Zoë had placed on Kaz's body, so she quickly replaced them, and he didn't even have to ask.

He loved what she did to him, how she made him feel. He loved that he'd been able to confess to her about his father blaming him for his mother's death, and that he hadn't wanted to run away and hide from her after doing so. He loved that she'd had to hurt him to make him finally feel and not want to push those feelings away, because feeling had healed him.

Being with Zoë had changed the way he thought. And that was everything right.

So he'd caught the vampire who had killed Ellen and Robert. Sort of. He didn't ever want to see Luc again. He could forgive a vampire who had been under the influence of a mind-altering substance, but he could never forget. He'd keep track of him via Zoë, and Vail had left him a text that Luc had contacted him.

As well, he'd stopped the distribution of Magic Dust when the dark faery had taken out Mauritius. The only way the streets of Paris would again see the addictive drug was if Zoë manufactured more of it. And she would never do that.

And with Mauritius dead, Zoë's use of molecular magic would not be discovered by the witches of the Light. Thus keeping her safe from the brand of warlock.

He'd achieved his goals and completed the job for the Order. On to the next job, the next vamp, another stake in the chest. It would never end. He didn't need it to end. Someone had to police the bloodsuckers, and he couldn't imagine working nine to five or wearing a business suit. The party never ended.

Yet what remained were Zoë's goals, and he wouldn't feel as if he'd completed all his goals if hers were not tidied up, as well.

She wanted to manufacture the faery poison. It sounded risky, but if it could cure vampires of their addiction to dust, then he was all for it, because there were always the crazies to deal with. Though he intended to be right there as bodyguard when Zoë started to interview faeries for the job.

But one thing remained that he really wanted to fix.

Zoë kissed his chest, and then playfully licked his lips before kissing him long and hard. Her slick, wet breasts slid across his chest and he held her tight, yet stopped the kiss.

Stroking his thumb across the scar on her cheek, he said, "If you can't heal yourself, maybe I can help some way? Like give some of my life to you to make it heal like you did for me?"

"Is it so important to you that I look a certain way, Kaz?"

"No. You're gorgeous just the way you are. I just, well hell, doesn't the scar make you think of violence?"

She nodded and dipped her head to press her forehead against his shoulder. "A warlock might be able to fix it, but I've refused Ian Grim's offer to try. I guess…I've always felt I needed to wear this as a reminder."

"A reminder of what? Nothing good. And you and Luc have put your bygones in the past. Don't you think it kills him to look at the scar, too? Come on, Zoë. Let's talk to the warlock. I want to help make you whole."

"I'd do anything to make you happy."

"No." He caught her hand and kissed her palm. "It's got to be because it will make *you* happy. If you are fine as you are then—"

"I would like to make it go away. I am a bit self-conscious about it...."

"Didn't you say something about your dad being a warlock? Maybe he can help?"

"I...don't know where he is. I wouldn't want him to see me like this, anyway. Let's stick with Grim."

"Are you and your father not on good terms?"

"As good as they can be when I haven't talked to him for a decade. Probably much better than you and your father— Oh, I'm sorry. That was horrible."

"It's cool. You and all your forgiveness kind of makes me want to look up the old man."

"Really?"

He shrugged, and flipped off the shower. "Maybe. Don't rush me."

He wrapped a towel about the two of them, and they didn't make it to the bedroom without having sex against the bathroom door, the hallway wall and finally, the bed.

As Kaz walked Zoë through the clutter of dried maple leaves littering the dark street, Zoë explained the love affair between her friends, Ian Grim, who was a warlock, and Dasha, who was—well, she hadn't a term for her beyond revenant. Which meant one who rises from the dead. Dasha didn't like the term, so she cautioned Kaz not to bring it up.

Zoë also explained exactly how she'd died. So when the

beautiful woman with long, black hair and bright green eyes answered the door, and Kaz's eyes went immediately to the red ribbon tied around her neck, he held back a wince. Dasha had been beheaded during the French Revolution for thievery. Seems the witch, Ian Grim—who hadn't been warlock at the time—had found her head attached to a new body, and well, from there it got even weirder. Grim had ransomed his status with the witches of the Light and had been ousted a warlock because it was against the Light's rules to keep dead things alive.

"This is Kaspar Rothstein," Zoë introduced.

When Dasha took his hand to shake, he was glad it felt warm. Mostly warm, anyway. He had a hard time getting his mind around who—what—she was. She was dead? But the warlock kept her alive with blood transfusions?

"Come in," Dasha said, leading them into a dark home that looked like something from Victorian times, replete with the silver-and-black-flocked wallpaper. "I'll tell Ian you're here, and with your new man. Oh, and Zoë, we've a surprise for you."

The dead woman disappeared down the hallway, her long Victorian skirts sweeping the dark cherrywood floors.

"So she's…"

"Save any questions for later, okay?" Zoë said. "Remember, be nice."

"I can do that. Nice is my middle name."

And he could, because despite having lived amongst the paranormal breeds for a decade, he was only now beginning to feel a part of it all. And he liked that. This hunter was changing, and for the better.

"I do like surprises," Zoë said, flashing him an eager grin.

"As long as it doesn't have fangs." He hugged her to his side and kissed the crown of her head.

* * *

"Daddy!"

Zoë rushed into her father's arms and the long-awaited bear hug took her from her feet. Didn't matter that she could barely breathe. He was here in Paris!

"What are you doing here? And why Ian Grim's home when you should be at my—"

Her father lifted a thick black brow in question.

"Doesn't matter. What does is that you're here." Zoë gave him another quick hug and they held hands, facing one another.

"You don't have a house, daughter dearest," Pierre Guillebeaux said. "Much to my horror upon arriving at what should have been your bright blue doorstep. What happened?"

"It's a long and strange story. I'm safe, and so is Sid."

"Sid? Is that…?" Pierre looked beyond Zoë at Kaz.

"Sid is my cat."

"Then who is this man whom I witnessed entering Grim's spell room with your hand in his?"

Kaz wrapped an arm about her waist, claiming her. She could even laugh at the discerning perusal her father gave Kaz. He'd left her only a few years after she'd reached dating age, and hadn't much chance to play the protective father.

"Kaz is my boyfriend," she said proudly.

Kaz offered his hand to shake.

Pierre held Kaz's hand a bit longer than usual, then dropped it. "Human. Bit of a disappointment, truth be told. You are in love with my daughter?"

"I am," Kaz said, hugging her closely. "It's nice to meet you, Monsieur Guillebeaux. Sorry to disappoint."

"Yes, well, you may yet grow on me."

"He's a hunter for the Order of the Stake," Zoë explained.

Both Ian and Pierre groaned at the same time.

"Really? Didn't realize how unpopular we knights were with the paranormal breeds." Kaz lowered his gaze.

"A human who hunts vampires," Zoë's father said. "I will give him points for that, but—no, only half a point. Kaz, eh? What sort of name is that?"

"It's Kaspar Rothstein," Zoë provided eagerly. There was no way she would allow her father to belittle Kaz when he had been out of her life for so long. "He's German."

"Oh." Pierre shrugged his shoulders and appeared to give that some merit. "I've just come from Berlin. Nice area. As are the fräuleins."

"Daddy, really? I haven't seen you in a decade and the first things you do are put down my boyfriend and extol the virtues of German women?"

"I'm sorry, Zoë." Her father kissed her on the cheek, then pulled back, touching the scar. "What's this from?"

"It's a long story, which I will tell you later, but it is also the reason I've come here today. It's an old wound, but I've decided perhaps I could attempt healing it."

"That'll take some powerful magic." Pierre glanced to Grim. "Ah. Well now, you've two warlocks. You want to give this a go, Grim?"

"Already working on it, Pierre."

After much thought and perusing his grimoires, Ian Grim finally invited Zoë to sit upon his spell table, and told Kaz to stand beside her. Zoë trusted Ian. Kaz, however, cast her a wary eye, but she gave him a look that reminded him to play nice.

Her father stood on the other side of her, acting more as an advisor to Grim, and agreeing when he'd pointed out various spells, or explaining how it could be done with more finesse. She was thrilled to see him again, but wouldn't hold out hopes that he was in town for long.

"This requires soul work," Grim announced. "I'll need a part of Zoë that is unselfish and strong and loving."

"Well, that's all of her," Kaz said.

Zoë caught his admiring look, and she felt the warm snuggles spill from the top of her head to her toes. Happily ever after felt so close, she could taste it.

"Right, but it needs to be an independent source," Pierre explained. "A part of her not within."

"I don't understand," Zoë said.

Dasha popped in with a tray of freshly baked cinnamon cookies.

"Not now, Dasha. We're working," Ian said, but in a kind way, not dismissive.

"Before you go…" Kaz grabbed a cookie from the plate, then two more.

Dasha beamed at him. Her father made that disapproving throat-clearing sound.

"I love cinnamon cookies." Kaz munched on the spoils and leaned nearer to Zoë. "Strength from not within," he said. "I don't get it, either."

"I am very strong on my own. I've healed Kaz many times," Zoë said. "He's been near death quite a lot lately."

"I expect so," Ian said. "That might explain your new hairstyle."

"Zoë, really, you've gotten that far with the molecular magic?" her father asked proudly.

She nodded.

"So you imbued molecular magic into the hunter?" Grim asked.

She nodded and then bowed her head. "Sorry, Kaz. I know I promised I wouldn't use warlock magic, but—"

"I love you," he said. "You can use whatever kind of magic on me you like."

She tilted her head against his. No one else existed when

she was in Kaz's presence. He smelled like cinnamon and licorice, and he was her hunter. All hers.

"Ahem," her father said.

"That should do it, then." Ian and Pierre exchanged looks. "You thinking what I'm thinking, Guillebeaux?"

"Yes. Unfortunately." Pierre tapped a finger to his bottom lip. "He does appear to give her strength."

Ian turned and sorted through some metal instruments on the table behind him, then spun around to display a gleaming steel knife, the blade as long and wide as his forearm. "I've always wanted to cut a hunter."

"Wait. What?" Kaz stopped midbite of the third cookie.

"He'll need some of your blood," Pierre explained. "Because, thanks to the molecular healing, it's got Zoë's life energy coursing through it."

Ian held up the blade. "You willing to bleed for this woman, Kaz?"

Kaz shrugged off his coat and flexed a biceps. "Tap me. But uh, does the knife have to be that big?"

With a smirk, the warlock gripped Kaz's wrist.

"Oh, let me do it, please?" Pierre reached for the blade, and Ian graciously handed it over to him.

"Now, Daddy, remember I love Kaz."

Pierre met eyes with the hunter, and even as the sun's reflection glinted on the blade and dashed across her father's face, he lost the teasing jest and nodded. "She's very special."

"You don't have to tell me that," Kaz said. "She's taught me a thing or two. Forgiveness being the most important."

"Fancy that," Ian said over Pierre's shoulder. "A hunter who knows the meaning of forgiveness."

They were both giving Kaz a hard time, but Zoë sensed Kaz took it with the same jocular intent in which it was given.

"Hold that goblet for me, Zoë," her father announced.

Pierre dragged the blade over Kaz's vein. Blood purled over the side of his arm and into the goblet. The hunter nibbled the remaining cookie, his eyes fixed to the macabre sight.

And Zoë leaned in to kiss him at the corner of his eye. "Love you," she whispered.

Chapter 24

Kaz stroked Zoë's cheek as they stood waiting for the Metro train to arrive. Her scar was gone. Her father had been the first to kiss her and pronounce her his petite mignon, a nickname she hadn't heard in a decade. It had been difficult to walk away from Grim's home while her father had strode away in the opposite direction. He was only in Paris for the week and had mysterious liaisons to engage, but tomorrow was all Zoë's, he promised.

Kaz kissed her on the cheek, then her mouth. They stood there, amidst the rumble of the approaching train, lips still against one another, yet heartbeats fluttering in sync. Her knight had rescued her, as she had him.

"Do I look better now?" she asked.

Kaz shook his head. "You've always been a stunner. I actually think it might take a few days to get used to the new you."

"You're not upset we performed the healing spell?"

"Are you?"

"No. This is good. It's erased a wrong—"

"That you don't need to atone for anymore. You got that? You and Luc are good. No one owes anyone for the pain they gave the other. You're even."

She nodded. "I'm cool with that."

The train squealed to a halt and Kaz tugged her on board and into the crowd.

"Where to now?" she asked.

"There's someplace I need to go. It's important. And...I need you to hold my hand."

She squeezed his hand. "I'd go anywhere with you, lover."

Kaz rang the doorbell, then stepped back to wait. Slipping his hand into his pants pocket, he curled his fingers about the old brass key. He could just walk in...

Not your home anymore.

At his side, Zoë gave his other hand a squeeze and cast her gorgeous gaze up at him. A soft confidence glowed in her expression, and it settled his nerves.

She'd taught him that forgiveness was essential to move ahead in life. To shed old scars that carry memories that were best buried. And though he knew she and her father had not parted on bad terms, watching them today had stirred up the longing in his core that he'd suppressed for years.

A longing for family that had been shattered due to circumstances no one had been prepared to accept or control.

Stepping back, he turned to look out at the street. It wouldn't take long to clear the block and be out of sight of the doorway.

"Forgiveness doesn't mean you have to forget," Zoë said softly, bringing his attention back around. "It means you're allowing yourself to move on, to shed the pain. I'm here for you."

He smirked and gave her hand a squeeze just as the door opened. Inside, a man who looked ten years older than he should stood tall and narrowed his eyes at the visitors.

Kaz swallowed and released Zoë's hand. He stretched out his hand in an offering to shake.

"Kaspar?" the man said finally. "My son. My prayers have been answered."

The men slapped their palms together in a firm grasp, and Kaz and Zoë didn't leave until three hours had passed.

"Thanks for that," Kaz said as he and Zoë strode through the Bois de Boulogne near the Jardin d'Acclimatation.

It was around eight in the evening and the sun had set, yet the neon lights from the nearby amusement park cast a golden glow across the fallen leaves and flower heads that had gone to seed. Neither had wanted to go home after leaving Kaz's father's home. The old man had begged Kaz's forgiveness and shown him his sobriety pin. Two years, thirty-six days and counting. He knew he'd messed up with his son, and had never forgiven himself for putting the blame for his wife's death on him.

Zoë had sat quietly, allowing the men to slowly gauge one another, and finally, when it was time to leave, father and son had hugged. Kaz hadn't told his father that he was a hunter, nor was it necessary. The relationship was yet fragile, but she sensed over the years, it would grow strong.

"There's no need to thank me," she offered, and paused beneath a streetlamp. Kaz wrapped his arms about her waist and pulled her in for a kiss.

"Let's do something crazy," he said.

"What did you have in mind?"

"I'm not sure."

"Slay a few vampires?"

"That's not crazy. That's just work."

She agreed with a nod. "Go on a trip?"

"I have to stay in Paris. I'm the only knight on call for another few weeks."

"We could...hmm...go dancing again?"

He slid his hands into hers and spun her beneath the glow. "I want to dance with you forever, witch."

"I like the sound of that. You know you've bewitched me."

"Right back atcha. How about this for crazy?" he said. "Let's get married."

The suggestion did not take her by surprise. In fact, it felt the perfect way to begin the next chapter.

"I do," she answered.

Kaz swept her up into his arms and spun her around. "I love you!"

* * * * *

I hope you enjoyed Kaz and Zoë's story.
If you're interested in learning more about
the vampire Vaillant, check out his story,
FOREVER VAMPIRE, available at your
favorite online retailer.
And watch for Rook's story,
GHOST WOLF, in October 2014.

REQUEST YOUR FREE BOOKS!

2 FREE NOVELS FROM THE PARANORMAL ROMANCE COLLECTION PLUS 2 FREE GIFTS!

YES! Please send me 2 FREE novels from the Paranormal Romance Collection and my 2 FREE gifts (gifts are worth about $10). After receiving them, if I don't wish to receive any more books, I can return the shipping statement marked "cancel." If I don't cancel, I will receive 4 brand-new novels every month and be billed just $22.76 in the U.S. or $23.96 in Canada. That's a savings of at least 17% off the cover price of all 4 books. It's quite a bargain! Shipping and handling is just 50¢ per book in the U.S. and 75¢ per book in Canada.* I understand that accepting the 2 free books and gifts places me under no obligation to buy anything. I can always return a shipment and cancel at any time. Even if I never buy another book, the two free books and gifts are mine to keep forever.

237/337 HDN F4YC

Name	(PLEASE PRINT)
Address	Apt. #
City	State/Prov.	Zip/Postal Code

Signature (if under 18, a parent or guardian must sign)

Mail to the Harlequin® Reader Service:
IN U.S.A.: P.O. Box 1867, Buffalo, NY 14240-1867
IN CANADA: P.O. Box 609, Fort Erie, Ontario L2A 5X3

Want to try two free books from another line?
Call 1-800-873-8635 or visit www.ReaderService.com.

* Terms and prices subject to change without notice. Prices do not include applicable taxes. Sales tax applicable in N.Y. Canadian residents will be charged applicable taxes. Offer not valid in Quebec. This offer is limited to one order per household. Not valid for current subscribers to Paranormal Romance Collection or Harlequin® Nocturne™ books. All orders subject to credit approval. Credit or debit balances in a customer's account(s) may be offset by any other outstanding balance owed by or to the customer. Please allow 4 to 6 weeks for delivery. Offer available while quantities last.

Your Privacy—The Harlequin® Reader Service is committed to protecting your privacy. Our Privacy Policy is available online at www.ReaderService.com or upon request from the Harlequin Reader Service.

We make a portion of our mailing list available to reputable third parties that offer products we believe may interest you. If you prefer that we not exchange your name with third parties, or if you wish to clarify or modify your communication preferences, please visit us at www.ReaderService.com/consumerschoice or write to us at Harlequin Reader Service Preference Service, P.O. Box 9062, Buffalo, NY 14269. Include your complete name and address.

PARA13R

SPECIAL EXCERPT FROM

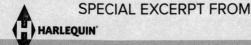

NOCTURNE™

Kai Faulkes, reclusive Sentinel protector of the wild Sacramento Mountains, is as untamed as the lynx whose form he takes; Regan Adler is on the run from her own nature. Only if they learn each other's secrets will they find their destiny together—and keep the mountains safe from a deadly enemy.

Read on for a sneak peek of

SENTINELS: LYNX DESTINY,

coming February 2014 from Harlequin Nocturne.

The fight had left him less staggered. Being *shot* had left him less staggered.

Kai Faulkes, thirty years old and never been kissed.

Never like that.

He made himself step back, made his expression rueful and his body still. Because he'd never known such *want,* and he'd never taken such liberties, and he didn't begin to trust himself not to take more.

Regan touched her mouth, her cheeks full of flush, her brows drawn together in a faint frown. "I—" she started, while he was still far from able to find words. *"You—"* she started again, and then shook her head, impatient with her own struggle. Then she shook herself off, pushing a wayward strand of gold away from her face. "Later," she said. "I'll deal with that kiss later. Right now, I've got too many questions."

For this, he met her gaze without flinching; he found words. "I might not answer them."

"We'll see about that. That needs care," she said, latching on to the most obvious need—looking at where the Core bullet had furrowed along the curve of his biceps.

But the arm would wait; it would heal faster than she could imagine. Other things wouldn't wait at all. For he needed to sweep through this area because the Core had finally infiltrated this remote and pristine place.

"Kai," Regan said, aiming a pale blue gaze his way with intent, regaining some of her composure—but not without the hint of remaining uncertainty.

Self-retribution slapped home. This woman wasn't Sentinel; she wasn't lynx. She wasn't born to be a protector. She'd been threatened and she'd fought back—but that didn't mean she wasn't still frightened.

She didn't need to walk back to the cabin alone.

She lifted one honey-gold brow, striking a note of asperity. "In case you haven't noticed, you're bleeding everywhere. If you faint from blood loss, I'm going to find my phone—" she glanced around, already looking "—and find a signal, and call for help. And somehow I get the feeling that's exactly what you're trying to avoid."

And Kai said nothing. Because Regan Adler saw—and heard—a lot more than she wanted to admit.

Even to herself.

Don't miss the dramatic conclusion to
SENTINELS: LYNX DESTINY by Doranna Durgin.
Available February 4,
only from Harlequin® Nocturne™.